THE GATHERING

THE GATHERING

SECRETLY SAVING THE WORLD

PART ONE OF THE HEDGEHOG CHRONICLES

Z.G. STANDING BEAR

Copyright © 2007 by Z.G. Standing Bear.
Cover illustration by Barbara Carter

ISBN: Hardcover   978-1-4257-8136-1
          Softcover   978-1-4257-8119-4

All rights reserved. No part of this book may be reproduced or transmitted in any form or by any means, electronic or mechanical, including photocopying, recording, or by any information storage and retrieval system, without permission in writing from the copyright owner.

This is a work of fiction. Names, characters, places and incidents either are the product of the author's imagination or are used fictitiously, and any resemblance to any actual persons, living or dead, events, or locales is entirely coincidental.

This book was printed in the United States of America.

To order additional copies of this book, contact:
Xlibris Corporation
1-888-795-4274
www.Xlibris.com
Orders@Xlibris.com
41336

CONTENTS

Chapter 1	Poisoned Earth	17
Chapter 2	The Journey Begins	24
Chapter 3	Rosie and Tadeusz	28
Chapter 4	A "Pigment" of Her Imagination	38
Chapter 5	Facing Reality	48
Chapter 6	Shadows of the Past	58
Chapter 7	The Circle of Sisters	68
Chapter 8	The Disciples of Anthross	79
Chapter 9	The Contraries	87
Chapter 10	Major General Spikers	100
Chapter 11	Spikers Travels North	113
Chapter 12	Bozeman the Spy	123
Chapter 13	Dungaree Rides the Bus	131
Chapter 14	Bozeman's Roundabout Journey	139
Chapter 15	The Gathering	150
Chapter 16	Bill the Bomb	158
Chapter 17	The Tactical Drill	174

With fond remembrance of these Grand and Ancient old friends who, through their brief time on this plane of existence had so much to teach . . .

To Flash and Thelma

. . . I am so glad I listened.

HEDGEHOG

The snail moves like a
Hovercraft, held up by a
Rubber cushion of itself,
Sharing its secret
With the hedgehog.

The hedgehog
Shares its secret with no one.
We say, *Hedgehog, come out
Of yourself and we will love you.*

*We mean no harm. We want
Only to listen to what
You have to say. We want
Your answers to our questions.*

The hedgehog gives nothing
Away, keeping itself to itself.
We wonder what a hedgehog
Has to hide, why it so distrusts.

We forget the god
Under this crown of thorns.
We forget that never again
Will a god trust in the world.

by Paul Muldoon
New Weather, 1973
Reprinted with permission.

67,000,000 SPRINGTIMES AGO (GIVE OR TAKE A FEW)

The blood-red sunset came crashing to a close. The youngsters all cringed as the ground shook, but their mother had a serene expression.

"Wow!" Little Petrov was impressed.

"Got 'im with the big horn!" Petrov's brother Vasily just looked up in awe.

"It's time you boys came with me to talk with your Grandfather," said their mother, Lalo. "You are getting old enough to hear what you must know for the rest of your life and the generations to come."

The boys were not that keen to sit down with their Grandfather, Bohuslava, the oldest and wisest of the entire Grootwhump. They were much more interested in the huge meat-eating dinosaur that had just come crashing down and blocked out the sunset. The teeth were huge, at least as long as the young hedgehogs were tall. There was blood all over. The scales were smooth and shiny. They'd never seen anything that big and fearsome so close up, a thing that would, millions of winters later, be called a tyrannosaur.

The normally mild triceratops that beat him just seemed to get in a few good licks with his spiky head. "Served the toothy one right," both boys thought, since he had just eaten and went after the triceratops seemingly out of meanness.

But Lalo insisted. "Now is the best time."

The twins waddled behind their persistent Mom around the blood-soaked teeth of the now dead tyrannosaur. The triceratops that had somehow won the contest snarled at them as they trudged past, but they didn't worry about the big fellow. He had never bothered them before. The red sunset was again visible.

Scurrying under protective rock ledges, the trio finally reached the small cave inlet of the Grootwhump Elder, Bohuslava.

Lalo, in her usual quiet way, addressed the most senior hedgehog. "My boys are entering being boys no longer. I ask you to tell them the secrets that will assure them long lives, for themselves and their children's children."

"Ah, yes, Lalo," said Bohuslava in a soft, measured voice. "But you must remember that I am getting very old and when I have myself traveled over the Bridge, you and your young men here must carry on."

"Yes, I know. It's a big weight to carry. But we shall do it," Lalo almost whispered. "I'll leave the boys with you now."

Old Bohuslava liked Lalo's two boys, Petrov and Vasily. A bit mischievous but spirited in a good way. They will be good messengers for those to come, thought Bohuslava.

The boys stood in front of their ancient elder respectfully, although both thought they'd much rather be playing outside and even exploring the giant dead tyrannosaur.

"Sit down, my young friends," said Bohuslava softly, "this is going to take some time."

The youngsters huddled together, resigned to their lesson, yet having no idea what to expect.

"Why is that great and powerful lizard lying out there dead?" questioned Bohuslava.

The boys suddenly came alive, for each had his own opinion.

"Because he was greedy!" exclaimed Vasily.

"Thought he was too powerful," added Petrov.

"You young fellows are going to be easy to teach," said Bohuslava, "you already show some wisdom."

"Our Mom is a good teacher," said Petrov. "She really takes care of us, and protects us well."

"Indeed she does," acknowledged Bohuslava. "One of the very finest hedgehogs I have ever known. She will carry forward the Instructions, what we call now the 'Original Instructions' with great wisdom."

"Why, then, Grandfather," questioned Vasily, "did Mom send us to you for these instructions?"

"Heh heh," chuckled Bohuslava, "perhaps she wants to me to think that even an old man such as I can still be valuable. But, on the other hand, she might think that you two roughhousing youngsters will listen more seriously to an old man than to your Mom. But, the real reason I think we, all of us hedgehogs, use this tradition of looking to the eldest ones of us for teaching is to be sure to respect the past, to learn from it, and to carry forward as much from our old ones as possible."

Vasily and Petrov sat silently.

"Our language is our medium and it defines us, lets us know who we are" began Bohuslava. "We will communicate in many languages over time, but the subtleties of the meanings of thoughts and words will define us, onto the perceptions of others."

"Like the big lizard defined the horned one?"

"Exactly, Vasily," responded Bohuslava. "The big lizard was bragging and braying, and coming upon the horned one, who was minding his own business by the way, positioned for a meaningless fight. All the horned one did was defend himself."

"He sure got in a good lick."

"A fatal lick, Petrov," answered Bohuslava. "All of what you have seen here today serves to teach you well. You have answered with wisdom even without being questioned. Now we must discuss the most important secrets of a long and rich life for you and those that will come after you."

"Those would be what we call the 'Original Instructions' Grandfather?"

"Yes, Vasily," answered Bohuslava. "This is secret and precious knowledge that you will carry forward to your children and them to their children, down through the ages. You both must be aware that there will come times when even after these ferocious giant lizards pass on, as they will, that other species, different in their form and different in their ideas shall dredge onto this planet their own methods of terror, and greed, and, yes, ideas of power. And like the dead and ferocious giant lizard you see before you today, those organisms of the future shall be dead of their own foolish and brave thoughts."

"Well, Grandpa, not to be too depressed about all of this," queried Petrov, "but what can we do?"

"Aha," answered Bohuslava. "Thought you'd never ask. It is the matter of the Original Instructions for a productive and wonderful life on this planet. Come with me back further into the protective rooms of this cave."

Vasily and Petrov followed their Grandfather back into the labyrinth of caves, hearing him begin "The Original Instructions are for all living things and are necessary for all the creatures of the planet to live in harmony. Without them, all is in disarray and discord. This is secret knowledge that you both will carry with you and pass along to your children. What I will tell you now conveys these instructions . . ."

Their voices faded off as they waddled further back into the cave.

6 YEARS AGO

Trudy Preston, nine years old, was doing what she liked most: Visiting the Botanical Gardens Park in Fort Worth with "Grandpa Mack," her Great-Grandfather. Grandpa Mack had seen a great deal of life, over eighty years of it, and had been, among other things, a decorated warrior.

"Grandpa!" Trudy shouted. "Look at the ants over there! They're fighting with those other ants!"

"Umm, I'm sorry to tell you, Trudy, that this is what much of our world is about. Everywhere around you, there's fighting. Those ants don't like the other ants coming into their territory. People do the same thing. They don't like strangers and like them even less if they look or talk differently. But look over there, under those bushes!"

"What's there, Grandpa?!"

"Heh heh, keep looking! They're hard to see."

"Oooh! I see some eyes! I think."

"Yes you do, three pair of bunny eyes. Looking right at us," Grandpa Mack said.

"Why are they watching us, Grandpa?"

"We're probably near their burrows, so they are curious about us. I don't think they like it at all."

"But Grandpa, we don't want to hurt them!"

"They don't know that, Trudy. The world is strange that way. So many different animals, each with their own societies, beliefs, and customs, and not a very good understanding of one another. So, often they fight."

Grandpa Mack looked down, gently stroking the soft green grass, saying softly "and we humans are the worst of all."

"Why, Grandpa?"

"Because we know no limits. We keep wanting more and more. At least other animals don't go off invading others and taking more than they need. People do it because they like power, or are greedy, or sometimes just to do it."

"No wonder the bunnies are worried," said Trudy quietly.

"No wonder," whispered her great-grandfather. "We humans think we're so smart, but there's so much we don't know. We're too new here. If we could only somehow speak with all of those animals. Those rabbits, those ants, wolves, beavers and muskrats. My, what they could tell us. But I think we humans are too full of ourselves to hear."

"Full of ourselves?" Trudy asked.

"We think we know it all, Trudy. And that which we don't know we make up stuff about. Then, if strangers come along and don't believe our made-up stuff, we kill them. Or they kill us. So we fight."

"I think the bunnies have secrets, Grandpa."

"And I don't think they're gonna tell us what they are," groused the retired Marine lieutenant general, "any time soon."

CHAPTER 1

POISONED EARTH

Thelma The Aged One

CHAPTER 1—POISONED EARTH

A scream! Loud, high pitched, unearthly. He had never heard such a sound. Yet he knew who made it. The stool slid out from under Pedro Cabrales and clattered to the floor. He caught himself sliding sideways and the oil change service form tore as he fell.

Pedro rounded the corner of the ancient glass and wood counter of one of the few service stations left in North America, a place he had managed for the last twenty years. He stumbled over the old, saggy chair with the chrome arms and ruptured plastic cushions, nearly falling as he cleared the door. The scream came again, other-worldly, but young. So young. A horror

"Maria! Oh God! Maria!"

Little Maria Sanchez, the peppy third-grader that visited with Pedro almost every day when she got off the school bus, was now lying in the sparse grass and dirt just to the rear of the station, at the beginning of the broad prairie-like field that lay beyond. Lying and writhing on the ground, and screaming.

"What is it, Maria?! What is it?!"

No answer! Only screams, as Maria's flailing arms clutched at her throat. Right by her side lay the paper cup that she'd held in her hand as she skipped from the station out to the back, as she did each time she visited after school.

Pedro knelt by the screaming girl, not knowing what to do. Her screams were more frequent now as she convulsed on the ground, now shaking and vibrating wildly. Her mouth open, gasping. Her eyes were wide with panic, fear.

"Oh my God!"

Pedro jumped to his feet and ran, half staggering, back inside the station. Fumbling with the telephone, he quickly tapped 9-1-1.

"The little girl here, she is, she is hurt bad! She is screaming! Gasping!"

"Quickly! Where are you?"

Pedro fired off the address into the telephone.

"OK, Sir! We're on the way."

The firm, assuring voice of the dispatcher calmed Pedro momentarily, and then he heard the sirens piercing the air.

"Thank God! Thank God!"

Pedro again ran around to where Maria, now gasping in soft sobs, lay. He knelt beside her, not knowing what to do. He thankfully heard the sirens growing louder. Then he looked up, across the field to the east, and his blood ran cold.

"Oh, my God!"

A hideous sight. The prairie dogs, the playful little animals that Maria loved so much, that she had always exited the school bus two stops beyond her home to play with were . . . were . . .

The sirens were deafening now. The paramedics pulled in first, two police cars close behind. Then a fire truck. Fire truck?

But Pedro's eyes were transfixed on the field beyond, in horror.

The paramedics descended on Maria. She still writhed and convulsed, but quieter now, less violent. Onto the stretcher and whisked away. Into the ambulance. Away. Away. The siren screaming back down the highway.

Pedro sat on the ground, staring.

A police officer put his hand on Pedro's shoulder, gently.

"Sir, did you phone in this call?"

"Si, err, yes," mumbled Pedro.

"Do you know what happened?"

"Look for yourself," said a sorrowful Pedro, gesturing toward the field.

"Damn!"

Other officers and the firefighters now stood just behind the crumpled body of Pedro, as all looked out over the field to the east. There, in twisted and grotesque shapes, with their eyes wildly open and the mouths agape in toothy, ghastly contortions were dozens, maybe hundreds of prairie dogs. All dead.

Pedro looked up almost pleadingly.

"The Plag! It is The Plag!"

#

Charles A. Rimson, MD, a pathologist by profession and the county coroner by election, usually enjoyed his forages into forensic pathology. It was a respite from the more mundane parade of endless tissue examinations under the microscope. But this case . . . different. Critical and stressful. The little girl had died suddenly on the way to the hospital in the ambulance. She had last been seen screaming and writhing on the ground at the rear of a service station north of town. Dozens of dead prairie dogs had also been seen in the area lying above their burrows in grotesque shapes.

The coroner asked to address the family of Maria Sanchez, although he knew nothing, at that time, of what had caused her death. There were rumors of The Plague, known to be harbored by prairie dogs. After seeing the horrific sights, Pedro Cabrales was convinced.

Dr. Rimson looked at the assembled crowd in the room. He asked if he could talk to Maria's family. No one moved. He asked again. Still, no one moved.

Finally, Joe Morales stepped forward and said, softly, "We are all her family."

Rimson asked, bewildered, "You're all her relatives?"

"In our neighborhood, we are all relatives, all family."

Rimson continued, "Maria did not die from The Plague. She died from something very sudden, not like The Plague, which works much more slowly."

"But the dead prairie dogs? Was that not The Plague?"

"We don't think so," answered Rimson, "too sudden. We must wait for tests."

#

A week later, the mystery was solved. Dr. Rimson thought it best that he address, before anyone else, the neighborhood "relatives" of Maria Sanchez.

"Maria died of an allergic reaction to gasoline poisoning," began Dr. Rimson. "She drank what she thought was water from the sink at the service station. But the water, from an old well not on the city water system, was full of gasoline. Most people would throw up the gasoline if drinking it accidentally, but Maria was allergic to it."

"But how did that gasoline get in the water?"

"Old gas station underground tanks," replied Dr. Rimson, "now decayed and leaking, poisoned the groundwater. We've notified the Environmental Protection Agency. They will investigate and order a clean-up. I'm so sorry this discovery had to happen in this way"

Pedro Cabrales raised a question: "What about the many dead prairie dogs?"

"The prairie dogs also were victims of the same groundwater poisoning as Maria. Their underground burrows were overcome with gasoline fumes, and most were killed by fume inhalation by the time they had escaped to the surface."

"They did not die from The Plag?"

Rimson answered, "no, they were poisoned by the gasoline in the ground, just as Maria was."

#

Old Man Muldraugh sat on his haunches eyeing the rest of the Council. "I'd like some suggestions! Before we all die!"

The Gathering

They all sat there motionless. Not a squeak.

"WHAT are we going to do!?"

"You're the Burrow Leader, Muldraugh, our Wise Elder," spoke Dalriegel softly. "We have always looked to you for answers to our biggest problems."

More were gathering around the main burrow where the Council met. None of the usual chattering. All was quiet. The families of prairie dogs in fifteen burrows, those closest to the big flatblack to the west of Muldraughtown had perished.

"We know that the Bigs poisoned the water in the burrows," offered Muldraugh, Jr., the old man's son. "Its scent is the same as at that Bigs place near the big flatblack, and you can smell it in the air near the rollers."

"It feeds the rollers," said Dalriegel. "It's in the ground and you can see the Bigs feeding the rollers at that place where that friendly little Big that visits us fell down."

"Maybe they're trying to kill us like they were when they used water down at the Southwest, at Boscotown," said old Muldraugh. "It's no secret the Bigs are trying to kill us."

"But what can we do?" Dalriegel, the Council member from the prairie dog burrows of Muldraughtown that were north of the Crosstown Flatblack, said, perplexed.

Muldraugh looked around at the Council and he felt as helpless as they. "We'd move, but I don't know that we'd be better off. I think we must council with others, possibly wiser ones than we."

"But who, Dad? Who are wiser than we? Many of the others are in as bad a shape as us. You should listen to the mice wail and moan. The muskrats down by the river just sit around and cuss all day. The marmots keep heading for the high country. The beavers are willing but very few, and the rabbits don't even want to talk about it."

"Ummm," mused Dalriegel, "and the bugs, when you can understand them, are blinded with rage. Y'oughtta hear 'em."

"Oh, great," answered Junior. "Bugs! I think you're the only prairie dog around here than can understand them hissing roaches and ants, Dalriegel."

"All you hafta do is listen real close. Get through the hissing. Really not hard to understand."

"Gives me the creeps," whispered Junior.

"Well, Junior, they're mad as hornets, and they say they're finally gonna do something. They're calling on mantises to organize things."

"Arrgh, mantises," moaned Junior, "meanest bugs around. Smart, too."

"Planners, as well," added Dalriegel.

"You wanna ask bugs? Mantises?"

Muldraugh the elder interrupted the exchange between Junior and Dalriegel. "Boys, I don't think our answers lie with the mantises, roaches, or ants, or any other bugs, for that matter. I may have a better idea, one passed to me by the squirrels over by the Big Oval where the Bigs go to school."

"Squirrels?!" Dalriegel let his mouth drop open.

"Squirrels?" Junior echoed.

"I know you don't think highly of squirrels," Muldraugh continued, "with their reckless behavior and all."

"Yeah, not to mention scurrying up trees when things start getting rough down here," Junior added.

"But," Muldraugh continued, "you've got to admit they are smart and their ears are always to the ground."

"Well, yeah," groused Dalriegel, "they're big on the rumor mill. So what?"

"There's a hedgehog over there," said Muldraugh quietly.

"A hedgehog?" Muldraugh, Jr., looked bewildered.

"How could a hedgehog be over there?" Dalriegel questioned. "Those old-timers don't even live on this side of the Earth!"

"Captivity," answered Muldraugh. "She's kept captive by the Bigs. The squirrels have spoken with her, told her about these problems. She already knew. She's real old. Old and wise."

"Already knew?" Junior asked, getting more confused by the minute.

"Said it's happening all over," Muldraugh continued, "all over the world."

"But what can she do? Captive and all."

"You know what she . . . and we . . . can do," Muldraugh lowered his voice.

"Organize?" Dalriegel asked. "Yes! Organize!"

"She has, through those squirrel friends of hers, already picked a spot for the few hedgehogs around here to organize. They'll all get sprung from their little prisons. You'll see."

"How do they DO that?" Junior asked.

"Just like we do, communicate by thoughts. It's just that they've been around longer than we, so many of them can do it between species. Cool, eh?"

"Well, yeah, I guess so," answered Dalriegel, "but what are they gonna do once they all get together?"

"I dunno, but the old one, Thelma, thinks they can communicate to the Bigs some sense of rightness about how they treat the world. But she did mention the bugs, too."

"The bugs?" Junior asked. "The Bugs and the Bigs! Yeehaw!"

"She's worried about the bugs."

"Aw, great!" Junior exclaimed. "NOW what?"

"You know that the ants lost hundreds of hills from this stuff in the ground. They're *reeeel* mad. The survivors, that is. Word has it they've called upon mantises to lead them against the Bigs."

"The Bigs are a horror," muttered Dalriegel, "but organized ants under mantises I don't even want to think about."

"End of the Earth, boys. That's why Thelma the hedgehog is worried about the bugs."

#

Archniss looked down at the tiny ant. "You're ssure you want to do thiss?"

"Yess, we all want to do it. We musst do it. All over our hillss are destroyed. Hundredss of them."

The towering mantis, a fierce presence backed up by eight other equally menacing brethren, lowered his gaze: "Unquesstioned obedience iss what we require. Upon pain of violent death. We cannot ssucceed otherwisse."

"W . . . we undersstand," stammered the ant, "but we cannot tolerate thiss desstruction any longer. Better to die on all our legss than by thesse fumes . . . Bigss chemicalss."

"Very well," replied Archniss, a mantis of great stature among warrior insects. "I will ssend your plea to the renegade leader of warrior insectss, the hedgehog Anthross."

The ant looked up in amazement, "Hedgehog leader?"

"Yess," replied Archniss, "hedgehog leader. He, like uss, knowss the Bigss must be eradicated, removed from the earth. He speakss with the mind of an inssect and hass forssaken the lesss enlightened hedgehogss. He iss alsso recruiting other hedgehogss for our causse. He will prevail. He will impresss you and all of the other insectss he iss bringing together to eliminate the Bigss from the earth."

CHAPTER 2

THE JOURNEY BEGINS

Flash the Welcomer

CHAPTER 2—THE JOURNEY BEGINS

Flash the hedgehog shifted her weight so as to expose a different expanse of fur to catch more of the soft, warm air that flowed up from the floor heater vent. She loved the vent and slept there whenever she could.

"Ahh, these humans got a few things right and forced air heating and floor vents was one of them," she thought.

"She was spread out over her all time favorite vent, the one in back of the living room under the blue hide-a-bed sofa. It gave her a secure place to hide and a clear view of the front door.

Tonight she was especially excited. Thelma was coming! Flash had never met Thelma but she knew from the conversations she had overheard from Jenna and Ivan, the humans that lived there, that Thelma was a very special hedgehog. Thelma was *old*! She was born in the Central African hedgehog homeland called northern Nigeria, in the human year 1993! She could hardly wait to meet Thelma, but she had some fears as well. What if the meeting failed? It could fail in so many, many ways. Flash tried to rid her mind of the "Original Instructions," but she could not. They had been around for countless Springtimes, over 60 million of them.

Jenna and Ivan were two humans, or "Bigs," that were OK for the most part, according to Flash. Both were teachers and seemed to love what they did. Although they were married to one another, they spent much time apart because Jenna traveled a great deal as a lecturer and educator while Ivan taught at a university. Once on a bike ride one Sunday, Jenna stopped at a local plant nursery as was her custom. She loved plants. As a promotional gimmick, the nursery advertised "Come see our two baby hedgehogs." Jenna did, and she was smitten. As these hedgehogs were not for sale she set out to find herself a pet hedgehog, and the rest, as they say, is "herstory."

She found one hedgehog, a little girl, in a pet store. When she brought the hedgehog home, Ivan objected, but Jenna simply proceeded to ask what the name of the new member of the family should be. While they were trying to decide, the hedgehog disappeared and was not found for several days. They decided to call her Flash, in honor of her ability to disappear in a "flash."

Ivan was getting weary of Jenna bringing home pet animals, such as the little squad of finches, and then going off on her educational trips, leaving

Ivan holding the pet care bag. But Jenna promised that this time things would be different, that the hedgehog would be going with her wherever she went. Indeed, for the first six months this was true, and Flash logged more frequent flyer miles than most humans do in a lifetime, although concealed in Jenna's pocket as she strolled through the airport metal detectors. Flash was good at lying low in transit.

However, things changed for Jenna as she began getting more international speaking contracts. She was afraid to bring Flash on international flights because she might be confiscated. So, as 1997 approached, Flash was essentially grounded. Although she seemed to miss the "jet set" life, Flash really liked her heater vent behind the blue hide-a-bed sofa.

And now, Thelma was coming! Flash was thinking hard as to what to say to Thelma, especially at first. She knew that hedgehog customs derived from the Original Instructions forbade any direct, intimate contact observable to the Bigs, but at the same time she longed for companionship. How, she thought, could she let Thelma know that she wished her to stay here without letting on to the humans?

Hedgehog customs were so hard to follow these days where there were Bigs around. Flash was sure that Bohuslava The Great, the hedgehog that had issued the Original Instructions so many Springtimes ago, was not thinking of the species of beings that would come to inhabit the Earth millions of years later. She thought, perhaps, now that this new species that knows no boundaries in their quest for greed and power is here, it is time to revisit the Original Instructions in order to deal with this new and murderous kind that call themselves humans.

Suddenly, a revelation came over Flash: She would just sit there! After all, Thelma was the far senior hedgehog. Yep, just sit there and see what would happen.

At 7PM the door was opened by Jenna and in strode Kelly, a college student that had cared for Thelma since 1993. However, Kelly was going into the Peace Corps and was not allowed to take her menagerie of a dozen small animals with her. So, here was the place that Thelma was supposed to go, providing, of course, that she got along with Flash.

Flash had come out from under the couch, as was her custom whenever the front door opened. The humans talked pleasantries for several minutes. Then they plunked Thelma right down on the floor, within a foot of Flash. Flash stood there frozen, not knowing what to do.

Thelma walked slowly toward Flash and, unbelievably, snuggled up to her and whispered: "We really need to be here, but I am afraid that if we fight or ignore one another, the Bigs will take me away."

Thelma continued whispering in Flash's ear: "We must somehow get organized because something very bad is about to happen!"

In a moment Flash was agreeing and yet bewildered. She thought to herself: "How can we, just small animals that have no voice to speak clearly to these humans, who are imprisoned in often terrible conditions, make any difference?" Not used to communicating so closely, Flash suddenly realized that Thelma was reading her mind, as hedgehogs do.

Thelma silently spoke, "There must be a way. We have been here for over 60 million Springtimes! What better testimony to our ability to survive? We will find a way. We must! We will be bringing many hedgehogs here to help us. They will all be very different, as you will see, and they will be coming from many different places."

Kelly, Jenna, and Ivan looked on in amazement. "What on Earth?" Ivan exclaimed. "Everything I've read tells me that these are solitary animals that do not get along, yet just look at these two!"

Understanding the exclamation, Thelma snuggled in closer to Flash and said "From this moment on we are going to be inseparable, young lady."

"Fine with me," said Flash, "fine with me. Come, let me show you my favorite spot."

The two of them darted under the blue hide-a-bed.

Ivan said, "I'll bet I know where they're going." As all three humans knelt on the blue hide-a-bed, leaning over the back, they could see two little hedgehog butts clustered close together, sharing the forced air heater duct. And so was born the union of Flash and Thelma, forever inseparable.

CHAPTER 3

ROSIE AND TADEUSZ

Rosie the Wanderer

CHAPTER 3—ROSIE AND TADEUSZ

Rosie knew that the end was near. The sparkling eyes that she had enjoyed for all of her life had dimmed and become dull. She sat there looking down at her dearest friend Sarah and gently stroked her facial fur and her quills.

"The melody is so lovely," Sarah whispered. "Beauty finally comes to me now after a life of fear and cruelty. I don't think those that hurt us can see beauty at all, ever. I sort of feel sorry for them. Even through my pain I always longed for beauty. Now I have it. Rosie, I hear it!"

"I can only faintly hear it," answered Rosie, "but it is surely beautiful."

Over the millions of Springtimes they have inhabited the Earth, hedgehogs, among the most ancient of mammals, have developed senses that have insured their survival. They communicate telepathically and hear the music of the earth in a great variety of its forms. The music Sarah was hearing clearly and Rosie was tuning in remotely was known to them as the Rainbow Bridge Song of Orestia. It is the song to assist a departing spirit over the Bridge to the next world, and it is the most beautiful song ever sung. It is even more beautiful than a hedgehog's personal song, which is a song unique to each and every quilled being, although many have forgotten their songs in this day and age.

"Farewell, sweet friend," Rosie quietly whispered as Sarah relaxed and her eyes, now lifeless, lost all expression. Sarah had traveled on to The Great Country of Souls.

It was cold. Too cold. Many of the hedgehogs were rolled up, some snuggling and a couple running in circles trying to get warm. Rosie sat in the middle of a metal tub, her head hurting and her skin crawling with some sort of dirty stuff. It felt as if she was in a death pit. Some of the hedgehogs around her had already died, others were near death and some had their legs torn off from fights. The air hung heavy with the smells of decay, blood, and hopelessness.

One hedgehog seemed to thrive on this misery. His name was Bowls, the swaggering male that wanted to boss everybody around and be the boyfriend to all of the girls. But the girls were sick! Sick and afraid and lonely and dying. Bowls' antics in the face of all this misery just made things more miserable.

Bowls came blustering through one more time shouting "Hey, Rosie, what you need is a strong boyfriend like me around!"

Rosie, a tiny and rather rangy Algerian chocolate hedgehog with quills that never seemed to quite lay down, simply rolled up in disgust wondering to herself "Where, on Earth, did this clown come from?"

"Aw, Bowls, get lost, will ya?" Ukuqambe, a spunky little male hedgehog, chimed up.

Ukuqambe, whose Zulu name could roughly be translated as "Gizmo" in English, was called "Qambe" by his friends. Specializing in hedgehog martial arts, even at just a tad over 200 grams, Qambe was more than the 450-gram bully Bowls could handle. Bowls had learned some time ago that messing with Qambe was not a good combat option, since Qambe had the deadly ability to roll up over the soft places of an adversary and gnaw away. Fortunately, Qambe was an honorable warrior and never used his skills unless they were truly needed.

Qambe was one of the most faithful followers of the Original Instructions issued by Bohuslava the Great, the legendary hedgehog prophet of immense importance to hedgehogs the world over. This secret knowledge has been the major factor in allowing hedgehogs to survive for so long.

"Bowls means no harm," piped up the tiny hedgehog Dolmen.

Little Dolmen was Rosie's favorite. If anyone had a gripe against Bowls, it was certainly Dolmen. Bowls constantly bullied him. But Dolmen was of another world, a kind and gentle world that one only dreams about. Dolmen trusted everyone, liked everyone, found good in everything. In hard times he shared food, often going without. He was a strange looking little hedgehog. His mouth was set in a slight, kindly smile; and one of his fangs had been sheared off at an odd angle. His quills were of the dark chocolate banded variety, quite common. What was unusual was that he had several bent quills on his forehead and one very long white quill just in front of his left ear that was bent almost in half.

"If everyone on Earth was like Dolmen," Rosie thought, "what a wonderful place this would be. Why are things so terrible?"

Rosie lay there in the squalor, thankful for the protective reinforcement from Qambe, and for the love she had for Dolmen. Not far from Rosie crouched Tadeusz, her friend and one of the wisest and gentlest hedgehogs she had ever known. Not a fighter and not as naive as Dolmen, Tadeusz was brilliant, impressing all others in this miserable environment with his wit and wisdom. Qambe looked up to Tadeusz with almost a godlike admiration. Tadeusz, in turn, always thanked Qambe for his adherence to the courageous defense of the right path.

"Do you ever think Bowls will come around to behaving himself?" Qambe queried. The question was directed to Tadeusz but said so that the whole circle of hedgehogs could hear. In matters of philosophy, they always deferred to Tadeusz. They were never disappointed.

Tadeusz reflected a moment and said, "In over sixty million years we've done well. Look at us! We have lived, survived, and let live. Our children survived down through the generations and we've never taken more than what we have needed. We're friends with so many other beings and live in harmony and balance. What more can you ask for?"

"But what of Bowls and his kind?" Qambe questioned.

"It is understandable because we are not creatures that are immune from interaction with others, including those that call themselves humans. We all learn habits from others. Bowls departed from our traditional ways and has picked up some human greed along the way. Maybe he will return to us, perhaps not. There are some with his attitude among us. We just have to realize this and know that when we depart from the Original Instructions, a few of us may become lost. The humans have never heard the Original Instructions, and now see what terrible things they have done, both to themselves and to the planet, and in such a short time! Only a few thousand Springtimes! In the last hundred Springtimes, these humans have truly begun to destroy the earth, killing themselves and others for their own convenience."

Suddenly everything tipped sideways and all of the 40 or so hedgehogs in the steel vat slid into a large pile of rolled up hedgehogs and assorted filth.

The human orchestrator of this disturbance, Jim Lonsey, muttered a few foul words and then exclaimed, "These sorry critters ain't worth the chow we're feeden' 'em!" With heavy leather gloves he scooped up groups of hedgehogs and threw them into cardboard boxes. Lonsey and his wife Melinda operated a small pet animal breeding operation, specializing in whatever pets were popular at the time. At the moment, hedgehogs, ferrets, guinea pigs, and a new item, sugar gliders, seemed to be where the bucks were. They had some 500 small animals in various metal tubs at the moment when Rosie's group was slid into a corner and thrown into boxes for sale to pet stores.

Jim and Melinda had been identified as a breeding "mill" and targeted from time to time by animal welfare groups. However, they always managed to stay one step ahead of trouble, mainly by getting tips from local law enforcement (Jim was a reserve deputy sheriff). They would hide the metal tubs in the woods behind their home when state or federal regulators called. They kept a few animals in a spare bedroom, properly documented, to satisfy the officials. But none of this was of any help to Rosie.

Rosie was tossed into a box that was both deadly and dangerous. She felt a hard, sharp pain on the right side of her head. Some sharp thing had stuck her in the right eye. It was a protruding nail. She momentarily screamed in pain and felt the warm flow of blood from her eye. She had been blinded in her right eye. As Rosie lay there, she realized something far more horrible: All of her friends were gone. Even her enemies were gone! Her dear friend Tadeusz was gone! So was Qambe! Dolmen was gone! Even Bowls the pain-in-the neck was gone!

She was in a box with five other hedgehogs. It was the "bottom of the tub." One was Sarah, a beautiful hedgehog with laughing eyes and a cheerful disposition. Another was Homer, a sort of sad little fellow that was scared most of the time. And they were all dead. Rosie was the only living hedgehog in the box. She sat there in that place of death and wondered what would become of her. She did not have long to wait.

Jim brought the boxes of hedgehogs to his pickup truck and, in order to make the animals more attractive to potential buyers, turned the boxes over one by one and shook the dirt, poop, and assorted filth through the holes in the top. Then he made the rounds of pet shops trying to sell his load of hedgehogs (next week it would be the bumper crop of guinea pigs). He had pretty good luck, but the dead hedgehogs were a definite bummer. So, after the first embarrassment of a pet store owner discovering a dead hedgehog (missing her two front legs, no less) in a box of a half dozen, Lonsey scanned the boxes before entering a pet store or mall and threw any dead hedgehogs into the nearest trash container.

By the time he got to the end of his rounds, the final box contained only Rosie and five dead hedgehogs. All five were tossed into a dumpster and Rosie was presented as the last "rare" hedgehog available to this pet store.

The pet store owner took one look at Rosie and her bloody punctured eye and declared that this hedgehog was "damaged goods." He offered Jim $1.50 for her, which Jim quickly accepted and began his journey home. As he left, Jim muttered "Well, I guess a buck and a half is better than throwing it in the dumpster."

Rosie was not a good pet store candidate. She was small and wiry and spent a good deal of her time rolled up in a protective ball. When unrolled, her missing eye was a definite turn-off to potential buyers. She was kept in a tiny Plexiglas drawer with dirty bedding material, a water bottle that hurt her teeth and mostly contaminated kitten food.

Her weight never got above 200 grams, just about seven ounces. In Rosie's fourth month at the pet store, a group of local school children toured the store on an educational field trip. They mentioned that their teacher had often talked about having a classroom pet. The store owner jumped at the chance not only to accommodate the group of children, but at the same time get rid of some deadwood inventory and get a tax a write off as a "donation." So Rosie became a school pet in Miss Emily Blodgett's middle school classroom.

Set up in a 20 gallon aquarium, Rosie realized that as bad as it was, these were most luxurious living quarters she had ever had. Her food was a low grade cat food that she disliked, and then there was that water bottle again. She lived in a bed of cedar wood chips that made her sick most of the time. The strong odor and the dust hurt her lungs and she had trouble breathing. But there was no escaping it.

During the day children in the class tapped on the glass of the aquarium and woke her up again and again. Nocturnal or not, this really did not matter for she had nothing to do at night anyway except try to figure out how to keep from breathing in those sickening fumes. "Certainly these humans should have learned about this by now!" Rosie said to herself.

Then, one day, after nearly two years of glass-tapping, cedar chips, bad food, and the terrible water bottle that hurt her teeth which had come with her all the way from the pet store, something changed. Rosie viewed it with renewed displeasure bordering on fright. Little did she know it would be her ticket out of there.

During a newly extended recess in mid-morning, the students had a little more time and freedom from supervision than in the past. Two boys, Martin Freed and Jerrold Adock, who were in one scrape after another at the school, saw an opportunity to engage in a little sport at recess: Indoor golf.

"What a nice driver this makes," said Jerrold as he hefted Miss Blodgett's umbrella.

"Hey, dude, we don't have a golf ball," Martin said.

"Yeah we do, man," as Jerrold pointed to Rosie's aquarium. "You remember that movie, what was it, oh yeah, Alice in Wonderful or Wonderland or whatever," Adock continued.

"Yeah, dude, like that queen or whatever was hitting a hedgehog around," Martin remembered. They went over to Rosie's aquarium and lifted her out. She didn't like any of this and rolled up in a tight ball, hissing and popping her loudest. Despite this, she was plopped on the floor and a few moments later whacked across the room with the umbrella.

"Hey, dude, let's see who can hit it into the wastebasket first," yelled Martin, kicking over a wastebasket.

Rosie stayed rolled up and became quite dizzy being hit across the floor with the umbrella, an ordeal that continued for about ten minutes, until recess came to a close. Freed and Adock's idea of sport went on each morning at recess for several weeks, until Becky Hancock happened to have forgotten her ball for the playground and returned to the classroom to fetch it.

Upon approaching the door, she overheard Adock and Freed laughing, along with a strange "thud" noise. Peeking around the corner into the room, she saw a round ball of spikes quickly roll by her and bounce off the side of an overturned wastecan. It took Becky only an instant to figure out what was going on. She ran to summon Miss Blodgett.

"They're torturing our hedgie!"

Miss Blodgett rounded the corner into the room just as the two boys were winding up their game. "What are you two doing?!" she shouted, snatching the umbrella.

Freed and Adock stood there, looking at the floor, giving the "evil eye" sideways towards Becky, who stood in the door with a smug expression on her face. Having placed Rosie back in her aquarium, Miss Blodgett pondered her next move. A disciplinary hearing for the boys would, of course, take place. But what about the hedgehog?

Rosie sat there breathing wood chip fumes and tried to figure if that was better than the cleaner air on the floor at the end of the swinging umbrella. She decided that both situations were equally bad. Still, she had heard of hedgehogs that lived a pretty decent life, she just wished she could enjoy some of whatever that was, some day.

She thought about what some of the wiser ones had told her, about hedgehogs living good lives both in the wild and in what they call "captivity." She remembered being told of her ancestors in Northern Nigeria really having it bad in the wild because, even though free to run, there was not enough food for the humans and the other animals, and there was a lot of killing. She also remembered tales about hedgehogs in England and Europe being treated very nicely in gardens and living good lives there, but then getting run over and killed by huge things the humans invented called rollers which traveled along hard ribbons of land called flatblacks.

Miss Blodgett was about to change things for Rosie. While in college, Emily Blodgett worked part time at a pet shop. She got on the phone to the shop's owner, a tall, rangy cowboy-type named Pete Crank. Pete's main love was horses but he also sold small pets and pet supplies in his horse supply and tack shop.

"Well, Emmy, I wouldn't want to sell no scrawny, half blind animule in my place," drawled Pete, but he hesitated and thought for a moment. Then he remembered, "there's this fella that bought a hedgehog we were goin' to put down 'cause two families brought her back and demanded a reefund 'cause she was 'too wild.' That was back in November," Pete recalled, "an' he ain't been back since 'cept to buy food. Got no complaint, I 'spose."

Emily was not following this and asked, "Pete, what are you thinking?"

"Waaal, I figger mebbe this guy might could take her in since he had no complaint 'bout the other one. I could give him a call."

"Could you do that?" Emily replied, knowing that the hedgehog classroom pet experiment had failed and wishing to get Rosie into a better environment.

Pete Crank telephoned Ivan. Ivan picked up the telephone to hear Pete ask about the "too wild" little female hedgehog that Ivan had purchased for a very substantial discount last November.

Ivan replied that the hedgehog, which came to be named Louise, was doing very well, "pretty wild but certainly not aggressive. Besides, I guess you can't have a Thelma without a Louise," he said, speaking of the older hedgehog named Thelma that he had inherited over a year before Louise joined the duo of Flash and Thelma.

"Howdja like another one?" Pete offered.

"Say again?" Ivan replied.

"Waaal," said Pete, "one of my former employees, now a schoolteacher, has a hedgehog that was a classroom pet that did not work out. Bein' teased by the students. Wants to find it a home. No charge."

"Well, I guess one more wouldn't hurt," replied Ivan, who by now had confined the hedgehogs to one of the bathrooms with a kiddie gate installed at the door. But then he stopped cold, and quickly asked "Oops! Is this a male or a female?"

"Female," replied Pete.

Ivan relaxed and told Pete he could take her in.

Rosie woke with a start. This was the sixth day of the seven day cycles she had come to recognize. The first five days were filled with noise and commotion and the last two were very, very quiet. It went on and on like this for a very long time. Suddenly she felt hands. Miss Blodgett's hands were picking her up.

"How unusual!" Rosie thought. "On the sixth day! Hmm. What's going on?"

She was put in a box, a small box. Hardly enough room to turn around. Rosie thought, "Now what!?" It was cold outside for a moment. Then into a warm car.

Rosie had learned the difference between a cold car and a warm car, especially in cold weather. Cold cars were associated with neglectful and abusive humans who did not care about how the hedgehog felt and warm cars meant that someone had cared enough to warm it up before the hedgehog got in. Miss Blodgett's car was always warm. Rosie went on the longest ride of her life. It was pretty smooth most of the way, but she had no sense of where she was going, because she was in a little box sitting on the front seat. The box had some oblong holes she could peek through, but it was difficult and all she could see was the inside of the car.

Emily Blodgett turned in to the small parking lot of the horse/tack/pet shop. She walked in with Rosie in the box. Emily expected a warm welcome from Pete, but Pete was very, very upset. As soon as she walked in the door, Pete said "Come see this! Damndest thing I ever seen here!"

They went to the back of the store. Pete's place was an odd collection of additions that had been built onto as the business expanded. It was a small store with many rooms and uneven floors.

In the back, under a counter where insects and small animals were sold, was the mangled corpse of some small animal. They didn't know what sort of animal it was because it had been skinned! It was nothing but a bloody mass of flesh that was being attacked by several species of insects. Pete pointed to the ear holes and speculated that the remnants of the ears were filled with mites and maggots.

Emily recoiled in horror. "What could have happened? Have you ever seen anything like this before?" she asked Pete.

"Never!" exclaimed Pete.

As Emily and Pete were staring at the lifeless mass before them, Rosie peeked through a slit in the box that Emily was still carrying. What Rosie saw made her blood run cold and her heart sink. She started to visibly weep and could not stop. She thought she would never stop. "What has this world come to? What has caused this horror?"

Upset at the sight, but nowhere near as upset as Rosie, Pete and Emily greeted Ivan as he arrived. Pete decided not to share with Ivan the sight of the corpse that he had found in the back room.

Rosie was taken out of the box and handed to Ivan. Rosie did not know what to make of all this as Ivan held her up and tried to get her to unroll. She was still trembling from what she had seen. Ivan held her carefully and stroked her still erect quills. Rosie relaxed a little. "Well, it can't get much worse," she thought, as she started to unroll and sniff the air with her hyperactive nose—a trait that all hedgehogs have. With hedgehogs, trust is evaluated by scent since the nose provides the most information of all their senses.

There were new smells here. What the Bigs called leather. A new human called Ivan. He held her carefully and stroked her still erect quills. Rosie relaxed a little. Then Ivan said, "What a tiny girl for an adult hedgehog." At that time being 2 years and three months of age, Rosie was fully an adult hedgehog, and would be about 36 years of age if she were a human. "She seems very scared," Ivan said, "we'll see what we can do."

The Bigs engaged in conversation and Rosie settled in and semi-snuggled into Ivan's hand. She overheard that there was someone named Flash, who seemed sick. Another hedgehog that was old and was called Thelmer. There was another called Louise that was crazy. Rosie wondered what lay ahead for her, and what kind of a place she was heading to.

Back in the box. "Sheesh, why can't I at least see and hear and smell where we are going?" Rosie thought. "Cardboard is too mushy-smelling, can't get by bearings." But the ride was short this time. Out of the car and into a building. A carpeted building. Doesn't smell too bad at all. Out of the box.
YIKES!
A face!
A HEDGEHOG face!
"Who are you!?" Rosie squeaked, startled. Hedgehogs almost never make audible noises, even though they are capable of a very wide range of sounds. After all, what's the use if you can mentally communicate?

Over millions of years, hedgehogs and other ancient animals have learned to communicate by mental telepathy. Humans sometimes call it instinct, but what do they know? As may be expected, communication across species becomes more difficult. Few humans can clearly communicate with mammals and communication between, say, insects and mammals, or reptiles and plants, or plants and birds, are difficult undertakings for all except the most gifted communicators.

"I'm Louise," came the answer. Louise was quite young, probably not over seven months old, peppy, and seemed happy. "Welcome," Louise said, "you are going to love it here. Plenty of room, good food, nice water you can drink from a bowl and not a tube, and very, very good friends. Even the Bigs are nice. Can you imagine that? But, best of all, there is Thelma, the old wise one. She will sooth your little soul. You are going to be all right. You don't look so good right now, but you are going to be all right."

Somehow, Rosie believed her. For the first time in a very long time, her thoughts went back to her old friends Tadeusz, Qambe, Dolmen, and their kindness and wisdom. She wondered if she would ever see any of them again. But she knew full well that one of them was gone forever.

CHAPTER 4

A "PIGMENT" OF HER IMAGINATION

Louise the Wild One

CHAPTER 4—A PIGMENT OF HER IMAGINATION

"Tell me more about Thelmer, the old, wise one." Rosie asked Louise.

"Well, she's so gentle and kind, you're going to really love her. But," Louise hesitated for a moment, "but, there's a scary part, too."

"Scary part?"

"I shouldn't bother you with it, Rosie," said Louise, "it's just that pogs* like Thelma not only talk through thinking in the present, like we all do, but can think and talk through time. They see things as they were long ago and sometimes see into the future. They have a bigger gift of time and space than we ordinary pogs do. That's why we look to them for advice. That's scary sometimes. Especially about the fierce monsters."

"M-m-m-monsters?" Rosie asked.

"Uh oh, looks like you're going up, Rosie," Louise exclaimed, "believe me."

Rosie looked at Louise quizzically and asked "What're you talking about?"

"You'll see, but don't be scared. You probably won't like it much, but you won't be hurt," Louise offered just as two big human hands came down and scooped up a startled Rosie.

"Bye, Lady," said Louise, "see you soon. Try to relax when the air comes at you, it's the best part."

Rosie was swept upwards and placed into some sort of bin.

"Two seventy," said Ivan the human, as he wrote the number on a clipboard holding a form. By now Ivan was getting organized, and he was displeased. Very displeased. It seemed a long time back when Flash had come to live with them in 1996, when he began reading up on pet hedgehogs. He had been involved in wolf rescue and came to be a real cynic when it came to the wealth of bad information out there in the public about wolves and wolf-dogs.

---

* Pog: A slang term for hedgehog. Some say the term is sort of a combination of the term pig and hog.

Now it seemed that the scene was repeating itself—more bad information. This time it was hedgehogs. Hedgehogs had become "fad" pets. Not only had their prices skyrocketed, but people were writing all sorts of "pet care" books about them that contained large amounts of outdated and downright harmful information on proper diet, environment, and other care issues. This misinformation, once discovered, started him on a "rescue" mission that was just beginning.

Rosie realized that Ivan was writing down her weight—270 grams. It was a daily ritual that would be repeated, day after day, for as long as she lived there. Pretty light for an adult African hedgehog, whose normal adult weight should be between 375 and 450 grams (which is just under one pound). But Rosie had always been a small, wiry girl.

She was not prepared for what was to happen next, as she was carried into a small room that was warmer than the other rooms and let down gently into a bigger bin. This bin had a strange device at the bottom that went up and down. Above was a large tube. Ivan called the thing a "sink." Rosie was picked up again. A stream of water began to flow from the tube.

Ivan adjusted the controls for the tube and Rosie was let back down into a pool of warm water. The water went all over her and she panicked . . . and ran . . . and ran. But the sides of the "sink" were slippery and she slid back over and over into the rising water. Suddenly the device at the bottom of the sink opened and the water ran out. But then it was closed again and the water rose. This happened several times and Rosie continued to run. Then, as she was getting a little tired, Ivan brought a bottle with soft sides over the water and squeezed it and a white liquid came out into the water. There was a sweet smell to this strange liquid, but Rosie did not feel in the least like tasting it and anointing.# She was too terrified of the whole affair. Then there were bubbles, lots of little bubbles.

This whole business was getting too weird! Holding her and splashing this stuff all over her, Ivan emerged with a small brush he called a "toothbrush"

\#   Anointing: Hedgehogs have several habits that are not found in other mammals, such as rolling up in a protective ball and the action known as "anointing" or "self-anointing." When a hedgehog encounters a new smell, s/he often licks the object carrying the scent, works up a froth in the mouth, and plasters the foam with the new scent over the quills with the tongue. Humans do not seem to know why hedgehogs do this, but some speculate that the purpose is to blend in more with surroundings or that the hedgehog may think that the new scent will provide protection is spread on the quills.

and began brushing her quills, front to back. This continued for several minutes and did not really seem all that unpleasant. In fact, were she not so scared, it could have been enjoyable. She felt the dirt and grime leave her and was really feeling better. The sink was emptied and Rosie was rinsed with clear, warm water, and brushed again. She had never felt this clean at any point that she could remember.

Ivan leaned over the sink and whispered, "I'm sorry, girl, but we have to do this."

Rosie was picked up and what she saw below did not look pleasant. Below her was a plastic tub containing water with brown "bubbles" in it. She was placed down into the tub and the oily water completely covered her.

"Well, this is it," she thought. But it only lasted for a second until she and the "bubbly water" were dumped back into the sink. Rosie quickly unrolled and tried to run out of the sink one more time. No luck. The sink was even more slippery than with the stuff Ivan called "shampoo." The device at the bottom of the sink opened again—Ivan called it a "drain"—and the bubbly water was gone leaving Rosie feeling very slippery.

Jenna briefly joined Ivan and asked "What was that all about?"

Ivan replied, "olive oil immersion bath—kills any mites that may be on her."

Jenna said "Well, she sure looks sort of greasy and forlorn."

Rosie agreed.

After a few more rinses, Rosie was wrapped up in a towel and she heard yet another strange new noise. A big sort of continuous "whoosh." Ivan dried her off with the towel and turned her over. She was having none of this and rolled up into as secure a ball as she could. However, the noise got the best of her and she peeked out to find a warm current of air blowing over her from a large device being held by Ivan several feet away. It was not a bad feeling, but Rosie had had enough of this for one day, so she stayed pretty well rolled up until the warm wind went away.

Finally, she was wrapped in the towel and gently placed on the floor in this warm room. Darkness came. Rosie rested and wondered what further strange things lay in store for her. Suddenly she thought about the last words she and Louise exchanged—about Thelmer and the monsters and speaking through time. It was all so weird.

"Hi, Rosie," came the voice. A new voice.

"Wha . . . what?" Rosie said, exhausted and thinking she was dreaming. "Who are you?"

She saw nothing in the blackness, but smelled a new, strange, scent. Hedgehog? Male hedgehog?

There was a hedgehog-shaped shadow up on top of the kiddie gate, of all places.

"I'm Bozeman. Not supposed to be here. Yet."

"Do you want to talk to me?"

"Yes. You're the only one who'll listen to me right now. You can help me when I need it. We think alike. I've heard how you act and speak, and I trust you. I can't approach the wise ones yet."

"Why can't you approach them?" Rosie asked.

"Because they think I'm crazy."

"Why would they think that?" Rosie pressed on.

"Well, because I am," said Bozeman. "But being crazy does not mean that I'm stupid. Anyway, there will be a time when they will need me."

"OK, Bozeman, you know I listen to everyone," answered Rosie.

"Of course. That's why I want to speak to you," replied Bozeman. "A bunch of us hedgehogs in a pet store have been approached by a some cockroaches and ants, and even a couple of mites who I could not understand. They wanted to talk to us about doing something with them."

"Gee, that's pretty crazy!" Rosie exclaimed.

"Umm, we've already discussed the crazy part," Bozeman replied. "They want us to assist them in killing Bigs. Millions and millions of Bigs. Maybe all of the Bigs."

"What's their problem?"

"They say that the Bigs are ruining everything and the only way to solve the problem is to get rid of them," answered Bozeman.

"Why did they talk to you about joining them?" Rosie asked.

"BECAUSE THEY THINK I'M CRAZY!" Bozeman shouted, exasperated. "Umm, sorry, shouldn't have yelled. Anyway, the other hedgehogs in the pet store told them I was."

"And what do they want you to do?" Rosie continued.

"Don't know yet. They were pretty vague. They want me to attend meetings. They said something about some of us hedgehogs acting as a diversion while they set up the mass killing of Bigs. I don't know what they plan, but they threatened me," concluded Bozeman.

"Threatened you?"

"They said they'd kill me like they've killed other hedgehogs recently, if I did not go along with them. They also said that more resolute hedgehogs, such as our leaders and wise ones would have to be killed if they got in the way, and that they were not even going to try to recruit them."

"What're you going to do?" Rosie asked.

"Act crazy, which is not a hard job for me. I'll try to learn what they are up to. Then I'll let the elders know and hope it's not too late. I just need you to stick up for me with the Dowagers and Seekers, Rosie. I'll try to let you know as often as I can. If they kill me, you can tell the others."

"How can they kill you, they're just bugs? Heck, we are insectivores. We eat bugs!"

"Now you know that we do not eat mites. Too small. And we do not eat cockroaches. Too yucky. The mites get in your ears. Way down in your ears, hundreds and thousands of them and they drive you nuts and out of balance. Then, when you cannot move, the cockroaches come in and eat you from the outside in. You may have heard about that poor fellow in the horse tack and pet shop."

With that, Rosie started to cry and put her head down on the soft towel. Everything was then quiet as Bozeman quietly scampered down the other side of the kiddie gate and waddled off into the night.

The light came back as swiftly as it had disappeared, a strange thing Rosie had become used to living in the captive human world of artificial light. Nothing was gentle about this human world; everything was abrupt. She was disoriented as she awoke and was distressed about a very bad dream she had about evil bugs, a crazy hedgehog named Bozeman, and memories of the horror she had seen at the tack shop. After exploring a bit, Rosie was back inside the towel. She was lifted up and Ivan removed her from the towel.

He stroked her quills and tried to reach up underneath her, but she stayed rolled up. "She feels warm and dry," he said to no one in particular and, carrying her back to the room where she first met Louise, gently placed her on the floor of the room.

It did not seem that Louise had ever left. "Hi," she said.

"What was THAT?" Rosie chirped.

"It's called a bath," said Louise. "Some of us really look forward to it. Flash loves 'em."

"I dunno," croaked Rosie, "might take getting used to. Pretty scary, but I didn't get hurt."

"I don't think you'll get hurt here. This is a special place," replied Louise, "but it's time you got to meet Flash."

Rosie wondered to herself what, on Earth, was going on here? Compared to her time at the Lonsey's animal mill, the horrible pet shop seemed OK and compared to the pet shop, the school was even better. But, all in all, it was all pretty bad. This place was absolutely unreal! She had only been here for 24 hours and it seemed absolutely crazy. That "bath" last night! That dream she had with the "visit" from a crazy hedgehog named Bozeman. BUT, of course, that visit was, well, just a . . . just a . . . well . . . "pigment of her imagination." And it sure was not a "figment," which seemed much more fleeting. Naw, this was a "pigment," which was indelibly inscribed into her memory.

That towel and the warm room! This strange Louise that she knew was a hedgehog but that seemed like a VERY strange hedgehog indeed with her nervous energy and very big ears. Not to mention the very long snout! What sort of weird hedgehog was Louise anyway? And now this Flash character!

But Louise continued, "It's better that Miss Flash introduce you to Thelma. I'm nervous around Thelma, she's just too deep and too far back in time for me. I'm just a simple, zippy, independent, ol' desert hedgehog. Don't get me wrong, I'm all for fighting for the welfare of us all, but what Thelma brings up is scary!"

"How's that?" Rosie asked, continuing the conversation that broke off just before she was snatched up for the bath.

"She thinks through time, Rosie," Louise whispered, "back through her ancestors, millions of springtimes ago, back through her ancient names, back to her old name of Xenortha. She speaks of horrible monsters with scales and tails and huge sharp teeth and, and . . ." Louise shuddered, "flaming red eyes that can see through you and burn."

Rosie gulped, "my goodness," as her remaining eye grew wide.

"And these big birds with razor sharp teeth that would come after us hedgehogs, millions of springtimes ago," continued Louise. "She tells of how we survived the red, liquid rocks and the deep, dark water, and the darkness and finally the great cold that killed almost everything else. It is terrifying," concluded Louise, seeming a little weary in the remembering.

"How does she know that?" Rosie asked.

"Like I said, she travels back through time," continued Louise, "and she is not the only one that does that. There are others, but only a few. They are the powerful guides that we have relied upon for millions of springtimes to keep us alive. One was Bohuslava The Great, whom we all know, the issuer of the Original Instructions over 60 million springtimes ago. But it gets worse, much worse."

"W . . . w . . . w . . . worse?" Rosie asked.

"Worse," continued Louise, "because we did not only survive but we discovered, or rather hedgehogs like Bohuslava and Thelma discovered, that also moving through time was a great evil, a dark destructive force. It was and is a force that counterbalances peaceful and happy lives and throws the world out of balance. Down through the ages beings were taken over by this force that seeks to not only destroy tranquility but the Earth itself, maybe all of creation. This is done on all scales, large as well as small."

Louise, seemingly growing even more weary, quite the opposite of her usually bouncy personality, struggled to a conclusion: "These forces are here today as they have been for millions of springtimes. The old scaly flying monsters with burning red eyes may be gone, but now there are metal flying monsters with burning red eyes called lasers. The horror has not departed. Thelma is concerned that within these new beings, the humans, this dark force has finally reached the capability to achieve the ultimate destruction. Anyway, Rosie, I think Thelma is here, in this very place, for a reason. You are the fourth hedgehog to show up here. She says that more are coming to this place. I think she is going to try to do something about all of this."

Rosie sat and pondered as Louise sauntered off for a moment. Louise' words echoed in her head in bits and pieces . . . evil . . . dark . . . all scales . . . red burning eyes . . . large as well as small . . . humans. Her thoughts traveled back to the hedgehog "mill" of the Lonseys and a bit of clarity came over her. "Dark and evil it indeed was," she thought.

#

They were in a room that was the largest and cleanest place Rosie had ever been in. It seemed to go on forever but it really was not all that big, perhaps seven by seven feet. It was actually what he humans called a "bathroom," and was reserved for the hedgehogs with the door being blocked by another of those things known as a "kiddie gate." There were no wood chips and the air was fresh and clean. Water was in bowls and not in bottles and metal tubes that hurt and sometimes broke your teeth. The food was pretty good, but all of it was dry food. There was a strange round device in the room that Louise called their "wheel." On the floor there were various things that Louise called blank newspaper and towels and hedgiehouses and logs. There were plenty of places to hide. Rosie was nervous but she was liking this place more than any place she had ever been. She kept saying over and over to herself, "What's the catch?"

Rosie eyed Louise and asked "What is that 'wheel' thing?" Rosie had seen things that looked a little like the wheel thing in the pet store. For a time she even had one in her tiny enclosure, but she could never get the hang of it. She had tried to get it to move like the gerbils and hamsters did, but her legs kept falling through the rungs. "Rodents," she thought, "are graceful and sure-footed." Sometimes she wished she were a rodent and not as clumsy and plodding as a hedgehog. The rodents seem to have so much fun on their wheels.

Louise said that the wheel was a special exercise wheel for hedgehogs. "It does not have those dangerous rungs that will break your leg. It's much more sturdy and has a plastic mesh floor. They are made in a place called Canada by a very kind human named Curt."

"Hmmm," Rosie mused, "seems like it's a little repetitious, running and not getting anywhere."

"Yeah," said Louise, "I guess it's this modern world we live in. All of the long-ago things we used to do have been replaced by machines. Goes for the humans, too. We used to forage and hunt for bugs and other food in the wild, but now our food comes in bowls and we have to run on a wheel thing to stay in shape. Humans do not hunt and gather any more and have to go to health clubs and use exercise machines. Weird, huh?"

As Rosie contemplated the wheel, Louise had disappeared and returned accompanied by a very large hedgehog with an astonishingly kind face. Louise introduced Flash to Rosie and Rosie just sat there and blinked with her remaining eye.

Flash immediately said, in an almost inaudible tone, "Welcome, Rosie, to your new home."

Rosie stammered, "I . . . I am glad to be here."

Flash and Louise sat motionless.

Rosie continued, "I've never seen a place like this before."

More silence.

Rosie spoke again, "Everything is so clean, everyone so friendly, even the human! Am I dreaming?"

Flash finally spoke, "No, you are not dreaming. This place is very wonderful compared with what we are used to, which is what the humans call 'the animal industry.'"

"Industry?" Rosie whispered, all of a sudden thinking hushed tones were in order.

"Yes, Industry!" Flash intoned much more loudly, "where the humans buy and sell souls as products!"

Rosie searched for words, stumbled around, and finally muttered, "Er, ahh, is that legal?"

"Rowww-Zeeee!" Louise exclaimed, sounding exasperated "Do the math, kid, where were you imprisoned, and sold and bought, and thrown away?"

Rosie hung her head and mumbled, "Well, yeah."

Flash suddenly raised her head and, with an air of authority, said, "in any case, here we are. We are at least in a fairly safe place. Here we are not going to be bought or sold or sent to a death place. Here we can, perhaps build something, something that can teach others about the survival that we have managed for so long."

Louise inclined her head. "And whom are we going to teach?"

Flash looked a little nonplussed and said, "first of all other hedgehogs, and then other animals, and even maybe the Bigs, the humans," and then added, "perhaps before it is too late."

Rosie's mind flashed back to the earlier conversation with Louise, of fierce red-eyed monsters and the Lonseys mill, and even the Original Instructions.

Louise reared back and shook her head. "Look, Flash, with all deference to your greater age and experience, and perhaps realizing that I am just a simple-minded Egyptian desert hedgehog, don't you really think that what you are proposing is ridiculous?"

Flash did not seem to be emotionally moved or impressed. Flash continued, "The Earth is failing, Louise, it is dying. We have survived on this Earth for tens of millions of years. The Original Instructions spoke to that survival and, yes, we were admonished never to reveal those instructions to other beings. To do so would bring us down into the pit of destruction where so many others have gone. Just look at what happened to the dinosaurs. But, over the millions of years since those instructions, things have changed. These new beings are among us now, these humans. They know no boundaries, and they know no respect for anything other than their own kind, and often not even then. They are destroying this planet. When they do they will take us with them."

"Oh, I don't know," Louise said, "perhaps it's best to be rid of them and we can hunker down for a few million years and wait for the planet to bloom again after they've gone."

Rosie just sat there taking all of this in. She thought that Flash's suggestions were certainly new and novel. Rosie had never entered into philosophical discussions with anyone, she had always just sat and listened. She had the most respect for the very wise hedgehog Tadeusz and always marveled at his wisdom, but had never heard such large questions put to him as Flash and Louise were now raising. She wondered how Tadeusz would respond to such questions and longed for him to be here to hear them.

Louise wandered off and scooted under the blank newsprint.

Flash looked at Rosie and said, "Louise is a very traditional girl. She is young and straightforward and she represents her ancestors well, her Egyptian desert ancestors. Few of her kind ever were brought to these shores. But she always impresses me with her devoted and strong views: The Original Instructions must not be shared, ever. That is the key to our survival as a species, she says. Many others agree with her. I do not, but I do not begrudge her those views, for who is to know who is right?"

"But come along with me now, because I have a lot to tell you before you meet Thelma," said Flash. "While you are going to like your surroundings here, you are probably going to become more scared and maybe even more sad than you were in those other places. You are going to find out some things you probably didn't want to know."

"About the red eyed monsters that burn?" Rosie asked.

"Perhaps," replied Flash, "the modern ones."

CHAPTER 5

FACING REALITY

Tadeusz the Thinker

CHAPTER 5—FACING REALITY

"There's awful things going on, Rosie," sighed Flash. "For the first time there are out of balance hedgehogs doing and saying the strangest things."

"You mean like Louise?" Rosie asked, bewildered.

"No, no, not like Louise," continued Flash, "Louise is simply a traditional. No, there are others who seem to have lost all sense of propriety and place. It's really worrying Thelma. Hedgehogs who, for the first time ever, seem like aliens and act in reckless and foolish ways."

"Well, many of us have a good sense of humor!"

"When I say foolish, I don't mean a sense of humor, Rosie," Flash said. "I mean foolish as in acting inappropriately and being impolite and seeming to forget all manners toward other hedgehogs."

"Oh," said Rosie, "I knew a fellow like that back at that mill place. His name was Bowls. Also, I had a dream the other night about a nutty hedgehog named Bozeman. He sure seemed off his rocker."

"Funny you should bring up Bozeman," replied Flash, "the crazy magician. Are you sure it was a dream? Bozeman comes up with such outlandish things, you THINK you were dreaming. Or you WISH you were dreaming!"

"Magician?" Rosie asked.

"Well, not really," Flash replied. "It's just that he does such outlandish things and can escape from almost any sort of place that we all call him a magician. He's just creative. And goofy."

"He spoke about talking with mites and cockroaches and killing all of the Bigs. He mentioned the skinned hedgehog found dead at the horse tack shop," as Rosie started crying again. "I hope that was only a dream, too."

Unfortunately that was no dream, Rosie," responded Flash. "It was a frightening act of violence that we do not understand. It has Thelma very, very worried."

Through the tears, Rosie asked, "What . . . what does such a horror mean? The hedgehog that had been killed was so kind, so gentle. He never hurt anyone."

Flash looked startled, "You knew that hedgehog? You knew he was a male? We knew nothing about him . . . or her, except for the horrible way in which he died. It was just reported to us by the Mouse Messenger Service, the MMS. The little mice were so scared they spread the word all over to all the hedgehogs they knew around here. We think they saw it happen but they were too scared to say, except that they knew it was a hedgehog that had been killed."

Rosie sobbed further, "Of course I knew him! The sheared off front fang was unmistakable. He was my dear little friend, Dolmen. From the mill. Dear, sweet Dolmen." She trailed off into sobs.

"I've lived with Thelma now for nearly two years," Flash continued. "Back in the beginning, Thelma was mainly interested in coming up with a way to try to teach the humans to live according to the Original Instructions. That's still her aim, but she seems more worried about something else right now. Terrible events like the death of Dolmen."

Rosie asked Flash, drying her eye, "Well, what if we share these secrets, the Original Instructions, with the humans? What good will it possibly do?"

"Possibly nothing, maybe everything. One never knows until one tries."

"How can we do it?" Rosie asked. "Humans can only communicate on one dimension—orally or by their symbols."

Flash mentioned that there are ways to communicate through special humans with extraordinary communication gifts or through their symbols, their talking leaves called books, for example.

"A few Bigs, very few," said Flash, "can communicate with us. Some much better than others. They speak as we do, through mental images. But only certain hedgehogs, the most imaginative and gifted, can engage in these communications."

"So, Flash," continued Rosie, "the Bigs are similar to us in that we both have only a few special and wise beings among us that can communicate between species?"

"Yes," answered Flash, "that's right. And other beings have their few that can speak to other species as well. It's all a grand mystery of the Universe."

Rosie still seemed skeptical, but she was not without fascination for this new friend she had made. "Such headstrong characters," she thought, "this Louise and Flash, so courteous towards one another and yet so distant as to what should be done."

But Rosie was curious about Flash, too, and wondered what her life had been like here at this wonderful place, before Louise and even before Thelma. Flash had been bought at the same pet store that had yielded up Louise and was the transfer point for Rosie, herself. It was also the same place where Dolmen had met his horrible death.

In the beginning Jenna had taken Flash with her everywhere she went, even by air. Jenna simply plunked Flash in her coat pocket as she walked through airport security and Flash was very good at lying low while in transit and was never detected. Of course, this was in the days before all of the heightened airport security.

Flash told Rosie, of course, that the Original Instructions had been around so long that hedgehogs around the world were naturally aware of them soon after they were born. They were as much a part of their makeup as self-anointing or rolling up.

"Many of the humans suspect we have secrets that we are not sharing," Flash continued, "they even write about it in their talking leaves. Some of them know that they are destroying our home with all sorts of foolish things. What they call industrial stuff. Stuff that leaves poisonous and tasteless food, bad water, bad air, almost anything you can name. Then they try to kill one another in huge numbers in events they call 'war.' Smart, eh? Of course, if they were to clear their minds, they could figure out the Original Instructions for themselves. But they won't. Maybe they can't."

This was all getting a little over Rosie's head. She never regarded herself as much of a philosopher pog. "Well," she told Flash, "I'm not sure I see the big picture but I sure have seen the bad side of life with the Bigs. How can they have so little respect?"

"I dunno," replied Flash, "that's beyond me, too. Seems they do not have much of anything but greed and viciousness. But, you know, us hedgehogs are beginning to argue among one another, too."

"Oh, I know!" Rosie exclaimed, recalling the bad times at Lonsey's "mill" and especially the belligerent hedgehog, Bowls.

"Well, it's bigger than that," Flash said, "there's a controversy as to whether the humans ought to be told the Original Instructions after all. Some hedgehogs say that these humans are going to kill everything on the planet and need the guidance before it is too late. Thelma says this, but Louise disagrees. Louise is much more traditional, not to mention independent. She says the Bigs will do what they are going to do and cannot take or follow advice. She thinks if we tell them of the Original Instructions they will devise ways to kill us."

"But why? Why would they want to kill us?"

"Because," said Flash, "it's an age-old fact about how Bigs think: What they don't know, they fear, and what they fear they try to destroy. Bigs only try to learn from one another and never from anything non-human. Why, they do not learn from one another very well."

"I guess I can see why Louise is suspicious of the Bigs," said a reflective Rosie.

Flash continued: "She thinks the Bigs are a part of the dark destruction that will end all life. She likes very few humans and she was almost killed herself just before coming here, just because she couldn't be sold in a pet store."

"But," Rosie said, "even if we decide to tell the Bigs of the Original Instructions that have kept us alive for so long, how can we communicate with them? They have such limited means of communication. All they can do is squawk and make talking leaves. And even in their squawking, their different groups do not even understand one another!"

"Umm, there are ways," Flash replied, "AGAIN, perhaps through some of the humans that have special gifts, perhaps through talking leaves. Our best thinkers can figure it out. Speaking of best thinkers, perhaps it is time you met Thelma."

"Thelmer?" Rosie asked.

"Yes," replied Flash, "our Grand Old Lady, our old wise one. All of the hedgehogs look up to her and treat what she says with respect. Even Louise, who is very independent and very traditional, still listens to Thelma with utmost respect. Although independent, a wonderful thing about Louise is how honest she is. She is always giving others credit for being smarter than she, calling herself 'only' a desert hedgehog with big ears and 'only' being a youngster. But she is much smarter than she lets on. And she is a good and loyal friend. A treasure."

Flash continued: "There are a human people native to this continent the big bunch of Bigs call 'Natives' or 'Native People.' Some of these Natives have a word for what I think Louise is like—'heyoka.' Heyoka means crazy, backwards, contrary, or someone who always calls into question whatever others say. That's why she's a treasure. No one gets away with anything that Louise does not call into question."

"Doesn't Thelmer get annoyed with Louise?"

"Oh no," replied Flash, "Thelma gets annoyed with no one. I think she is far above that. She is so kind and wise, she carries with her the wisdom of millions of years and is one of those rare hedgehogs that carries the weight of all time for us with such grace. It's amazing."

"You know," said Rosie, "I knew such a hedgehog like that once. His name was Tadeusz."

"I think there are a few such as that," said Flash, "and I think their spirits cross back and forth over the Rainbow Bridge that connects us to the spirit world, the Great Country of Souls, to come back and help us here on this difficult side. How else could you explain such old and wise spirits as Thelma and Tadeusz? So much wisdom could not be gathered in just one lifetime."

"Oohhhh, Flash," said Rosie, "you are losing me again. I'm just a simple little Algerian girl."

"Now you're sounding like Louise!" Flash giggled. "But you'll have time to learn and to live here in peace. You will be far from the horrors you have seen. There are a few humans who see to that. Now where Louise is a heyoka, an old English hedgehog known simply as The Elder seems to have laid a label upon old Thelma, calling her The Grand Dowager."

"Dowager?" Rosie asked.

"Yep, means dignified old lady, or something like that." Flash continued, "Far as I can tell, she's somewhere between the Dalai Lama and the Queen Mum, in human terms."

"Who are those?"

"Some wise humans," answered Flash. "We see a lot of the world around us and pay very close attention to all. These Bigs, for instance, have done a lot in their short time in this world, mostly bad. But they have done a few good things, too. We pay attention to all of it, the good and the bad. We learn from it all. Sometimes we take lessons from humans. Take General Spikers, for example."

"General Spikers?" Rosie asked. "Who or what is that?"

"Hmm, never heard of Major General Spikers, United Hedgehog Marine Corps, the famous warrior commander?"

"Nope," replied Rosie, "sounds impressive, though."

"Well, Major General Spikers, a fearless hedgehog in battle, has for years tried to convince the Dowagers that we hedgehogs ought to take a few lessons from silly, impractical, humans in the way they organized in military formations to stamp out organized bunches of other humans that were doing evil things. Spikers wanted to organize his own hedgehog military division to 'combat' something."

"What was it he wanted to combat?" Rosie asked.

"HAHAHAHA," Flash shook with laughter, "that was just it, he didn't know! He just wanted to combat 'something' and he felt that he needed a big bunch of organized hedgehogs and other animals to do it, whatever 'it' was. So he goes to the dowagers with this foolish idea and all of us were convinced that the dowagers would laugh him back to Nigeria . . . or even further away. But the dowagers often surprise us all in their wisdom."

"Did they not laugh him off the continent?" Rosie asked quizzically.

"NO!" Flash exclaimed, "quite the contrary. They gave approval to his idea and then allowed him to put together an organized hedgehog military group of his own."

"Couldn't he have done that by himself? Without approval of the dowagers?"

"Well, he COULD have," replied Flash, "but he was smart enough to seek approval of the old, wise ones, the Dowagers and the Seekers."

"Seekers?" Rosie asked, again puzzled.

"Male versions of the Dowagers," replied Flash matter-of-factly. "In order for us hedgehogs to be truly survivors, we must respect our community and those among us gifted with wisdom. Not all creatures of a species are equally wise. We know that. We look to those who are wisest if we know what is good for us. I'll bet you know some hedgehogs who are not wise, even though you have been isolated for a long time."

Oh, YES!" exclaimed Rosie, "there was that obnoxious hedgehog Bowls at that horrible mill where I lived. He seemed so strange and out of place. He really worried me."

"Hmm," reflected Flash," it's that sort of hedgehog that worries Thelma. It seems that she has heard of more and more of them showing up. Years ago, you hardly ever heard of someone like this Bowls character."

"I think I knew a seeker there, too," said Rosie. "Tadeusz. He was wise and kind. There was a fighter there, too, named Ukuqambe. But he was not like Bowls. He was kind and fiercely fought for good things."

"Sounds like Major General Spikers, who finally thought of something he could battle," added Flash.

"You mean that the Dowagers gave him approval to form a hedgehog military organization and also asked him to figure out what it was he was going to battle?" Rosie asked incredulously.

"Yes, they did." Flash replied. "You see, the Dowagers are wise beyond our comprehension. Useless to try to second-guess them. They may not have known about Spikers' scheme or if it would somehow work, but they did know Spikers. They knew he was an honorable hedgehog as well as a fearless one. They knew, as Thelma put it in her priceless way of saying things, 'that if something needed fighting, Spikers was the pog for the job.' So, they decided that he could be trusted to figure out what needed fighting. In the absence of anything bigger or more organized to fight, Spikers proclaimed that it was the mission of his new hedgehog combat division to fight animal abuse. The dowagers could not fault him there."

"And off he went to form up his hedgehog military organization modeled after human armies," sighed Rosie.

"Yes, he did," continued Flash, "but not just any human army. Actually only two human armies that we ever heard about. Those were the Boeotian army of ancient human Greece under General Epaminondas and the Third United States Army under General George S. Patton, Jr. Spikers was always muttering something about an army having to have a 'soul' and a just cause where the soldiers are also citizens. The Boeotian army of farmers defeated the professional soldiers of Sparta because they only wished to be left alone to raise their families and their crops. The U.S. Third Army fought against the evil human Hitler."

"Well, just one more little question," continued Rosie. "If Spikers was so impressed by these two armies, why did he opt to form up a Marine division?"

"Spikers had an answer for that, too," said Flash. "Spikers is a stickler for discipline and he said it was his opinion that no service had it tougher and had to be more disciplined than the Marines. Of course, he was quick to compliment the other services in getting tough jobs done, but it seemed his heart was always with the Marines. Earlier in his life, apparently he had trained as a Marine and had a human Marine mentor, an old retired general. Besides, he always said that in his opinion the toughest combat role was hitting the beach. And so it came to be that Spikers formed up the Second Hedgehog Marine Division (Mechanized)."

"Mechanized?" Rosie asked.

"Umm, yup . . . mechanized," Flash continued. "Spikers opined that he needed 'just a little' modern equipment if he had to do battle with animal abusers."

"Like that terrible place that I came from?"

"Yes," replied Flash. "Spikers set up his division in an ingenious way. All of the officers of the division, the commanders and the staff, were hedgehogs. All of the enlisted members of the division, the privates, corporals, and sergeants, were to be other mammals, possibly including humans, depending upon the type of operation."

"Why was that?" Rosie asked.

"Well, as captive beings in the so-called 'pet trade' in North America, we hedgehogs are maintained by humans. The soldiers and sergeants in the military actually fight and win the battles, for the most part. So while the hedgehogs will do the planning and the commanding, the more numerous humans or other mammals will and must fight the battles."

"Wow!" Rosie exclaimed. "Sounds like a good idea. I can speak from experience that there are some pretty cruel places around here that need combating."

"Except," added Flash, "that lately Thelma has been thinking of calling upon Major General Spikers and his Second Hedgehog Marine Division (Mechanized) to assist in some sort of new 'mission.' Thelma sees something terrible happening. Something beyond animal abuse and the general human misbehavior we have come to know and hate. Something worse than cities and pollution. Something really terrible. She is very worried and has not really been herself lately."

"I'm afraid to ask," said Rosie in almost a whisper.

"I, myself, am not sure what it is," said Flash, "but Thelma will tell us when she feels we are ready. There is one more thing you need to know, Rosie, before I take you to see the old wise one."

"I have heard much today," said Rosie quietly.

"I may not be with you much longer," said Flash also in a soft voice. "So little has been known about us by the humans up until now that many of us are sick from poor surroundings and food that is not suited for us. Don't blame Ivan and Jenna, because they did not know any better and had received bad advice. Even the books written about our care were bad."

"Wha . . . what happened? You look so nice and healthy," exclaimed Rosie.

"It was the food," sighed Flash. "Great stuff. We loved it. Yum! But it was awful for us. Lots of eggs. The care books on us said we loved the stuff, and we did! When I was not feeling so well, Ivan took me to a special human called a veterinarian. That's a human that is specialized in medicine for us animals. Like with everything else, some of these veterinarians are better than others. But this veterinarian specializes in us hedgehogs! She was very nice and really knew a lot about us. She really let Ivan have it when he told her what we had been eating. She put a cup over my face and I fell asleep. She said she examined me and took some blood. Later, Ivan talked with Jenna and told her Thelma and I were sick from what we were being fed. Ivan came and saw us and said he was sorry. He really seemed sad."

"But . . . but, Flash," whispered Rosie.

"Don't worry for me," reassured Flash. "Our visit here on Earth is really very short. I am so happy for my life here and my time with that grand old wise lady, and the zany Miss Louise, and you, too, Rosie. Even the humans, I love them, too. And they love us, as much as they are capable of, given their species. The veterinarians they call Doctor Lisa or Doctor Jolene did not have very good news for me, so I know my time is limited with you. It's my liver. It is sick and they do not think it will recover. Things are better for Thelma, though. She arrived later and is also older, so we think she will recover. The food is now no where near as much fun. That sure was good while it lasted. But I guess the new stuff is good for us now."

"Where do we go, Flash, when we leave?" asked Rosie.

"Another place, another world, Rosie" continued Flash, "a world where one recovers from the hurts and harm of this world. There is a Bridge that we all cross made up of rainbows. There are melodies that one hears that are the most beautiful you will ever hear. Thelma says that even a human has captured this music and has written it down, but you would have to ask her about that. Then, after you cross over that Bridge, all of the friends that have crossed before you will meet you there. No one is in pain any longer.

Although none of us wish to think about it, it's really all we have to hope for, after all. We shall all cross over some day. So don't feel sad for me, Rosie."

"Well, I will anyway because I love you, Flash," said Rosie quietly.

"Thank you, Rosie," said Flash. "And I love you, dear Rosie."

Flash waddled off in the general direction of the hedgiehut, probably to speak to Thelma. Rosie, alone with her thoughts once again felt very different than she ever had before. For most of her life she had worried about herself and her own safety. Now, now feeling safer than she ever had before, suddenly she worried about all hedgehogs and their safety, and this new set of fears facing Thelma. And she was worried for her friend, Flash, so bravely facing her last days among her friends. And she mourned for her little friend, Dolmen.

CHAPTER 6

SHADOWS OF THE PAST

Louise as a Youngster

CHAPTER 6—SHADOWS OF THE PAST

YIKES! Rosie was again startled as she was picked up from behind by Ivan. NOW Rosie wished she could speak directly to the human. "ENOUGH, already!" she would exclaim, "I don't need another of those bath things right now! I'm clean enough!"

But that was not what Ivan wanted. He sat down on the blue sofa bed with Rosie and just let her sit in his lap. When she relaxed a little, he softly stroked her quills.

"You've had a rough time, girl," he said.

"No kidding," Rosie thought to herself, knowing that the human could not possibly understand what she was thinking, but that she could understand the human's thoughts.

"Just know that we love you and that we will not let anything bad happen to you again," Ivan said.

Rosie relaxed her quills as he petted her, hoping he could understand just a little of exactly what that relaxation meant.

Ivan caressed and rocked her slightly and whispered, "I hope you understood me."

Rosie wondered to herself, suddenly, why the Creation was so complex. "Why can't we all speak the same language? And why can't we communicate better with the plants? Aargh! We can read the minds of mammals, but we are at a loss with trees and grass, and do not do very well at all with the beaky people the humans call birds, nor those with the skeletons outside called insects, nor even with those having scales. On the other hand, I did have a nice, although difficult conversation with a tortoise once."

Ivan sat with Rosie for a little over an hour in silence, softly stroking her quills. Rosie even relaxed so completely at a couple of points that she even dozed off momentarily. She was feeling pretty good and mellow when Ivan gently put her back in her room.

Rosie was startled to look right into Flash's eyes. "OH! I'm sorry! Guess I got pognapped."

"Time flows like a river, Rosie," Flash said, "and it is only relevant over millennia. It's something the Bigs have never learned. Seems like some of us hedgehogs are forgetting that, too."

Rosie tentatively replied: "Flash, I notice how easily you are picked up by these Bigs and how relaxed you are. I also noticed how even Louise behaves when picked up—running like crazy but still relaxed. I cannot seem to relax around these Bigs. Will I ever be able to? This Ivan seems as if he will not hurt me."

Flash, sighing deeply, replied, "Well, Rosie, you never know about Bigs. In times that go well for them, they may be your friend. But in times of difficulty, you may be cast off by them, perhaps even killed. These humans have proven themselves to be a very shallow species, largely uncaring about even their own, let alone others. I'm more comfortable around them because I've never been mistreated by them. You, on the other hand . . ."

". . . have seen some terrible things," Rosie finished the sentence. She then mused, "I wonder how I was lucky enough to finally find my way here."

Flash quickly answered, "Well, Rose, it may not have been as much of a chance event as you may think."

Rosie sat up in surprise: "What?!"

"The Dowagers and Seekers work in powerful and strange ways," Flash counseled. "It would not surprise me if Thelma somehow had you sent here."

"Of what possible use am I?" Rosie questioned.

"Well, Rosie," continued Flash, "we hedgehogs see the world in a very different light than most other beings, us being around for so long and all. Perhaps it is that the wise ones have figured out a very good use for you. But enough of our speculation! Let's go meet the Old One."

Rosie gulped. She didn't know if she was ready to partake of so much wisdom. Frankly, she was now a little scared of this legendary figure she was about to meet: The Grand Dowager.

Flash walked slightly ahead of Rosie to a large hedgiehouse. They both entered. There, toward the back of the house, sat a hedgehog. She was obviously not an ordinary hedgehog, if such could be said. She had the most penetrating eyes! Although she did not instill fear, she was to be held in awe, at least in the view of Rosie. The light was very dim. Dim light is really no problem for a hedgehog, whose eyesight is pretty poor anyway, living so close to the ground. Hedgehogs rely mainly upon scent, which is very keen, and upon hearing, which is fairly sharp as well.

Flash said quietly, "Thelma, I'd like to introduce Rosie."

Thelma looked directly into Rosie's eye, and said "Welcome, Rose, it is an honor to meet you. I have been expecting you."

"Y . . . y . . . you have?"

"Yes," said Thelma. "The Dowagers and Seekers speak freely across space and time. Tadeusz told me you were ready to come to us."

"T...t...t...Tadeusz?!" Rosie exclaimed.

"He is an old, or rather a young old friend," replied Thelma. "As contemporary age goes, Tadeusz is fairly young, but his lineage goes way, way back, even back to European hedgehogs from what we now know as Czechoslovakia—now divided—and Poland."

"But, why me?" Rosie asked.

"Tadeusz felt you would lend a spirit of depth to our undertaking here," replied Thelma. "A sort of experiential naivety."

"What?" Rosie exclaimed.

"The humans know very little about building communities, and yet much of their attitudes have rubbed off on us hedgehogs. This is mainly because these humans are so loud and crude about it. There is very little subtlety in how they act. Don't like it? Blow it up! Want what someone else has? Rob them or pick their pocket if you are poor. Cheat them out of it if you are rich," Thelma explained. "We hedgehogs have a far different approach. We bring together personalities that help us to see what the results of our efforts will be. We began this community over a year and a half ago. You are the fourth one to join us. Each has her or his job. Flash is a perfect mediator. She is wise and kind and, given time and wisdom, her spirit followers will be wiser yet, perhaps Dowagers themselves. Louise is the perfect, as they say it, *heyoka*. She questions everything! And you, dear Rose, represent the stark reality of life of what it is to be a hedgehog in the very worst of the so-called 'pet trade' in North America. You have seen the death and the pain from a number of different perspectives."

"Yes, I have," Rosie quietly replied. "But that does not mean I'm wise enough to offer advice."

"Your humility speaks volumes, Rose," replied Thelma. "You will be able to help us deal with these very serious crises we shall soon be facing."

All it took was a few moments and Rosie felt completely at home with Thelma. From the moment she laid eye on her, Rosie knew she loved her "Thelmer." Although she held Thelma in a certain degree of awe, she was more overwhelmed by her kindness and wisdom. Even just her appearance of kindness and wisdom. She was beginning to understand what hedgehogs like Tadeusz were all about.

"What are these crises, Thelmer?" Rosie, now more relaxed, asked.

"These crises are confounding even us Seekers and Dowagers, Rose," replied Thelma. "I am seriously thinking about it and will discuss it with those I trust as soon as I, myself, have a grasp of it. We have known for some time that the Bigs are ruining this home of ours. So, we have concentrated our planning and efforts about what to do about that. But recently, we have seen hedgehogs, not seekers or dowagers nor even pogs known to us as keepers of the Original Instructions, trying to gain approval to bring the Bigs to destroy one another. To me this was very disturbing. Now there is this horrible death of the hedgehog at the tack store. Flash tells me you knew him . . . Dolmen."

Rosie felt herself filling up again and choking back tears. "Y . . . y . . . yes. He was a dear friend."

Thelma gracefully but slowly got up and went to the door of the hedgiehouse, followed closely behind by Rosie. The pair stepped gently out into the wider outside air. Thelma turned around and looked at Rosie. Rosie froze in her tracks. Her one eye got very big as she stared, in disbelief, at Thelma.

There was no mistaking it, and once again Rosie was at a complete loss for words. Thelma broke the silence: "Why are you so alarmed, Rose?"

Her breath returning, Rosie gasped, almost inaudibly to Thelma, "You're Algerian!"

"Well, why not?" Thelma replied, matter-of-factly.

"But, but . . . ?" Rosie stammered.

"I guess we have been hanging around the Bigs for too long," replied Thelma. "It is a thing they call 'race' or 'racism,' or something like that, where one species thinks it is better than another species. Imagine that! There are some 14 species of hedgehogs, Rose. None better than the other. There are four 'genera,' or families of us. The bigger, browner hedgehogs that figure so highly in human folklore, are the English and European hedgehogs they call 'erinaceus.' Then there are the 'hemiechinus' hedgehogs, the desert hedgehogs, of northeast Africa and the Middle East. Louise is a desert hedgehog, as if you could not tell. Then there are the 'parachinus' hedgehogs of the Far East. Finally, there is us, the 'atelerix' African hedgehogs. Our family is of three species, Algerian, Central African, and South African. The humans like to try to preserve other animals that they have nearly wiped out. Guess they feel guilty about it. Among our hedgehog species only one the humans call 'endangered.' That would be the South African hedgehog, atelerix frontalis."

"Well, yes, but . . . ?" Rosie continued.

"Oh, there are no 'buts,' Rose," said Thelma, "life is the same no matter where or how or when it exists. Life only becomes widely painful when one species tries to dominate another. It has been going on for tens of millions of springtimes. It is hard to see the big picture of herstory, Rose. But let me say that we Algerian hedgehogs are no worse or better than any other."

"I never felt as smart as any of the others. Some of the others said bad things about us Algerians."

"You are truly smart in what you say and do, Rose," assured Thelma. "Depending upon who is in power, labels and bad words that are really meaningless are going to be spread and take on some sort of meaning. The humans, who are now the worst offenders of this, have killed and abused their own people for all of the centuries they have been here."

"Huh?" Rosie asked, a little overcome by all of this.

"Well," continued Thelma, "the humans that have come to this land from Africa have endured the identical hardships we have. They were kidnapped from their homeland, same as we were. They were forced into involuntary labor as field hands, we as pets. They were tortured or killed if they did not meet their captor's definition of 'domestication,' same as we. Louise was almost killed because some humans thought she was 'too wild.' You know, Rose, I have always been a little disappointed that the descendants of the African humans did not take up our cause. I wonder why that was?"

Rosie answered in her simple, direct, and incredibly wise way, "Perhaps they simply did not know our history. It's not like it was big news when we were arriving from Nigeria."

"Perhaps they did not . . . do not . . . know," responded Thelma. "That is a remarkable and yet simple statement, and it underlines the reasons we wish you to be with us. We need some more hedgehogs here with us as well. I think we will need another *heyoka* or two, some more contraries, perhaps older than Louise."

"Why would that be?" Rosie asked.

"Our work here heavily depends upon questioners of what we propose to do. Simply letting the Bigs in on the Original Instructions was one thing, but this new uneasiness is going to require some more drastic action. So I think we need at least one older, more seasoned *heyoka* to call us to task. Heh heh, the two of them ought to get along quite well."

"Oh, I never thought about that," Rosie said. "Do *heyokas* get along with one another?"

"Probably better than MALE hedgehogs do as a group," replied Thelma. "Isn't it interesting how the Creator has fashioned all of us? The fighting and the competition. Most of the time I cannot fathom it. What is the use of it?"

"Survival, maybe," offered Rosie. "Perhaps a way to have the weak not continue. But I guess some mysteries are beyond us."

"Indeed some are," continued Thelma. "But there are some more hedgehogs I feel we need to bring here. I think we need a keen spirit."

"Keen spirit?" Rosie quizzed. "Someone keener than Louise?"

"Oh, yes!" Thelma exclaimed. "Next to a keen spirit, all of us, including our vivacious friend Louise, are slowpokes!"

"My!" Rosie said, "THAT I've got to see."

"There is a hedgehog that lives south of here," said Thelma, "at a mass breeder's place. I think she will fill the bill. Her name is Angel."

"Ugh, mass breeder!" Rosie said.

"Well, ugh is right," continued Thelma, "but believe it or not, not all mass breeders are as bad as that place you came from. The breeder where Angel lives is a big improvement over where you were born. Angel was one of 18 hedgehogs taken in by this breeder from another breeder that got sick and couldn't take care of her animals. Angel will not last there. She is too contrary to breed. She won't mate with any male. She is too wild to sell. We will find a way for Ivan to take her in. Besides, the old *heyoka* is there, too, among those 18 hedgehogs. Her name is Grumpy. Lives up to her name, I might add."

"How did you find all of this out?" Rosie questioned.

"I guess you would say 'the Dowager Network.'" Thelma continued. "There is a Dowager there that also came in with the 18 hedgehogs. She is a very good breeding Mom hedgehog that I am sure this breeder will not let go until it is time for her to retire. Her name is Wumpling. But this breeder will not want to put up with Angel and Grumpy for long."

"Are there other hedgehogs you are thinking of bringing here, Thelmer?" Rosie queried.

"Oh, yes!" Thelma answered. "I suppose you have already heard of Major General Spikers and his Second Hedgehog Marine Division."

"Indeed I have." Rosie answered. "Can't say that I have ever entertained the notion of an organized hedgehog military force, though."

"Well, neither had any of the rest of us until Spikers came up with it," offered Thelma. "His idea to 'combat animal abuse' was attractive to us older Seekers and Dowagers. However, now I think we are facing something even more worrisome and may just need the skills that the old General may have to offer. As we all know, Rose, these humans, most of them anyway, know no boundaries, no limits on their greed. Well, what if some others, say, some animals, have decided that they are going to operate outside their circle of propriety? Go outside of their circle of life? Take more than they need? Deal with the humans in other than peaceful ways?"

"What would happen, Thelmer?"

"I don't know what would happen, Rose," Thelma said, "but I can think of what COULD happen. Keep in mind that the Bigs and us hedgehogs are far outnumbered by many species of animals. Even if we do agree to bring General Spikers all the way from Texas, we are going to have to see that his division is staffed with able commanders and staff officers, not to mention good human and other animal soldiers. I have spoken with the General about this, and he agrees on some of our suggestions, but vigorously disagrees with others. So, it will be interesting to debate these things with him when he finally shows up here."

"What could he disagree with?" Rosie asked.

"Well, as it turns out it seems that Major General Spikers is an old-time warrior soul that believes in military honor and chivalry, and all of that," remarked Thelma. "He admits the value of military intelligence in knowing about the enemy, but beyond that has little use for the kind of behind-the-scenes 'intelligence' of modern warfare. All he wants is a straightforward battle with little skullduggery. However, this new, strange, and shadowy enemy we are facing demands some deep undercover. I know of a few hedgehogs that are masters of escape, evasion, and undercover work. Spikers wants nothing to do with them. Calls them 'sneaky little creeps,' and other distasteful terms. The best of them is a young hedgehog named Bozeman, who just happens to be one hedgehog that the General despises."

"I'm beginning to get the drift," said Rosie.

"Of course there are others as well . . ." said Thelma as her voice trailed off and she disappeared.

"Now what?!" Rosie exclaimed, as she looked from side to side to see that Thelmer was nowhere to be seen.

"Evening weigh in," said Louise matter-of-factly, as she trotted up from the direction of the wheel. "Just relax and enjoy the ride.

A few minutes later, Thelma, as if by magic, reappeared, and Louise disappeared. Rosie finally discovered that Ivan was picking each one up and they were going straight up in the air. A few moments later Flash emerged from the shadows. It seemed that everyone knew what the exercise was, except Rosie, and so showed up for the trip. As Flash was put back down, Rosie was picked up and was placed gently in the gondola of the scale.

"Weight 272, up two grams," said Ivan a little absentmindedly. "At least she didn't lose any weight upon arrival. What the!!" Ivan exclaimed, as he shouted for Jenna, who was in the next room. "Jenna, could you grab that hedgehog that just escaped? She just ran around the corner into the living room!"

Jenna, apparently having gotten to her feet answered back that she did not see any hedgehog running anywhere.

Ivan, carrying Rosie, went back to the hedgehog room and counted all of the residents. All were present. "Must be seeing things," he mused. "I could have sworn I saw a hedgehog running around the corner."

Rosie was a little nonplussed by the whole thing. She was placed back in the hedgehog room and looked up at the large gate at the entrance to the room. She thought "how, on Earth, does anyone get through or over THAT thing?"

Louise waddled up to Rosie and asked what the commotion was all about.

Rosie replied that Ivan thought he had seen a hedgehog run around a corner of the room outside of the hedgehog room.

"Well, we're all here, aren't we?" Louise asked, as night fell and the light dimmed.

"Y . . . y . . . yes," Rosie answered.

SPLAT! Splat! splat!

Rosie sat bolt upright as the missiles hit around her. Louise was startled as well, as missiles came at them from the direction of the door.

Splat! splat!

A missile struck Louise on the quills and the black blob just stuck there like liquid tar. "Poop!" Louise declared.

"Poop?" Rosie answered quizzically.

"Is this someone's idea of a joke?" Louise exclaimed indignantly.

Louise ran toward the gate, followed closely by Rosie. "I can't believe that Ivan or Jenna would be flinging poop at us!" Louise said.

Louise stopped in her tracks, staring at the gate. Rosie stopped as well, but could not see very far due to her limited vision.

"Wha . . . what is it?" Rosie asked nervously.

This time Louise seemed nervous, also. "G . . . get Flash and Thelma," she whispered, "quickly!"

Rosie turned on her paws and waddled quickly toward the hedgiehouse. She burst in on Flash and Thelma and asked them to come quickly, that Louise has found something that was wrong, "maybe," she added.

Flash and Thelma accompanied Rosie to where Louise was still sitting on her haunches, stock-still.

"What is it?" Thelma asked.

"There, in the shadows by the corner of the door," whispered Louise. The poop missile still stuck to her quills.

Flash and Thelma strained to see what Louise had been pointing out. They inched a little closer to the gate and there could make out in the dusk the shape of . . . of . . . no, it could not be.

"A hedgehog?" Flash queried.

"I don't see how," answered Louise quietly.

"Whoever she or he is, there is no communication," said Flash. "How can that be? How can it be that you, Thelma, the Dowager, could not know that another hedgehog is here? How strange."

Splat! splat!
"That clown is throwing poops!" Louise offered.

Thelma waddled toward the hedgehog in the shadows while all of the others stayed back at a respectable distance. "Who are you?" Thelma said in a tone louder than Rosie had ever heard her use before.

Rosie's ears hurt a little when she thought she heard a strange, haunting voice coming from the creature beyond the gate: "Ssay swill ssoon gett riddd of yousss."

At this rather strange message, Louise shook her head in disbelief. The hedgehog beyond the gate, or what looked like a hedgehog, turned clumsily and went further into the shadows, flinging poop along the way at walls and furniture.

Thelma silently waddled back to the hedgiehouse. Flash removed the poop from Louise's back and sniffed at it delicately. "Diseases," said Flash quietly. "Salmonella and an outbreak of clostridia. Something is trying to get us sick or kill us."

"Clean up, everybody," said Louise. "How do we tell Ivan and Jenna?"

"Clostridium is an old friend of mine," mumbled Thelma, "I get an attack about once a month just from worrying about what we are to do. But the salmonella is really troublesome. We almost never have to deal with that."

"What WAS that thing?" Rosie asked. "What language was it speaking?"

"Whatever it was," answered Thelma, "I think it is the beginning of a very long experience of troubles for us. I fear that animals far more numerous than us are organizing as they have never organized before, and may be intent upon changing life as we know it on this planet. Perhaps we need to call upon General Spikers sooner rather than later."

CHAPTER 7

THE CIRCLE OF SISTERS

Little Flash the Successor

CHAPTER 7—THE CIRCLE OF SISTERS

Thelma waddled out of the Hedgiehouse, looking not in the least centered or in balance. Louise first noticed this and almost ran to Thelma. Rosie followed. "What's wrong?" Louise asked.

"It is within our circle, my Sisters," Thelma offered, "Our dear Flash is preparing to cross the Bridge. Soon she shall begin the journey. Let us go and be with her."

The threesome waddled laboriously into the Hedgiehouse where Flash lay looking rather tired. "I am sorry to let you down," Flash said, "but, as I knew and told you all about, it looks as if my time has come to cross over. I am so thankful that I was a part of this beautiful circle! Please keep this alive and please carry on our struggle to make this a better world! You know I will be with you as you struggle on!"

Thelma bowed her head and began to sob quietly. Louise and Rosie, not really aware of what was happening, simply sat and stared.

Ivan came by relatively early in the day and reached in and picked up Flash. He was worried that she had lost more weight and was lethargic. Ivan packed up Flash for a trip to the veterinarian. She was never to return.

Thelma got the information via the Mouse Messenger Service. She reported: "Our dear friend Flash died at the veterinary clinic at the young age of just under two years of age. Liver disease."

Ivan was saddened, really despondent, but also enraged. He was quick to realize that the information he had been getting from "pet care" literature was pretty much wrong. He was especially angry with himself.

Thelma was very stoic for several days. She seemed to be immersed in total grief. Finally she emerged from the Hedgiehouse and said: "Flash's spirit is somewhere out there and I need to find her. She has traveled back to us, I know it. I must go and find her again."

Rosie was very sad but pretty nonplussed by all of this. She asked Louise, "What is Thelmer talking about? Where is Flash? How can she come back from across the Bridge?"

"Oh, Rosie, these mysteries are too deep for me, too," answered Louise. "But Thelma knows great secrets and so we will see what happens.

Ivan was distraught with grief over the passing on of Flash. He blamed himself for not getting veterinary care sooner and seeking other opinions on diet. He was incensed that individuals were allowed to publish irresponsible nonsense about the care of hedgehogs and probably other animals as well. It was hard to tell who mourned the passing of Flash more greatly. It seemed that Ivan mourned her out of his own guilt for not realizing he was not providing a better diet. Thelma mourned because she had lost a friend and ally in this mission to save the . . . something . . . perhaps the world. Both Louise and Rosie mourned the loss of Flash simply as the loss of a dear friend.

A day after Flash had traveled over the Bridge, Thelma appeared in the center of the room and sat there, day after day, completely still as if a statue. "What, on Earth, was she doing?" both Louise and Rosie wondered.

Louise then let Rosie in on another observation: "Notice the poop?"

"What poop?" Rosie replied.

"Surely you must have noticed," Louise continued. "Thelma isn't pooping in her regular spot, she's dropping stuff all over. Green, slimy stuff at that."

"Yeah, but I figured it was because she was upset about Flash," said Rosie.

"Well, in part it is, but she is also sending a message," Louise continued, "a message to Ivan."

"To Ivan?" Rosie asked dumfounded.

"Yes." Louise replied, "The green, slimy, smelly poop in this case is just a clostridium attack. Clostridia are natural bacteria that we all have, but when bad things happen to us, they multiply and get out of control. Happens to Thelma all the time when she gets worried about something. Normally, she parks even her green poop where she normally does her business, in the litter pan. But now it's all over the floor."

"I noticed that, but I figured she was sad and had forgotten," said Rosie.

"Thelma never forgets, Rosie" said Louise. "Even the human Ivan got her message. He told Jenna to be careful and be sure to wash her hands thoroughly when handling the hedgehogs or cleaning up the hedgehog room. It was because of what happened the other night, when that scary, strange hedgehog showed up."

Thelma sat there for several hours, unmoving. Finally, Ivan came by and noticed Thelma in this odd position. He knelt down and looked directly into Thelma's eyes. He seemed to understand something, but that appeared too far of a leap of faith for a human. Surprisingly, he said, "Thelma, I think you need to seek the spirit of your friend."

That seemed to be an amazing statement from a human, both Louise and Rosie concluded. But Thelma still sat in a rigid position and did not move. She sat there all night.

At one point in the middle of the night, Rosie waddled up to Thelma and sat next to her. "I hope you don't mind," Rosie whispered.

"Of course not," said Thelma, "you are most welcome to be here with me. But you can not hear the melody, can you?"

"I don't understand," said Rosie quietly.

"Sound is amazing," replied Thelma. "When you stop to think about it, sound comes from all over and is made by everything in the Creation. We old dowagers and seekers, perhaps as a payment for having to bear the woes of the world, can hear the widest array of sounds. As our sister Flash is crossing over the Bridge, the crossing melody is sung. It is almost as if the Creator seeks to apologize to us for this sorrowful thing that is happening and provides us with this most beautiful of melodies. It is sad for us left behind, but it is so beautiful one cannot help but rejoice for the time that our friend Flash had with us. Our memories are rich, so much richer than if Flash had never been here."

"Far beyond the comprehension of the Bigs," sighed Rosie.

"Not necessarily," responded Thelma. "As with all of us in the Creation, some are better equipped to deal with the universe than others. Some humans can actually communicate and realize the truth of the world far better than others."

"Would Ivan be in this category?" asked Rosie.

"Not to a great extent, but just when I think he is a lost cause, he amazes me," said Thelma. "I am referring to those humans that are what they call 'artists:' The painters, poets, and musicians. Some of them have received direct help from the Creation."

"How do you know that?" asked Rosie.

"From what I have experienced, Rose," replied Thelma. "The melody for the Rainbow Bridge crossing was faithfully written down by a human. Other humans do this as well. In their home lands, they scare those humans that are in power and often they are persecuted, tortured, or killed. The artists speak to the boundaries of human convention and cruelty. They are a courageous group, and they stand up to cruel humans that are called dictators and despots. We hedgehogs like the musicians best because we can hear what they say. They speak in tones, and we can understand those."

"How do the humans know what music to write?" Rosie asked.

"I can't tell, but I suspect a lot of it has to do with pain, suffering, and fear," Thelma replied. "Some humans express it better than others. The descendants of slaves, people traditionally oppressed. Russians! Russian musical writers sure know how to express themselves better than most. And the people that were slaves here, and were brought here from our native Africa. They brought a lot of their music with them. Many times it was all they had."

"Was it a Russian that painted the musical portrait of the Rainbow Bridge?" asked Rosie.

"Yes, it was," Thelma replied. "He was not very well known. Other Russian musical writers that were much more famous wrote some great music for hedgehogs! The very best hedgehog dancing music is in the ballet suites of the Russian composer Dmitri Shostakovich."

"But who discovered the melody for crossing over the Rainbow Bridge?" asked Rosie.

"Later! Here we go!" Thelma said as two human hands scooped her up. "We're going on a journey."

Ivan had Thelma in a cage carrier in the car where Thelma could see out over the road ahead. Nearsighted as all hedgehogs are, she liked to see where she was going. Ivan settled back behind the wheel and outlined the day's events for her. "First we have a stop at the vet's to check you out for everything, including those green poops. Then we try to find you a new friend. I have a long list of places we can try."

The visit to the veterinarian was uneventful. Yes, she had raised levels of clostridium. Yes, she needed an antibiotic. Yep, the bubblegum flavored amoxicillin should do the trick. The second half of the journey had to be postponed for two weeks until Thelma recovered from the clostridium attack. This was something that annoyed her greatly, since she was also isolated from both Louise and Rosie.

But as soon as the quarantine was over, she was on the road again. Ivan knew that Thelma needed a friend. The next visit was to an apartment where a family advertised a female hedgehog for sale. Appointments had been made in advance. Thelma was placed on the floor and so was the other female, named Sonic. "Sonic," among pet hedgehogs, was sort of like the name "Smith" among humans. Sonic stood her distance from Thelma, and hissed considerably. Hissing is standard hedgehog vocabulary for irritation. Thelma asked Sonic how she felt, but Sonic only hissed in return. Finally, Sonic simply said to Thelma, "Your silly cause to reason with these Bigs is lost. These Bigs cannot learn. Give it up!"

Ivan gave up, and it was back into the car for another trip. This time it was to a so-called "backyard breeder." The house was a dirty mess, and the humans not much cleaner. The hedgehogs were kept in a set of several cages below the kitchen table. Surprisingly, the hedgehogs had cleaner environments than their human caretakers. There were two adult female hedgehogs, one group of four baby hedgehogs, and a combative male hedgehog.

Thelma was introduced to the two adult female hedgehogs. All three kept their distance. The two female hedgehogs wanted to know when things would get better for animals in general and hedgehogs in particular.

Thelma replied that she "did not know, but that we are trying to work on it."

The male hedgehog, named Rouse, looked disapprovingly at Thelma and muttered a few words, "Sso here you are, you fool. We are moving now and we will crusssh them, or better yet they will crusssh themsselves."

Thelma's gaze was distracted for a moment. What she saw on the other side of the kitchen, under the sink that was covered with a flimsy, dirty curtain made her blood run cold.

"What, on Earth?!" she thought to herself. She did not want to believe what she had seen. It was too crazy, too unbelievable. So much so that she even forgot the strange way in which the hedgehog Rouse spoke.

The next visit was to a pet store. Thelma was uneasy with the three female and one male hedgehog there. She wondered what was going on, and never had such a hard time dealing with fellow hedgehogs in the past.

The next pet store was the same. This time it was two hostile females. The tone of one of the female hedgehogs held Thelma's interest. She suddenly remembered the language Rouse used: "Why bother usss?" It was the hissing pronunciation that caught Thelma's attention. She had never heard this sort of language before from hedgehogs, until . . . until that night not too long ago when that mysterious hedgehog had flung diseased poop at the Circle of Sisters. Thelma looked up at Ivan, and he seemed to get the message: "Let's get outta here!"

A private home advertising a female hedgehog for sale was the next stop. The woman offering the hedgehog seemed a little disturbed and, for lack of a better term, deranged. She said that her hedgehog of about three years of age had been acting very strangely over the last nine months or so. Formerly a benign hedgehog, she reported that the hedgehog, Minnie, had become irritable and aggressive. Once again, Thelma was plunked down in front of Minnie. Minnie was a pretty hedgehog, but seemed disturbed at Thelma's presence. Again, the strange hisses and words.

"Your failed wordss with the Bigss amount to nothing," Minnie rasped, "Anthross has been right all along, and Anthross Disciples will cure thiss malady of Bigss once and for all. The planss are formed and under way."

"Who can I talk to?" Thelma asked.

Minnie replied "You will be sspoken to if and when the time comess. But your foolissh wayss are outdated, usselesss."

Sensing a standoff, Ivan packed up Thelma and off they went. Thelma wished Ivan could understand more of this, but knew he could not. At least now the strange group had a name—the Disciples of Anthross, whatever that meant.

The search went on all day. Thelma and Ivan visited pet shops, breeders, and two pet animal wholesalers. The experience was depressing. Most of the hedgehogs were hostile. However, toward the end of the day, Thelma and Ivan stopped at an old place where Ivan knew the owner. Yes, he said he had one hedgehog, a female. He brought out the hedgehog and placed her on the counter. She sat stock still, but did not appear to be nervous. She was a fairly substantial hedgehog weighing in at around 470 grams. Ivan took Thelma out of her transport container and placed her on the counter.

Thelma looked at the new hedgehog with disbelief. So very softly, she whispered, "Flash?"

The hedgehog just sat there for a few moments, and then waddled toward Thelma. They simply looked at one another for several minutes.

Ivan and the store owner looked on with curiosity. "I wonder what they're thinking?" said Ivan. "I've been trying to find a compatible hedgehog for Thelma all day with no luck at all. It looks like they are trying to stare one another down."

Of course, that was NOT what was happening. They were simply staring at one another, trying to figure out what was going on. They knew about traveling spirits but, as wise as Thelma was, there still were great mysteries in the universe that no one understood. After a time, she whispered again, "Flash."

"Something has come over me that I can't explain," the other said softly. "It's as if I had some kind of enlightenment or something. Somehow I knew you were coming here. How strange. I feel quite differently, somehow more centered.

At the same moment, both hedgehogs walked closer and snuggled with one another.

"Well," exclaimed Ivan, "it looks like we've made a match. You know, she does look sort of like Flash. Perhaps we'll call her Little Flash."

It was not long before Thelma, Little Flash, and Ivan were heading home.

Little Flash was still wondering what had come over her in the past few days. She had been in the pet store about two months and, still a youngster but big for her age, was all of four months old. "What do you think happened?" she asked Thelma.

"No one really knows," Thelma replied, "but there is that infinite cosmic world beyond the Rainbow Bridge where all sorts of magical things happen.

The Gathering

Spirits travel. I think a past spirit friend can send their spirit, or part of their spirit, or maybe a duplicate spirit back here to help us. This may have happened to you. Do you know where we are heading?"

"Not really," replied Little Flash, but I vaguely think there are other hedgehogs there, and . . . . and . . . . a blue sofa bed to hide under . . . where there is a heater vent that is very comfortable."

"Hmmm," said Thelma, "there is just so much that we do not know. So amazing. But I sure am glad that you are here.

"I'm glad to be here, too," replied Little Flash, "that pet shop was sort of grubby, but not too bad as those places go, so I'm told."

"One of our residents is Miss Rose." added Thelma, "now SHE has some stories about mills and pet shops."

"I don't think I want to hear them" said Little Flash, as the journey came to its conclusion.

Ivan unloaded the crew and went inside. Peeking inside the carrier he could see Thelma and Little Flash snuggled together at the far end. Ivan thought to himself, "what's the harm, I'll keep Thelma and Little Flash by themselves tonight and get a vet check for Little Flash in the morning."

"Hmm," offered Thelma to Little Flash," looks like we're being isolated from our friends until tomorrow."

"Why?" asked Little Flash.

"Well," Thelma replied, "normally he separates new pogs for 30 days to be sure we do not have anything, such as mites, that we could transfer to the other pogs. But I guess you'll join us all after a check-up at the vet."

Thelma and Little Flash talked through the night about Thelma's concerns. She had been aware for some time about changes she had seen among many hedgehogs: Their hostile behavior and strange speech, a sort of distant speech made with hissing sounds. She told Little Flash about the "Anthross Disciples" business, and their plan to kill Bigs.

"What is going on?" Little Flash exclaimed.

"There is something else," said Thelma, "something that I noticed on the journey to pick you up I still cannot make sense of."

"Do I really want to hear this?" Little Flash responded.

"Might as well, you are in this up to your quills whether you like it or not," Thelma said. "Besides you are here for a purpose. You have inherited Flash's Spirit here on Earth. Her Earthly Spirit found a good home. You will have the courage to carry on her work."

"I hope I'm worthy of that," replied Little Flash.

"Do not worry, you have the courage," replied Thelma, "giving Little Flash's face a snuggle, typical hedgie behavior.

"At one of the places we went in search of you," Thelma continued, "I was placed with two very worried and scared female hedgehogs who wanted to know about this new, strange business. They wanted to know if all hedgehogs had forgotten the Original Instructions and were now thinking strange, new, harmful thoughts. They seemed terrified. I had no answers for them. Then, in a nearby cage was a male hedgehog named Rouse who spoke in that same, strange way, that hissing way we are hearing more and more. His message was the same. Our message for the Bigs was too late and we were foolish to think we could do anything. But then, Little Flash, I turned and looked under the sink of this place. Under a flimsy curtain. On the floor. I could not believe my eyes."

"W . . . w . . . what was it?" asked Little Flash, not really sure she wanted to know.

"Roaches!" exhaled Thelma with a sort of gasp. "Hundreds maybe thousands of cockroaches!"

"Yuck," exclaimed Little Flash, "I've always preferred crickets myself. 'Sides, roaches can make you sick. Never know where they've been or what they have been eating. Sort of like slugs. You can get sick and die from eating those guys from all of the poison chemicals they eat."

"Well," continued Thelma, "many of us insectivores in captivity do not even dine on insects any more. Many of us have become vegetarians. But that is a subject for another time."

"Thousands of cockroaches?" asked Little Flash, getting the conversation back on track.

"Yes, thousands," continued Thelma, "which, of course, is not particularly strange in grubby surroundings, and these surroundings were definitely grubby! However, it was what the cockroaches were doing with made my heart almost stop."

"What were they doing?" whispered Little Flash. "The Watusi?"

"That would be pretty funny if it were true. I see you have also inheritedFlash's sense of comedy. They were all just standing there, in rows and columns, absolutely still and silent, all facing in the same direction!" Thelma nearly gasped.

What!?" exclaimed Little Flash, "I've never seen any kind of bug do that, except maybe ants or sometimes bees!" Are you sure they were cockroaches?"

"No doubt about it," continued Thelma. "Not only that, at several places at the head of the columns were large palmetto bugs, the big flying roaches pacing back and forth seemingly clicking and hissing at the huge assembly of smaller roaches. The order is like nothing I have ever seen, not even among ants or bees. They were lined up like a big bunch of guinea pigs. You know how guinea pigs will line up with their backs against the wall? But these cockroaches were also lined up in ranks. I could not believe my eyes."

""What can you make of it?" asked Little Flash.

"I do not know," continued Thelma, "but as I looked around in disbelief, the hedgehog Rouse seemed to pick up on my bewilderment. He screamed at me "We are organizzzed and we are ready!""

"What did he mean?" mused Little Flash.

"I got the impression," continued Thelma, "that he was in some way connected to this organization of cockroaches. Also, as I looked closer, there were cockroaches and a palmetto bug or two standing in a circle around Rouse himself in his cage. He seemed frozen there, unmoving."

"I wonder what's happening?" queried Little Flash.

"I do not yet know," answered Thelma, "but it is not at all natural, nor is it in line with the Original Instructions. My worst fears are that these insects are organizing, in a way never before thought about. You know, they outweigh and outnumber everyone. An intelligent plot on their part can wipe out all life as we know it on Earth. THAT has me gravely worried. When we get through with your appointment at the veterinarian's tomorrow, we will discuss this with Louise and Rose. I have been able to set up a way for two more hedgehogs to join us. They are very hard to put up with, but they will be a great asset."

"Hard to put up with?" asked Little Flash.

"Yes!" continued Thelma, "among the worst! They arrived a short time ago from a place called Nebraska. They and sixteen other hedgehogs. Their names are Grumpy and Angel. They are two of the most independent little cusses the world has ever seen. If I thought Louise was a *heyoka*, believe me, she is a mild mannered lady compared to these two."

"Why invite them here?" asked Little Flash.

"Because we need their spirit and their fire!" Thelma replied. "I need their help for some of the big decisions I'm going to have to make. I am thinking about calling up that big old fighting military hedgehog, Major General Spikers and his Marines. That is a very big decision, and I need to get the advice of the strongest *heyokas* I can find to see how and even if I should try to do it. You see, we dowagers gave permission for Major General Spikers to form his Marine division to 'combat animal abuse.' Well, that was logical and innocent enough. I mean, all his Marine division had to do was to call in artillery strikes on abusive pet stores and breeders. That was about it. A worthy undertaking."

"Artillery strikes?" asked Little Flash.

"Heh heh," continued Thelma, "well, sort of. We call it the 155mm howitzer United States Department of Agriculture unannounced inspection in violation of the Animal Welfare Act. It's the hedgehog version of heavy artillery. Almost all of these pet stores are not licensed to sell hedgehogs under this law. So, if they are abusive or neglectful, we call in USDA inspectors. They get inspected, cited, and sometimes fined or shut down. It's a good use of 'artillery' for us."

"And now you want him, this general, to do something else?" asked Little Flash.

"Perhaps," continued Thelma. "These strange new developments, these oddly acting hedgehogs that are so confrontational, these cockroaches lined up in ranks, all of these strange events, seem to require some extreme measures. But I do not know what is the right course. Perhaps these extreme *heyokas*, Grumpy and Angel, can shed some light on this.

"Hmm," mused Little Flash, "we may be biting off more than we can chew."

"Maybe," replied Thelma, "but I do not think we have a choice. Anyway, the wheels are in motion now and Grumpy and Angel will be on their way soon. So fasten your seat belt and enjoy the ride."

"Groan," sighed Little Flash, "some ride!"

CHAPTER 8

THE DISCIPLES OF ANTHROSS

Bowls the Bully

CHAPTER 8—THE DISCIPLES OF ANTHROSS

In a place not far from where Flash and Thelma lived with their ever-growing group of hedgies, another group of animals huddled in the shadows of an unfinished new house.

"Thiss isss ass closse ass we can get to them." said Archniss, deputy to Anthross, leader of an ever growing army of insects.

Archniss was addressing an odd assortment of creatures which included two hedgehogs, one of which was Anthross himself and the other was Bowls, who had been recently recruited. The remainder were insects, most of whom were praying mantises like Archniss, but there were also a few small groups of cockroaches and carpenter ants, as well as a few palmetto bugs.

Anthross replied, "Thiss isss the perfect place. Closse enough to thosse that will causse trouble and in a place where we will not be detected. No humansss are in thiss place at night. You chosse thiss well, Archnisss."

"But let me tell you why you are here tonight, Bowlss," Anthross continued, "becausse we are going to need to do ssome sserious work. Thesse Bigsss, thesse humanss, musst be sstopped, and we are going to have to do it."

"What are these Bigs doing," asked a curious Bowls, here on his first visit.

"You already know what they are doing," said Archniss, "desstroying thiss whole planet with their poissonss and their mechanical devicess and their sslaughtering of all ssortss of non-Bigss. Why, they even sslaughter one another!"

"Yeah," said Bowls, "but what can we do about it?"

"We have a masster plan," said Hisstolo, another of the mantises. "We are going to have them wage war againsst each other."

"It will come asss no ssurprisse," added Archniss, "ssince they do it all the time anyway."

"But how can we have them do this?" Bowls asked.

"We will have the mosst powerful group provoke the otherss!" Hisstolo exclaimed.

Bowls thought to himself that this really sounded pretty stupid. Here were a bunch of bugs and a couple of hedgehogs sitting in an empty human house plotting to have all of the humans wipe each other out.

"HAWHAWHAWHAWHAW!" Bowls bellowed.

Bowls suddenly found himself surrounded by mantises. He got a look up reeeel close at their razor sharp jaws. A thought suddenly came over him that even though hedgehogs are classified as insectivores, that ENOUGH insects could turn the tables very quickly. It was a wise thought. Bowls wiped the grin off of his face.

Anthross spoke, "Thesse are sserious timesss, Mr. Bowlss. I would ssuggesst that you not mock or anger thosse determined to ssucceed in thiss misssion. To do so would be hazzardouss to your health. Very hazzardouss."

"I get the message," said Bowls seriously. "But have the Bigs really done that much damage?"

"Jusst look around you," said Archniss, "everywhere is death and destruction. Mosst of the Bigss are sstarving and a tiny few are blindingly wealthy. What other animal do you know that behavess like that? They wage warss againsst eachother everywhere and develop hideouss weaponss. What other animal do you know behavess like that? SSome of them hijack transsports of the other and kill passsengerss. When wass the lasst time you ever ssaw a gorilla or a rabbit or a dung beetle hijack an airplane or rob a bank? They make everything ssick, from horssess to treess to even themsselves with their fumess from everything they usse for their convenience—vehiclesss, heating, appliancess, factoriess. What other animal doess that? They try to wipe out almost every animal and plant on Earth by making what they call pessticidess and inssecticidess and herbicidess! What other animal doess that? Look at how they wasste sstuff! What other animalss have landfillss, toxic wasste dumpss, dead riversss? Then, what other animal hidess everything so they do not have to ssee what they have done? When they eat ssomething that hass been killed, they inssisst on never sseeing the killing. Insstead they want it in a box. How inssane is that? Thesse guyss are nutss!"

"Guess, so," said Bowls, who was never a hedgehog that was too quick to pick up on social causes.

"Sso are you with uss?" Anthross asked.

"Well," asked Bowls, "I'm wonderin' how you guys are going to pull this off? Also, why you need to get hedgehogs involved? I mean, like we are just a small group of animals kept as pets by the Bigs in North America."

Anthross squinted at Bowls: "We cannot tell you all of the planssss until we think you are ready. However, we feel hedgehogss can be ussed effectively ass decoyss to attract humanss into momentarily abandoning their dutiesss. Long enough for usss to get into their facilitiess and begin the conflict between them."

"What do you want me to do?" Bowls asked.

"We'd like you to recruit hedgehogss," said Anthross, "perhapss 70 or 80 of them to act as decoyss to the Bigss while the inssectss carry out their misssion of sstarting the fightss between the Bigss."

"This might be a blast," responded Bowls, "but I got a few questions."

"By all meanss, assk them." Anthross said.

Well, first," asked Bowls, "where can I recruit hedgehogs?"

"Thingss are a little ssparsse here in Colorado at the moment, not many hedgehogss being bred for the pet trade," said Anthross, "but there iss a good recruitment basse in Texass. Bessidess, the airport at Dallass-Fort Worth hass an excellent transsport terminal for ssmall mammalss. Not very good for inssectss, though. The rat that commandss the air transsport there doess not permit inssectss to usse the place. But we will take care of him and hiss helperss."

"Rat?" Bowls asked. "Commanding air transport?"

"Yesss," answered Anthross, "they've been doing it for yearsss. They ssneak ssmall animalss on planess and sships, sometimness bussess and trainss. But they don't like inssectss getting in their vehicless. They alwayss give uss a hard time."

"How do I get there?" Bowls asked.

"We will fly you there," Archniss answered.

"But how can I recruit, if I do not know what the overall plan is?"

"It'ss an eassy ssell, Bowlss," said Anthross. "All animalss want the Bigsss gone, so we can return the Earth to itss natural sstate."

"In the end you will be a famouss hedgehog," added Archniss. "You will be admired and ssought after. The earth really doess not have much of a choice."

"Well, this sounds sort of OK," said Bowls, "but who are these ones that will cause trouble you were talking about? They're somebody other than the Bigs, right?"

"Yesss," answered Anthross. "They are a group of hedgehogss that fancy themsselvess better than otherss. Call themsselvess the 'Dowagerss' or the 'Sseekerss.' They believe in telling the Bigss the errorss of their wayss according to ssome ancient code of theirss. We know and mosst other animalss know that they are a bunch of foolss and that the Bigss will kill them if they try any of thesse kindss of communicationss. You know that Bigss kill what they do not undersstand, and they do not undersstand animalss, and do not want to. No, Bowlss, the Bigss have to go."

"How do I recruit these hedgehogs?" Bowls asked.

"You go where they are," responded Hisstolo, "into homess of Bigss, their pet sstoress, and, of coursse, into thosse pet millss like where you came from. Millss are the besst place to recruit from, becausse they are the cruelesst placess for animalss outsside of sslaughterhoussess. Millss are alsso the eassiesst placess to esscape from, becausse they are sso poorly kept."

"Yeah, I can see what you mean about the mills," replied Bowls.

"You usse the reassonss we told you about ass why the Bigss musst be done away with," said Archniss. "They will lissten to you. You will become their leader."

"Sounds good," said Bowls, "but who are these 'Dowagerss' or whatever you call them?"

"Theyre the older hedgehogss that fancy themsselves wisse," responded Anthross, "but we know better. They can be dangerouss to our causse becausse they do not agree with us. We are here becausse we wanted to be closse to them to keep an eye on their mosst resspected and powerful one. Her name is Thelma, and I think sshe is wisse to our planss. Archniss and Hisstolo tried to talk to her and sshe refussed to go along with usss. Sshe may try to fight uss."

"If she is just one old lady," asked Bowls, "how can she fight you?"

"Sshe'ss ssmart," said Archniss, "and many hedgehogss will follow her lead. There is one troublessome old hedgehog now down in Texass who is very dangerouss. He iss a military hedgehog known ass Spikerss who headss up a bunch of hedgehogss that fight againsst pet sshops that ssell hedgehogss."

"Should I try to get this Spikers guy on our side?" Bowls asked.

"Don't wasste your time," said Anthross. "Ssince I am a hedgehog and I know thesse players, I can tell you that Sspikers is a losst causse. He getss hiss military authority from thesse Dowagerss and lisstenss to them. He iss too old to change, too opinionated."

"OK," said Bowls, "so what do I do with these hedgehogs once I recruit them?"

"Firsst, you train them to be charming to the Bigss," said Anthross. "Teach them cute and endearing behavior. Then you train them to sspeak ass we do, in our accent sso that we can recognize thosse who have been trained. You had better work on it, too."

"OK," said Bowls, "makes sense, . . . err, makess ssensse to me."

"You musst also train them to fight other hedgehogss that opposse uss," added Archniss.

"Then, when they are trained," continued Hisstolo, "you ssend them here to our location on the transsport planess out of Dallass."

"But didn't you say, uh, ssay that the airport ratss running that sshow will not cooperate?"

"The airport ratss do not permit insectss to travel," said Anthross, "but hedgehogss are welcomed by them becausse hedgehogss are the oldesst of mammalss and the ratss resspect them."

"Do the rats, er, ratss, run all of the air transsport?" Bowls asked.

"Mosstly yes," answered Archniss. "They have traditionally done sso all over the world. We inssects do not get along with them, but their day iss coming."

Bowls liked his new role. Being in charge of things was neat. He wondered how this Anthross guy got the bugs to go along with his plan, whatever it was. But Anthross and the bugs seemed to agree on the scheme. The only thing that looked a little strange to Bowls was Anthross' appearance. He was one strange looking hedgehog. Sort of thin, but his eyes were sunken, red, and kind of watery. Seemed as if something was wrong with him. He had heard of red eyed hedgehogs before and there were even a few of them, white ones called albinos, at the mill that he came from. He also remembered one or two apricot colored ones that had red eyes. But, still, Anthross seemed weird, and the red eyes on a chocolate colored hedgehog did not detract from that odd appearance. In the end, Bowls simply chalked it up to his feeling that Anthross was a very old hedgehog, none of which Bowls had ever seen in his lifetime. At the mill where he was born, the young hedgehogs left there for pet stores or they died. No one ever got old in an animal breeding mill, including the hedgehogs used for breeding.

Bowls received further indoctrination from Archniss and his team of mantises. They trusted him only slightly and told him just a few of their strategic plans of having the Bigs wipe one another out. Apparently it was through an exchange of the Bigs own weapons. Missiles. The hedgehogs were to be decoys at these missile sites so that the insects could do their work, whatever that was.

Then came the day that Bowls departed for Texas. In the first leg of his journey, he was escorted by Hisstolo to a regional airport about 40 miles north of town, hitching a ride on a bus.

"Say, how come we have to go north to this little airport and not south just a little further to the big airport in Denver?" Bowls asked.

"Too dangerouss," replied Hisstolo. "It'ss eassier to get on the planess at the ssmaller airportss then once you get to the bigger airportss you are already insside."

Once at the regional airport in Wyoming, Bowls was given instructions on approaching the old rat that lived there. "The rat'ss name is Henry," said Hisstolo, "he iss harmless, very old, and cannot ssee very well. Communicate clearly with him. He is sso old he ssurely will be caught by the Bigss very ssoon. They have a cat here that is ssuppossed to hunt mice and ratss, but the cat likess old Henry, sso he is ssafe. Inssectss get to fly out of here, too, but that iss becausse Henry cannot ssee uss. Denver iss a different sstory, much more dangerouss. The large airportss are too full of Bigss and the rissk of disscovery too great. Disscovery meanss that the Bigss call in special murdererss, death ssquads called 'exterminstorss' who usse all sortss of evil methodss, like trapss and poissonss, to maim and kill."

"Yep," thought Bowls to himself, "gotta get rid of the Bigs, er, Bigss."

"What happenss when I get to Denver?" Bowls asked.

"The ratss will come into the cargo hold where you are and give you insstructionss," said Hisstolo. "The rat terminal manager at Denver is an Englissh rat named Worthington-Kent. Almosst all of the rat airport managerss are Englissh ratss."

"How come English, er, Englissh?" Bowls asked.

"I don't know," said Hisstolo. "They have been doing it for a very long time, from the time of ssailing sshipss when England ruled the ssurface of the ssea. But Henry, here, is a local rat."

"Awright," said Hisstolo, as they approached the small airport terminal, "Henry's over there under that overhang below the downspout. Just walk right up to him and say you want to go to Dallas."

"Right, see . . . er, ssee you later." Bowls replied.

Waddling up to the elderly rat, Bowls saw that he was stooped over, a little unkept, and was blinded by cataracts. "Hello, Mr. Henry, I'm looking for a plane ride to Dallas."

"Eh?" Henry the rat asked.

"I'M LOOKING FOR A PLANE RIDE TO DALLAS!" Bowls shouted.

"Oh, heh heh," replied Henry, "hearin' ain't what it used to be, eyes are shot, too. 'Bout all I can do now is feel along by smell and vibrations. Dallas, Eh? Gotta go through Denver, y'know."

"YES, I KNOW," said Bowls, "CAN YOU HELP ME?"

"Sure, sure, young fella," Henry replied. "Plane due in this hour, let's get over on the tarmac."

Once over on the runway side of the terminal, Bowls heard the engines of an airplane landing and the craft touching down, although his naturally poor eyesight only permitted him a blurry view of the plane.

"It's the biggun," said Henry. "Thirty passenger Brasilia rather than the smaller Beech 1900. Can't see 'em any more but can tell by the vibrations. Better for you 'cause it's easier to hide in there. You go up the stairs fast after the passengers are off and get under the rear row of seats. Don't go back in cargo—no heat in there."

As Bowls followed Henry across the tarmac, they scurried under a parked truck. Henry crept back out to gauge the positioning of the plane and passed by Phoebe, the aging airport cat, who was calmly sitting in the sun enjoying the warm weather.

"Good afternoon, Mr. Henry," said Phoebe.

"Good afternoon, young lady," Henry replied. "Fine day, isn't it?"

Before Phoebe could reply, a steel toed boot swiftly swung and caught Phoebe in the midsection, sending her flying for about ten feet and tumbling earthward, to run in the opposite direction from the Big who had kicked her.

"Stupid, sorry damn cat!" exclaimed the airport baggage handler. "This here rat walks right by and that dumb cat don't do nothin'!"

"Yep," thought Bowls to himself again, "gotta get rid of these Bigss!"

CHAPTER 9

THE CONTRARIES

Angel the Contrary

CHAPTER 9—THE CONTRARIES

At the Hedgiehouse, it was early, where Thelma and Little Flash had just settled in after a night full of conversation when they were jolted awake.

"OK, girls, time for a trip to the vet!" It was Ivan.

"Well, he's right on time," said Thelma. "Maybe I can tag along."

Across the house in the hedgieroom, Louise and Rose were vaguely aware of what was up, but were eager to meet their new roommate. Little did they know the resident population was going to increase very soon.

The trip to the veterinarian was considerably shorter this time. Thelma wondered why.

"New vet, girls, closer to home," Ivan said, solving the mystery. "Our wolf vet."

"Oh, great," thought Thelma, "a wolf vet! Like wolves and hedgehogs have a lot in common! Well, four legs, two ears and a mouth I guess."

It turned out that the new veterinarian was an experienced zoological and wildlife vet recently retired from the local veterinary medical college.

Thelma and Little Flash were whisked to the back of the clinic. Ivan's hands came into the carrier and gently picked up Little Flash and plunked her on the scale.

"Four hundred and seventy grams," he said as a technician wrote down the weight. "Just a tad over a pound, not bad at all."

A moment later smaller, more delicate hands picked Little Flash up and cradled her for a moment. Then began some vibrations from the fingers that caused Little Flash to giggle.

"Heeheehee, that tickles," squirmed Little Flash.

Cilla the veterinarian, gentle and very experienced with all manners of wild animals, had a soft spot in her heart for hedgehogs. Over the years she had read just about every book and article about them. "What a pretty little girl," she said, looking over Little Flash.

Little Flash relaxed in her hands, feeling confident that no harm was going to come to her. Like Thelma, Little Flash had a trusting nature, which was probably not a good trait for survival in Nature. But this was not Nature. Nature, for the tens of thousands of hedgehogs in North America, was half a world away.

The veterinarian peered into Little Flash's eyes and said, "We've got a sweet one here, I don't think we will even have to put her under."

"Under" meant a dose of the anesthetic gas isoflurane, something that Thelma regarded as dangerous.

"Oh, good," thought Thelma, "I don't trust that stuff. Gets you all dizzy and makes you sleep. Feels bad when you wake up. Blechhh."

Cilla poked, prodded, and peeked at Little Flash: Eyes, ears, mouth, legs, skin, quills—everything except a blood draw.

After the examination, Cilla said, "She seems fine. No evidence of masses or mites. I don't think we need to put her under for a blood draw. She seems alert enough and her poops check out fine."

Once free of the veterinary clinic the ride home was uneventful. Except for the stop at the pet supply store. The pet supply store was a rather new phenomenon on the American scene. Like it's compatriots in the general merchandise and office supply arenas, these pet supply stores were cropping up all around the country and with their mass merchandising driving all of the smaller independently owned pet supply stores out of business.

Patrons at the pet supply store were urged to bring their pets inside, so in went Thelma and Little Flash in their carrier. No sooner had Ivan cleared the door on the way to find a supply of his favorite brand of shampoo for the hedgehogs when he was stopped by a store patron, who was there with a large shaggy dog and several children.

"Watcha got in that there carrier?" bellowed the man, as the children crowded around and the dog began to whimper.

"Hedgehogs," said Ivan nonchalantly.

"HEDGEHAWGS?!" roared the man.

"Hedgehogs!" mimicked the children.

"ARF!" went the dog.

"Lemmesee lemmesee lemmesee," began the children's chorus. More people gathered around.

Ivan reached into the carrier and extracted Little Flash. Little Flash took one look at the assembled mob of Bigs, and rolled up just a little.

"Harumph," she thought, "an entire crop of both big Bigs and little Bigs. The little ones are almost as ugly as the big ones. Not very well behaved, either."

One little girl began screaming and jumping up and down, "OOHHHHLOOKY, a PORKYPINE, a PORKYPINE!"

"Yikes!" thought Little Flash, rolling up a little more, "these Bigs are nuts."

Another little girl exclaimed, "LOOK! LOOK! It's rolling up in a ball!"

An adult woman shouted, "How KYOOT!"

A little boy yelled, "WAY COOL!"

In the carrier, Thelma was laying low. She thought to herself "Maybe the cockroaches are not so bad, after all. Sheesh!"

"Is it pokey?" asked one of the girls.

Ivan, apparently used to these sorts of encounters, said "Oh, just a little. You can pet her if you like."

The small girl timidly put her hand out, withdrew it several times, and finally, at the urging of the adult man, tenuously touched Little Flash's quills. Normally a very mellow pog, Little Flash could not resist and when the little girl finally managed to touch her quills, she jumped and popped.

"AIEEEEE!" screamed the little girl at the top of her lungs, "IT POKED ME, IT POKED ME!"

The other children backed away as if terrorized.

The little girl continued to scream, "THE PORKYPINE POKED ME! THE PORKYPINE POKED ME!"

Ivan gently placed Little Flash back inside the carrier. Thelma looked rather disgustedly at her and whispered "You just had to do it, didn't you. The Bigs are not rational, especially the small ones. Just remember not to do that if one of them is holding you or you'll get dropped unexpectedly and you might get hurt."

"Umm, sorry," said Little Flash, "Couldn't resist."

Ivan wheeled the cart to the shampoo aisle and exited through the register line, stopping to bring out either Little Flash or Thelma on three more occasions.

Back home, Little Flash was put through the bath routine, which was just about identical to the experience Rosie had upon her arrival. Little Flash really enjoyed the bath, however, and especially the soft, warm flow of the hair dryer. She laid back spread-eagled, put her head back and closed her eyes, letting the warm air flow over her tummy fur.

Ivan, the operator of the hair dryer, called for Jenna to come and see. "Come have a look!" he exclaimed, "Little Flash is having an 'out-of-quills' experience!" They both looked and giggled as Little Flash carried on her escapade, thoroughly enjoying herself.

Once warm and dry, Little Flash found herself plunked down in the hedgieroom, where Thelma had already returned and was in the hedgiehut talking to Louise and Rose about her adventure of the last two days. Worried that it may be too much for them, she minimized the part of the row after row of cockroaches.

Little Flash was introduced to Louise and Rosie and all began a friendly and lively discussion about their backgrounds. As this was going on, Thelma suddenly sat up.

"There's the call!" Thelma exclaimed.

"What call?" asked Rosie.

"Ivan's getting a telephone call," answered Thelma. "Soon they will be on their way."

"Who?" Rosie asked.

"Our new friends, Grumpy and Angel," replied Thelma.

Ivan listened on the telephone as Marilyn went on in her English Cockney accent. "Aye was given yer number by the vet down 'ere, ya know. Take in wayward 'edgeoggs, do ya?"

Ivan replied, "well, yes I do, I suppose. Hadn't really planned on it, but, yes, I guess I do."

"Jolly good!" Marilyn exclaimed. "Got me a couple 'ere that eye can't do nothin' with, y'know. Won't breed. Too ornery to sell. Hate to dispose of 'em, though. But I'm not all that well heeled. Can't care for unprofitable animals, you know. You can 'ave 'em if you want."

"Ummm," trying to think fast, Ivan responded, "are they female?" He thought he had an "out" if they were males since it was not Ivan's intention to take in any male hedgehogs. He was not interested in breeding and felt he did not have the room for any more in the house.

"Right-O, females they are!" Marilyn exclaimed.

"Well, OK," Ivan responded, wondering what he had gotten himself into.

The trip to Marilyn's breeding operation took about an hour and a half. A widow, Marilyn was the only human living at her place. She did, however, have permanent company in the form of some 200 ferrets, 40 hedgehogs, a few dozen guinea pigs and a few assorted dogs and cats.

Marilyn, an outgoing and robustly cordial woman, invited Jenna and Ivan into her home, which was stacked to the ceiling with all manners of cages. Guinea pigs were in the living room, ferrets in the den/family room, and the hedgehogs were in the cellar. Marilyn explained how she had come by 18 new hedgehogs from a friend who was a breeder in Nebraska who fell ill and could no longer care for her animals.

"Ere's one of 'em, as grumpy as they come, she is," said Marilyn, as she held up a medium sized gray hedgehog.

"PFFFFFT!" went the hedgehog as she rolled up in a ball and when put down, much to Ivan and Jenna's surprise charged them with her head down much as one would expect from an enraged bull.

"Wow!" exclaimed Ivan, "I guess there is no other name for this girl other than Grumpy!"

"Yep, Grumpy she is," seconded Jenna.

"She's two years old," said Marilyn. "Born on June 15th. Absolutely will not breed. Runs the males off, she does. Her little white pal is the same way, 'though much younger."

When Marilyn emerged with the other hedgehog, Jenna remarked "Oooh, she looks like a little angel."

"Might look like one, but she's just as bad as the other one when it comes to breedin'," Marilyn said. "Wants nothing to do with the males. She's six months old. Been keepin' 'em together. They seem to get along. The white one is nowhere near as grumpy with people as the gray one, but she has one other annoying habit where I can't even sell her to a pet store. Too bad, too, since these albinos bring a pretty penny."

"What sort of habit does she have?" Jenna asked.

"You'll find out soon enough," said Marilyn, "but I can't bring 'er to the pet store chain I sell to and have her pull the same stunts that little rascal named Bozeman pulls. Store can't sell 'im because he's gone all of the time!"

"Gone?" Ivan queried.

"Gone!" Marilyn exclaimed. "Lord knows what he's after, but he escapes from whatever they put him in every night! Scurries around on the floor of the shop during the day and no one can catch 'im for a week or so. Store manager said 'e'd stop buyin' from me if I ever sent him another one of those. Well, this one's the same way. Gets out of the cage every night! The next mornin' she's up with the ferrets, or the guinea pigs, or in the bathroom! Lord knows how she gets up those stairs, them being bare wood and all."

Ivan was beginning to think he was losing his senses, but with the two hedgehogs in a carrier, Ivan asked if he could see the other hedgehogs.

"Right-O," responded Marilyn, as she led the pair downstairs into the basement, which was warmer than the rest of the house. "Got to keep 'em warm, y'know."

There were about 40 hedgehogs in a basement room, also in medium sized cages similar to the guinea pig cages in the living room.

"Got 'er prize breedin' male," said Marilyn, as she held up a tiny albino hedgehog. "Don't look like much but he's a real Casanova. 'Bout two years old, so he's going to be around for some time."

"He seems to be very sweet tempered," said Jenna.

"A real charmer, 'e is," remarked Marilyn. "'Ave a look at Big Mama over 'ere," as she hefted a very large female chocolate colored hedgehog.

"Wow!" exclaimed Ivan, "I do not think I've ever seen a hedgehog that big."

"Rightly even bigger than most English 'edgehogs," said Marilyn, "about two and a half pounds she be."

"Are you going to sell her?" asked Ivan.

"Oh, no," said Marilyn, "not for now at least. She's a very good Mum. I might think about it about six months from now when she reaches retirement age. Don't want to breed 'em too old, you know. Not healthy."

"Well, maybe you could let us know when you retire her?" Ivan asked, feeling that he was slipping down some sort of a slippery slope.

"Will do," responded Marilyn. Name's Wumplin' but I think it was supposed to be Dumplin.' Her first owner made a typo on her computer when she sent the name to her friends and put a W there instead of a D. Imagine that, named by a typographical error."

"We will keep that in mind," said Ivan, as they gathered the carrier with the two new hedgehogs, Grumpy and Angel.

Inside the carrier, Grumpy and Angel were wondering what was going on.

"Now what?!" exclaimed Grumpy, as they were loaded in the car.

"Didn't you tell me that a Dowager that lives near here wanted to see us?" Angel asked.

"Yes, I did," replied Grumpy, "but I am not sure this is the right crew. It is old Thelma, from the Old Country, but I thought she was living with a young human college student. I guess she knows what she's doing. Fine old lady. Very wise and diplomatic. If she wants to see us you can bet it's important."

"Well, she may want to see you, but I don't know what she could possibly want with me," said Angel. "I'm too young to know anything."

"Don't sell yourself short, Kid," said Grumpy. "Those old ladies have ways of finding uses for you that you never even knew you had."

Grumpy and Angel were unloaded and put in a large plastic container with translucent walls. In there with them was a water bowl, food bowl, blankets, a few toys, and one of those exercise wheels.

"Well!" Grumpy exclaimed. "These digs are certainly more room than at Marilyn's place."

"Look it this!" Angel shouted, letting out a clearly audible squeal. "A wheel! A Curt Decker 10 inch! Not too shabby! Wonder what I can get it up to."

"Sheesh," sighed Grumpy, "just don't poop on the thing! I like my wheel as well as the next pog, but some of you guys are just plain gross."

"Hey, Grumper," said Angel, "you are too much of a neat freak. All the pogs say that."

That night, Angel wheeled with abandon and, of course, got poop all over the wheel. For weeks she had been searching Marilyn's house for a wheel and found none. The next morning, Jenna and Ivan came downstairs and were preparing to take Grumpy and Angel to Cilla's veterinary clinic.

"Oh, gross!" Jenna exclaimed, taking a look at the poop-covered wheel.

"Wow, that's pretty ripe," added Ivan.

Angel was dead to the World, with a very contented smile on her face. Grumpy, on the other hand, was disgusted.

"Never thought I'd be agreeing with Bigs," she fumed quietly to herself. "Blechhh."

After noticing that Grumpy was absolutely spotless, Ivan decided to give her a bath anyway, so he could see if her to see if her toenails needed clipping. Amazingly enough, they did not. "What an extraordinary hedgehog," Ivan noted. "Never seen one so clean."

After drying off from their baths, Angel and Grumpy were plunked down in the center of the hedgehog room. Both sat stock still as Ivan and Jenna watched in silence to be sure everyone got along.

The first hedgehog to greet them was Louise, who had heard the commotion and had tunneled out from under her newspapers. "Hi!" she greeted, "you must be Grumpy and Angel!"

"Those we are," answered Grumpy, "heard we were called by a Dowager. Can't say I'm displeased by the surroundings. What's wrong with your fur?!"

"My fur?" Louise answered.

"Your fur!" Grumpy exclaimed. "It's all gray!"

"Oh," answered Louise, "it's from the newsprint ink. Harmless stuff. Made from soybeans. I stay under the papers so I can take off in any direction. Don't like to have my exits blocked."

"Well, I can appreciate that," said Grumpy, "but that paper is unacceptable. You look crappy. We'll have to get some blank paper."

"How do you do that?" Louise asked.

"Easy," replied Grumpy. "The newspaper company has what they call 'end rolls' that are blank paper at the end of the press run. They can't run out of all the paper on a roll or it will mess up the press. So there's always some blank paper left."

"Yeah, but how can we get some?" Louise asked.

"Easy," Grumpy answered. "I know a pog in California whose human caretaker has a Dad that works at a newspaper. I'll have her send Ivan a roll of it. Hopefully he'll get the message."

"Say," asked Louise, "haven't the Bigs declared hedgehogs illegal in California?"

"Hedgehogs and a whole bunch of other so-called 'exotic' animals," answered Grumpy, "but my friend out there lays low. Her human caretaker is pretty quiet about it."

"You are welcome to join me under the papers," offered Louise.

"Thanks for the offer, but no thanks," replied Grumpy, "I'll wait for the blank paper to get here. I'll be able to find a spot until then."

During this conversation, Angel was looking around at the environment. At the doorway was a rather tall "kiddie gate" that did not look too terribly difficult to scale for an accomplished and motivated climber, which she certainly was. But why escape when you had wheels to run on? And there were two of them there, another Curt Decker 10 inch, and an absolutely high speed Jennifer Young redliner bucket wheel! Angel bet she could get that Young wheel up to 100 miles per hour. Angel figured she was in pog heaven.

The whole scenario was interrupted by the arrival of Little Flash and Rosie, who had waddled up from the Hedgiehouse to greet the newcomers. Friendly greetings were exchanged and the group sort of sat in a huddle long enough to convince Ivan and Jenna that all was well among the new additions to the group.

After exploring the area for a few hours and sniffing every thing in sight, Little Flash suggested that they have a meeting with Thelma, and get down to some serious business. They met in the dim light of the Hedgiehouse.

Thelma began: "I cannot thank both of you enough for coming. We need dedicated contraries, *heyokas*, here during the difficult times ahead."

"Hmm, you don't get any more *heyoka* than Grumpy!" exclaimed Louise happily. "I'm so glad to see you here! And the little Olympian *heyoka* Angel is an added plus."

"I agree," continued Thelma, "good *heyokas* are essential to these problems that are before us. Although I do not know all of the details yet, many insects are fed up with the Bigs and are devising ways to have the Bigs in this country attack Bigs in other countries with their highly dangerous weapons. The bugs then know the Bigs in the other countries will retaliate with similar weapons. Their aim is to have the Bigs wipe each other out."

"Have you tried talking with these bugs?" Angel asked.

"We have tried several times," answered Thelma, "but they have been hostile and unresponsive. Worse yet, it seems that these insects are not only set on doing this, but they are led by a hedgehog!"

"Whaaa . . . t!" Angel exclaimed.

"A hedgehog?" Grumpy asked, surprised. "What hedgehog in her right mind would do such a thing?"

"I appreciate your alarm," continued Thelma, "and he seems to be a rather strange hedgehog as well."

"I 'spose he is!" Grumpy said. "What a freak! Leading bugs around to destroy the Bigs. Hang around this planet long enough and you'll hear everything!"

"His chief henchbugs are mantises," added Thelma.

"No surprise there," said Grumpy. "Mantises, besides having absolutely NO sense of humor, have been grumbling about the Bigs for as long as I can remember."

"Their hedgehog leader, who calls himself Anthross, attacked us the other night by flinging contaminated poop at us" said Thelma. "Apparently he wants us gone along with the Bigs. We've had to double the field mouse guard and listening posts around the place."

"So what are you planning to deal with this . . . this . . . horror?" Angel asked.

"We've been thinking of asking Major General Spikers to mobilize his Marine Division for all-out combat," replied Thelma.

"Whew!" Angel exclaimed, startled. "That's pretty drastic. No other way to deal with this Anthross guy?"

"Not that we can see," said a dejected Thelma. "I think that their plan, if carried out, will destroy the entire planet and everything on it."

"These sure are strange events," offered Angel, after the group had been sitting in silence for a while after Thelma had finished.

"Not so strange," said Grumpy, who continued: "Trouble with you, Thelma, is that although you are a very wise Dowager, you are also much too trusting. Your reputation of wishing to convince the Bigs to clean up their act by letting them in on the Original Instructions is noble but there are a good number of hedgehogs that think the Bigs will only exploit that and probably try to eliminate us. Bigs do not handle criticism well and they certainly will not curb their greed and desire for unlimited power."

"Well, I know the controversial aspects of that," answered Thelma, "but I think the notion has promise and hope for the world. What I really cannot figure out are these strange events, and most notably the involvement of hedgehogs."

"You cannot figure them out because you think too well of everyone and every thing," answered Grumpy. "But the events are quite plain to me."

"Care to explain?" Little Flash asked.

"Of course." replied Grumpy. "The strange hedgehog behavior is exhibited by hedgehogs that are on the fringe of our moral grounds. They are often the lost ones that must be shepherded along. I know several of them. They are weak, from weak environments. Weak individuals make up for their weakness by craving power when and where they can find and wield it. They scheme and manipulate, for they lack the courage to confront real problems head on. As has been said by many—only the weak are cruel, gentleness can only be expected from the strong. Rosie, I'll bet you knew several in that mill place where you were born."

"Yes, I did," answered Rosie. "They were sorta pitiful. They had little courage and were very scared most of the time. They were often bossed around by the likes of that obnoxious hedgehog Bowls. And, you know, Bowls himself seemed lost and possessed only of the courage of a bully. He seemed shallow and really a coward underneath. Often I even felt sorry for him."

"These strange hissing accents come from the world of insects, not mammals," Grumpy said. All of this is the product of some source outside of our realm of hedgehogs that are following the Original Instructions. I don'tt know exactly what it is yet, but I can tell you it's not good. Anything that runs counter to the Original Instructions is not good! Hearing this speech in various places also tells us that they, whoever they are, are organized."

"And the cockroaches under the sink?" Louise asked.

"That is the most serious part," said Grumpy. "Cockroaches do not mass in formations like that. Ants sometimes, bees maybe, but not cockroaches. They are massing for a reason and I don't think it's a coincidence that hedgehogs speaking in these strange accents were nearby. This is an organized effort. It's not good! There's danger afoot! I can smell it!"

"So you agree that we need to call in Major General Spikers and his Marine Division?" Thelma asked.

"That's the very least we need to do!" Grumpy replied.

"We need to do more?" Rosie asked. "What?"

"You need to realize some things about Major General Spikers," continued Grumpy. "I know him well. He's a grand old warrior whose courage is unexcelled. But, like all of us, he has a weakness or two. He's a brilliant tactical fighter. He knows battle and the importance of swift movement, transportation, and logistics. But he's such a scrupulously honest soldier, he hates dishonesty and deception. So, he never likes to use spies, or even clandestine forms of 'military intelligence.' The 'Old Man' drives me nuts with his disdain of clandestine work. So, we'd have to convince him that he needs a strong intelligence faction, what the military calls a G-2. This is going to be a big battle!"

"Well, I know General Spikers, too, and I agree," offered Thelma, "he is definitely not a 'sneak-around' kind of guy. Do you really think he will need that much 'military intelligence?'"

"Absolutely," replied Grumpy, "from what I've seen this Anthross group is very secretive, not to mention nasty. We can't fight something we don't understand. Intelligence is the key. Fer cryin' out loud General Spikers does not even HAVE a G-2. The G-1 Administration guy fills in as the G-2."

"Where would we find such a, er, . . . spy?" Rosie asked.

"Not to worry, I have a couple in mind," said Grumpy, "indeed probably the best there ever was."

"Who might that be?" Little Flash asked.

"A character named Bozeman," continued Grumpy, "sneakiest hedgehog that ever lived. The guy is amazing. Escape from anything, anywhere, any time."

"Do you think General Spikers will put up with him?" Thelma asked.

"No." Grumpy said. "It will be a very hard sell. Also, there are some other holes in the 2d Marines staffing that we will have to look after. General Spikers has done the best he could down there in Texas, but he has not been challenged with this kind of a mission before. For the animal abuse combat he has been concentrating on artillery and infantry field forces. For this mission he will also need good staff officers and a few special units."

"Anyone else in mind?" Thelma asked.

"A few," responded Grumpy. "There is an old hand named Shakespeare that would make a great regimental commander for prairie dogs. There's also a crazy guy called Critical Bill that will take on any mission. Ideal for the staff are two old-timers. Ms. Tiggywinkle is a logistical genius and the best bet for the G-4 supply chief, and old Clyde, the unflappable master tactician is a shoo-in for the G-3 operations staff chief. Also, there is a young but very talented warrior named Ukuqambe that is really impressive—restrained but real tenacious."

With the mention of Qambe, Rosie sat straight up: "Where is he? He's an old friend, a fine, fine old friend!"

"Some of these pogs are going to be hard to find, Rosie," said Grumpy. "But we'll find them. 'Qambe is a fine pog, a real traditional. His dislike of the Bigs is a little extreme, though. He'll make a fine field commander."

"How do you know all of this military stuff, Grumpy?" Rosie asked.

"Umm, she's a colonel in the Marine Reserves and is General Spikers' Chief of Staff of the Division," said Louise quietly. "Now you know why her gear is always so squared away."

"Oh," said Rosie, "learn something new every day."

"How does a militant feminist like you fit in with the Marines?" Little Flash asked.

"Very compatible," said Grumpy. "Both require a fighting spirit, and you do not want to get in the way of either one."

"Then it is settled," said Thelma. "We call up General Spikers and the Second Hedgehog Marine Division."

"Semper Fi!" Louise said.

"Oooo-Rah!" Grumpy exclaimed.

CHAPTER 10

MAJOR GENERAL SPIKERS

Major General Spikers, United Hedgehog Marine Corps

CHAPTER 10—MAJOR GENERAL SPIKERS

Major General Spikers, United Hedgehog Marine Corps, awakened after his customary four hours of sleep to reconnoiter the area. No change, he observed. No action either. This was getting old. He was camped out here in Texas with little to do since he had been assigned to Dallas to battle animal abuse in pet stores. But now there was new information!

Word of his transfer had come via MMS, or Mouse Messenger Service. Unbeknown to the more crude humans, which included almost all of them other than the so-called "animal communicators," animals communicated using a very wide range of couriers and telepathy. The MMS was generally the "end user" couriers because they can most easily get in and out of buildings. Over land and air, all manners of animals relayed messages and each had their strengths and weaknesses. Ferrets, for example, were both fast and reliable, but tended not to be trusted by other small messengers, such as mice and prairie dogs because they often saw the other couriers as a potential lunch. Chipmunks were very accurate, but they would not go long distances. They took forever to get from one point to another as they spent most of their time frolicking. Prairie dogs goofed off too much and always wanted to socialize. Squirrels were good messengers as long as they did not get distracted by food along the way. Then, of course, there were the rats. Rats refused to deal with messages at all, saying that they had enough to do running the transportation system.

Many years ago with the advent of transportation by horse and sail, the rats assumed the role of animal travel agent. Small, agile, and strong, they developed skills of stowing away on virtually any form of transportation. Down through the ages, rats have mastered all new forms of travel. Although they will accommodate traveling messengers, they, themselves, will not carry messages unless the messages are for the transportation system, which means, for other rats.

At the time the first message arrived, Spikers was commanding his Second Hedgehog Marine Division and, as he had originally proposed, was combating animal abuse. This was mainly carried out through infantry attacks (notifying state and local authorities of abusive pet stores) and artillery strikes (firing U.S. Department of Agriculture inspectors) at abusers.

The job really was not as exciting as Spikers had originally envisioned it. Actually, it had gotten pretty routine. Spikers was getting annoyed with being a "desk general." He needed a beach to hit somewhere! He envisioned himself as a pog of action and here he sat in Fort Worth, Texas directing infantry and artillery strikes from his office. Spikers had grown a little too heavy for his own satisfaction and felt that he needed to get out in the field for a while.

"Squeek!"

"Huh!?" groused Spikers, as he looked up and saw the tiny field mouse hunched a safe distance from Spikers' camouflaged hedgiehut.

"Squeek," repeated the mouse, "m . . . m . . . m . . . message for you, Sir."

"Well, out with it young fellow!" Spikers bellowed in his usual authoritative tone.

"W . . . w . . . well," continued the mouse, "t . . . t . . . this is from Dowager Thelma in Colorado. She wishes for you to come to see her and Colonel Grumpy for a special mission. A dangerous mission. She also said that you should not attract much attention in how you come there."

General Spikers squinted at the mouse, and then said "What channels did that message come through, young man?"

"I'm a girl, Sir," squeaked the mouse. "Name's Madeline."

"Oh, sorry, young lady," said Spikers, and then grumbled under his breath, "Arghh, mice, can't tell 'em apart."

"It came from field mice to prairie dogs in Colorado, then through a marmot network along the mountains to New Mexico, then more prairie dogs to a squirrel runner service to Dalhart. I think some coyotes brought it to Lubbock, although that is not too clear. Then it was handed off to another squirrel outfit, and then to me. Only took about a week. Not bad."

"Harrumph!" Spikers grumbled, "two sets of prairie dogs. I guess I'm lucky it didn't take three months with those clowns. Alright, young lady," Spikers raised his tone, "I have an assignment for you!"

"Yes, Sir," squeaked Madeline, "be happy to help. We mice appreciate your work to stop neglect at pet stores."

"Well, I've got to get out of here legitimately and without suspicion, so I'm going to have to call in some fire on my position. Here's what I want you to do. The humans that live here go to Hulen Mall on Tuesday evenings to shop. The kid that is supposed to take care of me has been whining for a more cuddly pet. So, get your friends to somehow hustle a chinchilla into the front window of the pet store in that mall. Got it?"

"Chinchilla in the window?" Madeline replied. "We can do that. I have lots of friends at the mall."

"Good! Ought to work," said Spikers, "then that kid Malcolm will beg his momma for that chinchilla, and here he will come."

"Then what, Sir?" Madeline asked.

"Well, then the kid will neglect me and his momma will raise cane, and off I will go." Spikers explained. "They will get on the Internet and try to sell me or give me away. You know what humans are like. Souls bought and sold."

"Isn't that dangerous, Sir?" Madeline asked. "The boy's mom may not notice that you are being neglected."

"Risks of war," answered Spikers, "but I could stand to lose a few grams anyway."

Madeline scurried off and it was not too long before a chinchilla by the name of Fifi was delivered into Spikers' environment. The chinchilla chatted on and on about how this very special little boy had picked her out as someone special. Of course, she WAS in the window of the pet shop at the mall and had wondered how she suddenly got to be in the showcase.

"Hello, there, Hedgehog," Fifi swooned, "I am Malcolm's new pet. I guess you are passe around here, aren't you?"

Spikers let out an audible groan and managed a strained, low, "pleasedtameetcha."

The chinchilla babbled on about room decor and adequate dust baths, as well as the finer quality of dust bath products.

Spikers just sat there and wondered to himself what he had done. "OK," he thought to himself, "I tried this 'neglect' shtick to get out of here, but I did not deserve THIS." Then he said to Fifi, "Say, you seem a little more fashion conscious and sophisticated than most chinchillas I've met?" He tried to make his voice drip with sarcasm, but it went right by the chinchilla.

"That is very observant of you to notice, hedgehog," whined Fifi, "we chinchillas become more sophisticated the closer we live to Dallas."

"Howzat?" Spikers asked.

"Proximity to Neiman Marcus, of course," droned Fifi, sounding a bit bored.

"Oh, shoulda known," said Spikers, opting to terminate the conversation before he became ill.

As predicted, Malcolm spent hours playing with his new pet and left Spikers alone to the extent that he began forgetting to provide food and water. After about a week, Malcolm's Mom noticed that Spikers' cage was looking dismal. This was helped along by Spikers himself, who made sure things were noticeably disheveled. Spikers did not like this one bit, as he prided himself on being squared away. All in all, it was a miserable time for the Old Man.

#

The depressing state of affairs caused Spikers to sit idly by and reminisce upon his past and how he came to be in this place at this time. He remembered his amazing beginnings on that bright morning in the pet shop where he was offered for sale as a youngster.

"He's a fine looking little fellow!" the woman exclaimed. "Just what Mack needs! A bristly little companion that won't be too much trouble."

"Yes, Mrs. Tarr," answered the pet store clerk. "And he's guaranteed against any illnesses plus we'll take him back if Mr. Tarr decides he's not the pet for him."

"I appreciate that, young lady, but I think Mack will just love him. We used to have big dogs, but you know they are terribly hard to keep up with once you get on up in your eighties."

Joan Tarr, walking slowly and relying heavily on her cane, exited the pet store with her new friend, an as-yet unnamed baby hedgehog that was to be a gift for her husband, Macklin "Mack" Tarr, age eighty-seven, Lieutenant General, United States Marine Corps, Retired.

Joan and Mack Tarr, married upon his graduation from the Naval Academy and now celebrating 65 years together, knew one-another very well. Through three major wars and over forty years of active military service, the couple weathered the trials of long separations and the possibilities of death in combat. For most of her life, Joan was employed by the Red Cross and had come to specialize in disaster relief, herself a well known and respected executive throughout her career.

In their younger days they had kept horses and loved big, wooly dogs. Now, in their later years, both were in the state of frail health that great age brings. Joan had visited her physician a week ago and received some bleak news. The brain tumor that had been discovered six months ago was advancing. She knew it would not be long now. Joan had long talks with her two daughters and all three agreed they wanted to get Mack a companion animal of some kind—someone to keep him company in the lonely void that would occur when Joan departed, as she knew she soon would. The search became an obsession, as Joan and her daughters scoured the newspapers and the pet stores, for they were not even sure what kind of pet they wanted.

Then they saw him. A little white ball of quills in a pet store aquarium.

"What, on earth, is THAT thing?!" Joan's daughter, Marie, asked.

"It's a hedgehog," said the clerk, "kinda gruff at first but a little softie once you get to know him."

Joan stared off into space and said slowly, almost mechanically, with tears beginning to well up in her eyes: "Kinda gruff at first but a little softie once you get to know him."

On the way home in the car, Marie asked, "Do you really think Daddy will take to that little thing you just bought?"

"Oh, yes," replied Joan, as she held the little hedgehog in her lap, "they're made for each other." As usual, Joan was not wrong in her assessment. Mack was overjoyed.

"Say, look at this little trooper!" Mack exclaimed. "Well, now Lieutenant Spikers, naming him instantly, what a fine fighting Marine you'll make! Not every day a new trooper comes with his own armor!"

And so it went, the newly commissioned hedgehog went everywhere with the aged general. As Spikers gained in size, weight, and age, he was promoted up through the ranks as the General thought Spikers was ready to take on new responsibilities. At his reunions of old military buddies, Spikers, also known in those circles as "Little General Mack," became well known. Several of the old-timers, veterans of World War II, got hedgehogs of their own to care for and induct into the "hedgehog military."

In his travels to visit old friends, he even came across several that already had hedgehogs. Spikers got to interact with some of his peers on these trips. Among them included a few up in Colorado—youngsters named Roscoe and Bill, and a rangy little fellow named Shakespeare. Down South, he got a chance to stay with an independent little character named Sergeant Gunny Prickles, where he learned a good deal about escape and evasion.

Mack's preferred pastime was reading in his library of past military exploits, especially obscure publications produced by individual units, such as battalions, regiments, brigades, and divisions. As he read, Spikers was always at his side or in his lap. Mack and Spikers were the inseparable recipients of long forages into military history. Although they studied military exploits through all ages, they spent most of their time on the BIG war, World War II, where Mack had commanded a battalion in combat. He had also been highly decorated, winning the Navy Cross and the Silver Star for valor, as well as four Purple Hearts for wounds.

One of Spikers' favorite times were the Sundays when the old General's great-granddaughter Trudy visited. Now fifteen years of age, Trudy seemed wise well beyond her years. She was devoted to her great-grandfather and adored Spikers. They always sat and talked at length while sitting in a pair of upholstered blue rockers facing a sturdy inlaid coffee table in the center of General Mack's study. The study was large and lined with many bookcases filled to the ceiling with a vast array of volumes, mostly of military history, but also of art, music, and philosophy. On the floor were several oriental carpets, mostly Heriz, which Spikers loved to traverse. The carpets, all fairly old and well traveled, comfortably fit his paws. Spikers had free range of the study and the adjoining bathroom.

"Grandpa!" Trudy exclaimed. "Do you think Spikers understands us?"
Spikers looked up at the two of them and thought to himself, "Uh, oh."
"Well, Trudy," replied Mack, cautiously, "he comes from among the oldest mammals on Earth. They must have learned a great deal in those tens of millions of years. So let's say they can understand us. Why should they let us in on that secret? What have we humans done to deserve that kind of trust? Precious little, I'm afraid. When our kind has tortured and killed in anger and greed, the wounds we make . . ." he stopped and gazed out the window, then resumed "the wounds we make . . . never heal."

"But I think he understands us, Grandpa. And I think he knows we love him and would never give away his trust."

He gently placed Spikers down on the carpet in front of his rocker. "Captain Spikers, you know where the 102d and 103d Infantry Division histories from World War 2 are shelved. Would you mind trotting over there and showing Trudy where they are?"

Spikers continued to sit on the carpet in front of General Mack and looked up. It was a big decision to comply with this request. It would prove that he understood. "Why not? Maybe a violation of the rules. But this is a fine family I have!"

Trudy sat there, unbelieving, and thinking, logically, that her great-granddad was possibly getting too old to make much sense. But deep down in her heart she knew better. So she just sat there in awe and stared at Spikers, who continued to sit stock still, looking up.

Then it happened. Spikers broke and trotted over the carpets to the ceiling-high bookshelf at the west end of the study. He climbed up on the bottom shelf and pawed at two volumes shelved there, among a wide expanse of books arranged numerically by military unit.

"My goodness!" Trudy exclaimed.

"Go look, Sweetheart," General Mack said, perplexed and relaxed at the same time. "Just go over there and pull the books from the bottom shelf that Spikers just pawed."

Trudy got up and went over to the bookcase. Spikers sat there and looked up, not moving. She gently pulled the two tall volumes from the bookshelf and opened the cover of the first. She read the title page: "With the 102d Infantry Division Through Germany, Edited by Major Allan H. Mick, Washington, Infantry Journal Press, First Edition, 1947." Then she read the dedication on the following page: "To the officers and men, our friends, who died that we might live and hope for a better world." Replacing the volume on the shelf, she opened the cover of the second volume and read: "Report After Action: The Story of the 103d Infantry Division, by Ralph Mueller and Jerry Turk, Artist Bill Barker, copyright 1945, 103d Infantry Division."

Silence.

Spikers trotted back to his favorite spot on the carpet under the coffee table.

Trudy stared at her great-grandfather.

Silence.

"Grandpa," Trudy softly spoke, "he **knows!**"

"Yes, he does," answered Mack. "He . . . they . . . always have."

"I'm trying to figure this out, Grandpa. You trained him, right?"

"**HA!**" Mack exclaimed loudly, surprising himself, Trudy, and Spikers, who jumped straight up and hit his head on the bottom of the coffee table. "One thing I've learned about hedgehogs is there's no training them!"

"Then why did you pick books on the bottom shelf?"

"Well, Sweetie," said Mack resignedly, "if I picked a division on the top shelf, say the First Infantry Division, Spikers would have had to get a hedgehog-sized extension ladder to climb up there. Figured something on the bottom shelf would be suitable without having to request logistical support."

"Grandpa, I still think you trained him."

"Look, I'm as surprised as you are. Old as I am, I still don't know what to make of it. So, let's see. Why don't you go around the library and pick a spot. Don't stop, just look at the books on the bottom shelves and memorize a title."

"Grandpa, this is really goofy!"

Silence.

"I think."

Silence.

"OK, I'll do it!"

Trudy crawled all over the large study on all fours, peering at the bottom shelves of books as she went. Mack and Spikers followed her visibly. Finally she got up and plunked herself down in her rocker. "OK, I got one."

"Well, what is it?" Mack asked of his great-granddaughter.

"It is a gray book with red letters in a slipcase . . ."

"Say, listen up Spikers!" Mack jovially exclaimed.

". . . with the name 'Bonhoeffer' on the spine," ended Trudy.

Spikers looked up and thought to himself, "Hrummph, she could have picked a less depressing book! THAT book is far worse than even war." He trotted over to the other end of the study and climbed up on the bookcase base and pawed at the spine of the Dietrich Bonhoeffer book, "Letters and Papers from Prison."

"He *has* to know!" Trudy exclaimed.

"Told ya, Sweetheart," Mack said. "Is this a very special gift for us, or what?"

"It is. It IS! But what can we do with it or make of it? Who shall we tell? This is a big discovery, Grandpa!"

"I'm afraid we cannot tell anyone, Trudy."

"But Grandpa, this is important!"

"Yes, it is. Probably the most important thing I have ever learned in this long life of mine. But, Trudy, where we have been given a very special gift, it is also a secret."

"But, but . . ." Trudy stammered.

"Others would not understand. They would call us crazy."

"But we could SHOW them!"

"No, we can't. Young Spikers won't do that for others. I can guarantee that. Don't you see that he did this just for us? Did you see him hesitate before he trotted over to those books?"

"But, Grandpa!"

"Don't try too hard, Trudy. We humans are so very limited in our ability to understand too much of anything. Just rejoice in what has happened to us just now." His voice trailed off, "In all my life and for all I've seen, I have never . . . never . . ."

The old general stood, straightened up, and carefully and formally saluted the little hedgehog. Mack and Trudy swore they saw Spikers raise his right front paw in a return salute.

#

As she knew it was coming, Joan Tarr traveled on her journey away from this world when Spikers was about a year old. She had been right. Mack had Spikers in his pocket at her funeral service and at graveside. As he was helped back from the grave site by his daughters, grandchildren, and great-grandchildren, once in the car, Mack gently placed Spikers in his lap. Marie overheard him say, "Well, it's just you and me now, Old Man," as he petted Spikers gently.

One day just over a year later, Marie was looking in on her father as she did at the end of each day and found him relaxed in his favorite chair in his study. He had joined Joan in her journey over the Bridge to the next world. In his lap lay open a book about the World War I history of the Thirty Third Infantry Division—the Division of the Golden Cross. Just above the book, snuggled up on his side was Spikers, Mack's companion to the end. Unfortunately, at the time of General Tarr's death, his great-granddaughter Trudy Preston was away at a school camp.

In the initial commotion surrounding the death of General Mack, Spikers was quickly handed off to an old family friend who agreed to take him in. He was almost immediately disposed of by being sold to a pet store. For cash. No questions asked.

Most distraught about the hedgehog was one of the great-grandchildren, Trudy, who wished to take in the hedgehog. Her parents told her to forget about it, citing too many pets already and Trudy's need to study for college. Trudy knew that they did not understand, and at this point could not understand. Why, they did not even know the name of the hedgehog! Why should they? No one really cared.

#

Unbeknownst to Spikers, Trudy persisted in her pursuit to recover him. After some two months of cajoling and relentless avenues of persuasion, her parents finally relented. After all, by any standard Trudy was a wonderful kid. Bright and energetic with a strong moral code, she was focused on a career as a zoologist from as far back as anyone could remember.

Her heart sank when, finally permitted to make the phone call about Spikers, she was informed that he had been sold to a pet store in Dallas about two weeks ago. Trudy finally got an uncle to drive her to the Dallas pet store.

"Nope, don't have no hedgehog," said the store manager a second time, after Trudy had questioned several clerks in the shop.

"But there must be some mistake!" Trudy insisted. "My cousin's friend said she brought him to this very shop two weeks ago and you paid her thirty dollars for him."

"That's not possible 'cause we cain't legally buy or sell hedgehogs. Fed'rul law."

"Look," said Trudy, "I just want him back. I'll pay whatever you want. I know she brought him here. Her parents came with her."

"You got a ree-ceet?"

"Her folks said you paid her in cash and there were no receipts."

"Cain't sell what I don't have," replied the manager.

Things got worse for Trudy, because she never believed anyone in her family would sell her great-grandfather's home. But everything was put up for sale—the home and everything in it. The old rugs went to a carpet merchant and the books, all of Macks treasured books went to a bookseller who bought the books by weight! Trudy pleaded with her parents to let her have at least the things in Grandpa Mack's study. Once again she was dismissed as a "child." She vowed that some day she would find and bring home her great-grandfathers special place in the world—Spikers and that magical library.

#

Spikers suspected that his sale to the pet store manager was a secret transaction. He knew he had no rights and no protection. He knew he could be killed at any time and no one would know, and few, if any, would care.

From that point Spikers lived in several "homes" and pet stores. He truly missed the old General and Trudy. During his despair at one pet shop he wondered to himself, "how difficult life is when you cannot make your own choices."

A woman, wealthy by almost any account, was attracted to the strange animal in the plexiglass container. Her son Malcolm was always interested in "weird" pets, she said. None of those humans had any idea of what the reality was. How could they?

#

Madeline the mouse showed back up again to look in and see how things were going. This time she brought a couple of friends, Stanley and Mona.

"Squeek," Madeline sounded her customary greeting, and then got wide eyed at the mess she saw before her, which was quite a contrast to what Spikers' environment looked like just a few days ago. "Ewww, what happened?"

"Harummph," snorted Spikers, "a pog's gotta do what a pog's gotta do."

Stanley the mouse piped up, "They're on the computer now."

"What ARE you talking about?" Spikers growled.

"Trying to find you a home," said Mona. "The mom is chewing out the kid for not taking care of you and telling the kid she's going to find the hedgehog a new home."

"Yeah," said Spikers, "I figured the end was near when she tossed some food in my place last night. She didn't seem too happy."

After a few days, Malcolm's mom found a woman over in Dallas that billed herself as a "hedgehog rescue." Emails flew back and forth and the woman, Heather, volunteered to take in Spikers.

As they were going out the door, Spikers nudged the corner of his carrier, and it opened, depositing Spikers in the grass. Knowing how to provide the proper set of nudges to animal carriers was a skill that Spikers got very good at in his younger days in Marine Escape and Evasion School. He had learned from the very best, Sergeant Gunney, one of the few hedgehogs who insisted upon being a sergeant rather than an officer.

"I work for a living!" Sergeant Gunney often said.

Spikers took off in the direction of the porch of the house. As Malcolm screamed for his mother that the hedgehog had escaped, Spikers called for Madeline under the porch. Almost immediately, Madeline, Mona, and Stanley presented themselves in front of the General. Now there were no physical barriers between them and the enormous hedgehog, who looked menacingly down at them from under his helmet with the two stars on the front. He looked at them for a short time and then saluted them with his right front paw. "Mission accomplished!" he exclaimed. "You are brave troopers! And you believe in the welfare of all animals. You have my gratitude . . . and salute!"

The three tiny mice stood tall and proud. Such a recognition from a senior commander of the very oldest animals on Earth was to be treasured. General Spikers then fished three tiny mouse-sized commendation medals from under his helmet and presented them to each mouse.

Major General Spikers then slowly marched out from under the porch, to be scooped up by Malcolm and was placed back in the carrier.

Spikers was delivered to Heather's Dallas apartment and at the time of delivery the total elapsed time since the message had been delivered by Madeline was just under 30 days. In Spikers' estimation, that was not bad timing seeing as how it was a fairly elaborate scheme. However, he still had to get to Colorado.

The accommodations at Heather's were more spacious than at Malcolm's. There were also other hedgehogs there, some six in all. Most were "rescues" but two were used for breeding, as Heather considered herself both a breeder and rescuer.

Major General Spikers was mainly interested in two "rescue" hedgehogs at Heather's, an elderly female named Blackberry, and a rather strange fellow called Dungaree. Dungaree was quite angry most of the time and constantly complained about the Bigs. He groused about how they had messed everything up and had to be done away with. He did his part by biting every human he could.

"Death to the Bigsss!" Dungaree would often say in a strange, hissing tone.

Blackberry was a different story altogether. She was the senior hedgehog in terms of age at Heather's rescue, and had near Dowager qualities. She was very gentle and wise, and kindly to all of the beings in the home, including

Dungaree, who was known by the other hedgehogs simply as "DD" which stood for "Disagreeable Dungaree."

"What's the drill?" Spikers bellowed, which was his favorite question when entering into any situation not involving combat. In Spikers' mind, anything not involving combat was drill preparing for combat. He got that straight from General Mack.

Blackberry answered Spikers in her customary soothing tone. "There is a great deal of strife around and Grand Dowager Thelma has requested you join her in Northern Colorado for a serious conference. I am not privy to all of the details, but Dungaree just left this morning. I guess these are opportune moments because Heather's fiance is causing difficulty for her.

"How so?" Spikers asked, lowering his normally blustery tone.

"Well," continued Blackberry, "theirs is a fairly tumultuous relationship in human terms. He is on a power trip and she is trying to recover from a very painful background. Humans! You know, their own worst enemy. Yesterday he told her she had to make a choice between him and all of these hedgehogs."

"Hmm," said Spikers, "not much of a choice there. Naturally she chose the hedgehogs."

"Not quite," said Blackberry, "she agreed to send some of the hedgehogs away to calm him down. Looks like it is you and Dungaree for now. But that is OK because you are both going north on an airplane and that is what we want, right?"

"Well, it's what I want," said Spikers, "but I'm not sure where this Dungaree fits into it. Guy gives me the creeps. I hope they don't assign him to my command. I do not need new discipline problems."

"You leave tomorrow, General," continued Blackberry. "A human named Ivan is flying through Dallas from Austin on his way to Colorado and is going to take you up there."

"Humphh," grumbled Spikers, "I hope it's in a carrier I can get out of. Riding in the cabin with the humans is plush, but I have to make some liaison visits in the airport before we leave."

CHAPTER 11

SPIKERS TRAVELS NORTH

Major General Spikers, United Hedgehog Marine Corps

CHAPTER 11—SPIKERS TRAVELS NORTH

As was the norm, Heather was not on speaking terms with her fiance on the following day. Since she had no automobile of her own, Heather had cajoled her father into taking her and Spikers to the airport.

General Spikers was fairly livid for three reasons, all of which had to do with the small cardboard box in which he was being transported. First, he had no way to escape and do his business at the airport. Second, the box was stuffy, small, and uncomfortable. Third, he could not see where he was going.

Heather was a sweet soul, thought Spikers, as humans go. Her fiance, on the other hand, could use a direct dose of artillery.

Once at the airport, Heather and Spikers went to meet Ivan at his arrival gate, but were stopped cold at the metal detector. "No animals beyond this point without a ticket," droned the security guard. Heather brought the box holding Spikers back to her father in the lobby, and then went on to meet Ivan.

Ivan, however, had brought a carrier for the trip that was measured to specification in order to fit under the airplane seat. Once meeting up with Heather and accompanying her back to the lobby, Spikers was transferred from the box into the carrier. As they were making small talk walking through the lobby toward the security checkpoint, suddenly the carrier came apart, and this very large, white hedgehog, made a beeline for the airline ticket counter.

Spikers rounded the corner of the counter and, looking up and down the counter quickly, heard a voice. "In here, Old Man!" came the voice from a crevasse under the counter.

People had been staring at the event, and wondered what that large white thing with spikes was, moving along the terminal floor. Embarrassed, Heather and Ivan went to airline officials and explained the situation.

In the meantime, Spikers was being treated like royalty.

"Matthews, here!" said the rat in a definite British accent. "Station manager, you know."

They were inside the ticket counter, which was decorated with various works of art in addition to the usual equipment one finds at airports. Spikers was impressed. His Spartan military preferences usually shied away from luxury and opulence, but this was very nicely done. And from rats, no less.

"Care for a spot of tea and a slice of Dundee Cake, General?" Matthews intoned in that crisp upper class British accent of his.

"No, thank you, the Bigs will panic if we do not conclude our business very soon," Spikers replied, "but thanks for the hospitality." He wondered out loud how a rat with a British accent ever got to Dallas, Texas.

"Thank you very much," continued Matthews, "I understand the need to press on, with you traveling in the human cabin and all that. As it happens, transportation is a long-standing specialty among British rats. Goes back to the days of sailing ships, actually. Since we can move about the world with utmost dispatch, it is not unusual to see us in distant lands."

"Impressive," said Spikers, "as is that large painting over the lounge area," referring to a large oil painting of a rat.

"Yes, quite," said Matthews, "Scabbers, you know. Famous, you know."

"Oh, yes," said Spikers, "very brave account for himself on that train outside of London some years back. But didn't he sort of lose it some time later?"

"Quite," continued Matthews, "but then you must take it in the context of the times. Our main interest was his heroic actions on transportation. Besides, heroes among rats are rather difficult to come by, what?"

"I suppose," said Spikers, "which brings us to the matter at hand: Military transport of hedgehogs for combat operations."

"Yes, quite, and for a briefing on that we will call upon our transportation military attache, Sergeant Major Brundish, said Matthews. "SERGEANTMAJOR!" Matthews bellowed, as loud as a rat could bellow, that is.

"SAH!" shouted another rat who had marched up and stood at attention.

"Transportation briefing for the General!" Matthews said with authority.

"Sounds as if you've got some military background, yourself," said Spikers, quietly commenting to Matthews.

"Yes, quite," said Matthews, "long line of military rats back to the humans World War II. With Montgomery in North Africa, you know. Desert rats, you know."

They went into another room where Sergeant Major Brundish explained the rat air transport system. He went into considerable detail as to how rats could smuggle passengers into the pressurized freight holds and even into the human compartments. He unveiled the map of North America showing airport locations and added that not all airports could serve the transport system because planes serving those airports did not have pressurized and heated freight compartments. The briefing concluded by both Matthews and Sergeant Major Brundish assuring General Spikers that the rat air transport system could provide complete assistance.

As they shook paws preparing to depart, Matthews remarked "Already begun your troop movements, eh? Hedgehog fellow came through 'ere yesterday. Odd fellow, I must say. Rather strident, if you will. Chap named Dungaree. Not very courteous."

"He's not one of my boys," said Spikers. "But I agree he's an odd one. Gives me cause to wonder what, on earth, is going on. But I guess I will find out soon enough. Thank you for the excellent briefing."

As they went back toward the entrance to the rat Transport Operations Center, Matthews remarked that in a dire emergency they could short out the wires under the computer consoles if a flight ever needed to be delayed to get an important passenger aboard. "But that is dangerous work both for the rat electrician chewing on the wires and for all of us in that the humans may tear apart the console looking for the trouble before we can restore it. There is one other thing, somewhat troubling, that I probably should mention, General."

"What's that?" Spikers asked.

"Happened yesterday when that Dungaree chap boarded his flight," said Matthews. "The escort rat was besieged with what had to be a hundred or more bloody cockroaches! Too many to fight. He was seriously bitten over and over. He killed a few of them but wound up a bloody mess and is down the hall in the sickroom now."

"Can we visit him?" Spikers responded.

"Right-O," answered Matthews, as Spikers, Matthews, and the Sergeant Major went to the sickroom.

A gray rat was lying on a bed being looked over by a rather portly mole, who Matthews called Dr. Snout.

"Ah, Matthews," Dr. Snout said, "troublesome case here. Infected bites. Nasty little fellows, those cockroaches. We have a very sick rat on our paws here."

"Thanks, Doc," said Matthews, "I'm sure you are doing all you can. This is General Spikers, and of course you know the Sergeant Major. We'd like a few words with Gnarley, here."

"Pleased to meet you General," Dr. Snout said. "Try not to talk too long, he's really quite weak. Needs rest."

"Quite," said Matthews, "we will be brief. Can you tell us about it, Gnarley?"

In a very weak voice Gnarley the rat spoke: "Well, as you know I was escorting that hedgehog Dungaree up into the pressurized animal hold, when these cockroaches also tried to board. Must have been two dozen of them. I began to chase them away because our requirements against transporting insects."

Matthews turned to Spikers and said "Queen's Regs, you know. No insects on board."

"Is this the Queen of the rats?" Spikers asked, not entirely familiar with the hierarchy.

"No, no," answered Matthews, "the Rodent Queen, actually, since some years back we consolidated rodent activities. Efficiency measures, you know. Improves communications and travel, what? The present reigning rodent monarch is a gray squirrel, actually. Queen Rizabeth the Second. Fine lady. Actually had an audience with her once. The rest of us rodent species have leftenant governours-in-council. System works rather well, you know. You hedgehog chaps should give it a go."

"Well, it certainly sounds effective," said Spikers, "I may suggest it to the Seekers and Dowagers."

"Well now, Gnarley, poor chap, what on Earth happened?" Matthews inquired.

Gnarley continued: "As I was chasing them off, it seemed like thousands more attacked me, coming from all over. I disabled a few but I was overcome. They bit and tore at me. You can see my fur is ripped to shreds, and I'm lucky I'm not dead. I've never seen so many—and all of them concentrated on me. I blacked out and woke up here. I have no idea where they all came from . . . or where they went."

"And the hedgehog . . . Dungaree," asked Spikers, "did he assist you in warding off the attacking cockroaches.?"

"That's the strangest part. He just stood there! He did nothing. I looked at him and even tried to speak. But he did nothing. I thought surely he would help me."

"I wonder where the cockroaches went?" Matthews questioned. "When Gnarley was found bloody and unconscious, the rats that found him reported no sign of cockroaches or insects of any kind."

"I think it's quite clear," snarled Spikers in a low voice, "that those cockroaches boarded the plane. They were all going somewhere."

"Rather unsettling, what?" Matthews remarked. "Massed insects! Quite dangerous! Together they outweigh all other moving creatures on Earth!"

"Rest assured we are trying to get to the bottom of this," Spikers said. "I thank you heartily for your hospitality and willingness to do a difficult job, and do it very well. I hope I can return for a visit in the future, under better circumstances."

"Yes, quite!" Matthews said. "Come back any time."

In the terminal, there was anxiety and chaos among the humans, mainly airline ticket personnel, Ivan, Heather, and Heather's Dad. In getting to know hedgehogs better, Ivan had come to appreciate their ability to disappear seemingly into thin air for extended periods of time. Although, Rosie and Angel escaped regularly, it was odd that Thelma, Little Flash, Louise, and Grumpy never tried to do so. And now this Spikers takes off and disappears in the airport, of all places.

Just as Ivan was having anxieties of missing his flight, there he was—Spikers—just sitting there at the corner of the ticket counter! Everyone breathed a sigh of relief as Ivan scooped up Spikers and re-installed him in the carrier, this time being sure to fasten it securely.

Spikers felt he could now sit back and enjoy the ride. He had made contact with the transporter rats and was out of that crummy box. The carrier had little windows all around so he could get a good view of things. This time he went right through the security point with the small green ticket that Ivan had purchased from the airline.

Leaving a tearful Heather behind, Major General Spikers was finally on his way to Colorado and his meeting with The Grand Dowager and Colonel Grumpy.

The trip to Colorado was uneventful except, as usual, the flight attendants all wanted to see the hedgehog. After the attendants made a fuss over Spikers, several passengers, especially those with children, wanted to see him, also.

Once at home, Ivan went through the usual bathing procedure with Spikers as he did with all other hedgehogs entering. Spikers found himself ensconced in the upstairs bathroom where the baths were given. They were spacious quarters with a "kiddie gate" at the entrance. Now tipping the scales at some 700 grams, Spikers considered himself a tad too heavy to try scaling the wall and going over. But he did remember his engineer training and could easily use leverage to move the gate to the side on the bottom to effect an exit. This he did about 3AM when all was quiet except for the faint noise of exercise wheels coming from the downstairs bathroom.

"Ahh . . . piece of cake," Spikers thought to himself as he rounded the corner and viewed the carpeted stairs. Uncarpeted wood stairs would have been a lot more difficult, not in getting down, but in getting back up. Carpets were a cinch. He sort of half-rolled down the long flight of stairs, enjoying himself for the first time in a long time. Bouncing down the stairs was sort of fun, invigorating, as long as he could control the speed. Now near the entrance door, Spikers quickly scurried around to the kitchen and the bathroom off the kitchen where the main group of hedgehogs were housed.

"Oh, my!" Rosie gasped as she spotted the very large silhouette of a hedgehog past the gate. She ran to get Louise and, collaterally, Grumpy, speaking in rapidfire: "T . . . t . . . there's a hedgehog beyond the gate!"

Thinking that Rosie was reporting the reappearance of the strange hedgehog that was firing germ-laden poops at them, they both responded, unknowingly running over Angel, who was still fast asleep, and who awoke with a start and ran along after them. All four stood staring at the gate and the shadow beyond.

"Much bigger than the other hedgehog," offered Louise.

"I'm worried," said Rosie. "Danger seems to be lurking everywhere."

"No good strangers have come up to that gate lately," offered a sleepy Angel.

Suddenly, a commanding voice pierced the air "WHAT'S THE DRILL?" Spikers bellowed.

"Yes! It's General Spikers!" Grumpy shouted.

All of the hedgehogs ran to the gate and wedged a corner open, and Spikers strode inside. Ms. Grumpy gave him a sharp salute, and Spikers returned the compliment.

"Ahh, you're too fast for me, Old Girl," he said, "I've always tried to salute you first."

"Well, General, it's an old game we play," responded Grumpy, "it's so good to see you!"

"I understand the Grand Dowager has some serious concerns," said Spikers.

"Yes, indeed," replied Grumpy, "but first we will talk a bit, and you must meet the hedgehogs that have come together here."

For a long time Spikers visited and talked with the hedgehogs in residence. His most ingoing and interesting conversation was with Rosie, who naively asked question after quesion. Spikers was ready for her.

Rosie began earnestly and incisively, "How can you support war, or any sort of military action? We hedgehogs have survived, thanks to the Original Instuctions, for so long without that."

"A simple set of facts, Ms. Rose," General Spikers said "leads us to do this. There is an evil that deserves attention. The Dowagers and Seekers commissioned me to combat animal abuse. Many of these humans are a tragedy to the planet, but also, like any living things, can be highly instructive. Sometimes, great evil must be faced in an organized manner, especially if that evil is, itself, organized. This is one rare instance where we can learn from the humans. Now there is apparently some large evil lurking now, even more evil than abusive pet stores."

Rosie pressed on, "But why a military force?"

"Because the evil, especially that concocted by humans requires an effective offensive or counter-offensive," continued Spikers, adding that "humans have waged war against one another for thousands of Springtimes. Why not learn from their successes and mistakes?"

"Perhaps," sighed Rosie, "but how do we find a competent and ethical human military commander to emulate?"

"By studying history," said Spikers. "The greatest commanders are few and far between. It's a difficult job, leading soldiers in combat. You must be sure your cause is just and there are no other ways to solve your difficulties. You must often fight far from home and so your supplies must be available, even over long distances, with no interruptions. Then, although you must conquer the enemy as your primary mission, you must do so at the least cost in lives and suffering for your own troops. Finally, you must realize that generals do not win wars, soldiers win wars! You must take care of your soldiers! Sometimes that includes placing their welfare above your obligations to your own superiors, especially if your superiors make bad decisions in battle. Few human generals had these qualities, only a handful, and they merit study."

"Who were they, General?" Rosie asked, ever more curious.

"Well, Epaminondas of Greece who led his farmers to defeat the professional military of Sparta was one. This was some 2,300 Springtimes ago. More recently in the large event known as World War II, I always loved that old grump "Howlin Mad" Smith of the US Marines in the Pacific. Now although such well known generals such as MacArthur and Patton had very illustrious names, I am afraid my most prominent heroes are a little less well known. One was Major General Ernest Harmon of both 1st and 2d Armored Divisions. And my all time favorite was Major General John S. 'Tiger Jack' Wood of the 4th Armored. General Wood, never getting promoted further because he would not kiss up, was the most fiercely loyal commander a bunch of soldiers ever had. In the field he never lived at a standard above his troops. If they were in the mud, so was he. Anyway, you see, we can learn from others. Now in the case of humans, unfortunately, most of what we learn is what NOT to do."

"How do you know when it is proper to commit your troops to battle?"

"That is among the most difficult decisions to make. It requires counsel and thought, unlike the humans, whose military must often charge off at the whim of some power mad or vengeful leader, committing lives to battle some group that does not deserve or need to be attacked. We hedgehogs that adhere to the Original Instructions have checks and balances that only commit troops when essential. We have our Contraries that question our every move. Our military leaders do not go blindly on, but question the reasoned use of troops. The Dowagers and Seekers themselves are in those roles because they are wise. Above all, they reason and they listen."

"Do you know what this evil is that you will be fighting?" Rosie asked.

"Not yet," replied Spikers, "not until I talk to the Grand Dowager. But I suspect it will take a far more coordinated and active effort than the neglectful pet stores."

Little Flash appeared and introduced herself to General Spikers. "Thelma wished for you to meet our little community first, General," she said, and then added, "perhaps we can speak with her now."

"Affirmative!" Spikers said, as he bowed to Rosie and accompanied Little Flash into the Hedgiehouse.

After a very warm greeting, Thelma asked General Spikers if he wished the meeting to be private or in the company of the other hedgehogs in the community. Without hesitating, Spikers replied he'd like the meeting to include the other members of the group. The hedgehogs were called in and sat in a circle.

Thelma began, describing all of the strange events they had observed. The other hedgehogs chimed in regarding their individual experiences. General Spikers sat silently the took all of this in. At the end he added the strange experiences he'd had with Dungaree. They all wondered what to make of it.

Thelma then brought up a very delicate subject. "General, we all know that you are a very straightforward, old-school warrior pog. You have done us great services in commanding your division in the war against animal abuse and combating neglectful and abusive pet stores. But this is a new battle about which we know very little."

Spikers leaned forward a little, and said "What're you driving at? If I may ask?"

"Well," continued Little Flash, as if she felt obliged to deliver the "bad news," thus sparing the Grand Dowager of the chore. "It's felt that these special circumstances merit a special attention to military intelligence. Specifically, we think we need a very skilled set of intelligence officers on board."

"In your division," she hastily added.

Spikers looked suddenly stern and glum at the same time. His expression did not foster optimism among the council of hedgehogs. Everyone sat in silence for what seemed to be a very long time. Finally he spoke.

"You all know how I despise spies, sneaks, subterfuge, and all of that," Spikers said. "I am an old honorable warrior that relishes a strong, straightforward battle."

The hedgehogs in the circle were bracing themselves for another one of Spiker's "battle nobility" speeches. They got something quite different.

Spikers relaxed and said, "I am not so hidebound and foolish not to realize that we have a very serious emergency before us. I know there is something almost inexplicably evil here we must fight. I also know we do not know exactly what it is. So, I agree we need military intelligence to clarify exactly what we are to fight. I do not acknowledge this need lightly, for you all know how I think. I stand ready to implement the augmentation of this element to my division, and although I don't have to like it—it's necessary. We will recruit the best officers in this field that we can."

At the end of that bizarre revelation, Thelma reflected, "Well, General, that certainly was the most honest and brutally frank expression I have heard in a very long time. You do not mince words!"

"Try not to," answered General Spikers. "I will take these guys in. I won't like it, but duty demands it."

Rosie waddled off and felt a little better. She really liked Major General Spikers and looked up to him as a very courageous soul. But the controversy about the "military intelligence" thing had her a little confused. What was all of that about? Why was it a controversial issue? It would not be long before she found out.

CHAPTER 12

BOZEMAN THE SPY

Major Bozeman, United Hedgehog Marine Corps

CHAPTER 12—BOZEMAN THE SPY

"Why do you have those rocks on top of the hedgehogs?" Ivan asked, looking at a small aquarium holding two male hedgehogs, one chocolate colored and the other an albino. He was standing in the same old pet shop fom which Little Flash had come.

"You want him?" Jim, the owner, replied. "Because I have had it with that little chocolate-colored rascal."

"What's the matter with him?" Ivan asked.

"Even those rocks will not keep him in there!" Jim exclaimed. "He still escapes. Sometimes I can't find him for days at a time. I told the breeder I want no more like him. I don't know what it is with him. Never saw a hedgehog like that. I think the other one, the albino, is his brother since they came in at the same time. The albino stays put, behaves himself. Both of them are very friendly, but I can't stand these escapes any more. He gets out every damn night!"

Ivan had gone to the shop to buy hedgehog food, as he had become disenchanted with the food he was formerly using—too high in fat and too low in protein. Jim was carrying a different brand of hedgehog food that was favored by the veterinarians. Ivan eyed the little chocolate hedgehog through the glass and at that moment both hedgehogs stirred and looked right at him.

Ivan thought to himself "Oh, great, just what I need—another hedgehog!" In taking in Major General Spikers, the first male hedgehog had arrived, there being only female hedgehogs on the scene up until that point.

"Where'd he come from?" Ivan asked.

"The breeder I use near Denver," Jim replied. "But I think his Mom came from Bozeman, Montana. The Dad maybe from Omaha. Look, you want him you can have him. Free, no charge. But if you take him I don't know what you can keep him in because whatever it is he will get out of it."

Ivan removed the rocks on top of the aquarium top screen. He picked up the little chocolate hedgehog, who remained calm. Turning him over, the hedgehog remained unrolled and crossed his front legs, completely relaxed, staring right into Ivan's eyes.

"Well, he certainly is a friendly little fellow," remarked Ivan.

"Sure is," said Jim, "but I don't dare sell him. Customers'll bring him back every time and demand their money back. Why, they'd come back and demand their money back even without the hedgehog because he was missing. It's already happened three times!"

"Well," said Ivan, "what's one more. Five or six, not much difference. We've got Spikers in the upstairs bathroom. We can put this one in the bathtub, if he doesn't get along with Spikers," as he placed the chocolate hedgehog back in the aquarium.

"These two seem to get along," said Jim, "but I'd have to charge you full price for the albino. He's good natured like the chocolate one, but he doesn't try to escape."

"No thanks," said Ivan. "I have more than enough. But I'll take the chocolate one."

Inside the aquarium, Bozeman and his brother Waylon sat hunched together, hoping Ivan would take both of them. Life in a ten gallon aquarium was almost intolerable for animals used to foraging from four to seven miles per night in search of food and romance (not necessarily in that order).

"Don't think it's going to work," whispered Bozeman. "You should have escaped more."

"I guess so," replied Waylon, "but I'm just not as antsy as you are. Not only that, most of the time I cannot even figure out how you do those things. Oh, well, watch for me and we'll get back together."

"Nothing to it. You just have to plan ahead. Like that time I threw in that stick we hid under the shavings. Knocked off those rocks just fine. You have to keep that stuff hidden, or the Bigs will get wise to you."

"Ummmnnn... Bozeman, I get tired just listening to you," groaned Waylon.

The humans returned and Ivan scooped up Bozeman once again, but this time he was put in a cardboard box.

"Adios, pal," Bozeman communicated to Waylon, leaving his brother behind in the aquarium.

"Bye, Boze, I'll miss you," said Waylon. "We'll meet up again."

On the way to his new home, Bozeman saw that the box, a specially manufactured "pet carrier" made expressly for bringing small animals home from pet shops, was a laughingly simple device that could be easily breached.

"Well," he thought to himself, "might as well get in some practice," as he fiddled with the cardboard flaps and was soon out of the box and over the side of the seat.

Once home, Ivan thought the box was very light. Suspicions confirmed a moment later: No hedgehog. He searched the car in painstaking detail. No hedgehog.

Knowing what would follow upon discovery of the empty box, Bozeman had waited by the car door and darted outside as soon as it opened. He was now under a shrub in front of the house.

"Let's see now," Bozeman thought to himself, "either slip in through a mouse route or just sit on the porch until this Ivan fellow comes back outside," when his thoughts were suddenly interrupted.

"Hallo," came a voice from under the bush, "are you here for the meeting?"

"Uhh . . . sure," mumbled Bozeman, not knowing about a meeting nor who was speaking to him.

"We musst hurry, then, or we'll be late," said the voice, "I am Ssstaley, who are you?" As the voice came closer, Bozeman was surprised to see a hedgehog emerge from under the bush.

"Hedgehog's the name, do you think we will learn anything more at this meeting?" Bozeman queried, not knowing at all what this Staley was talking about.

"Of coursse," said Staley, "we're going to get briefed by the Commandant himself."

"Oh, of course," replied Bozeman, not even knowing about a commandant. Maybe it was just another way to refer to Major General Spikers, to whom he was supposed to report for a military mission. The field mouse named Oblivion had delivered the message to Bozeman while he was in the pet shop.

Oblivion specialized in delivering messages to caged animals in pet shops. His name used to be Frolic, but the local Rodent Judge, as usual a kangaroo rat, changed his name to Oblivion, which is where he would have wound up if he got captured in a pet shop. Pet shop work was dangerous. The humans who operated them were always on the lookout for escaped animals and were skillful in trapping them. Getting captured meant being locked up in a cage and having to settle for pretty bad food and then being sold to other humans. This could be deadly, especially for a small rodent, who might wind up being food himself. Oblivion, although a chance-taker, drew the line at being a snack for a snake.

The message was from the Grand Dowager, urging Bozeman to come to their assembly area and be called to active military duty as an intelligence officer. He was asked to be on his most charming behavior for this human fellow Ivan, who would be at the shop to buy hedgehog food. No mention was made of his brother, Waylon. The message also stated that he would be serving on the staff of Major General Spikers. This he did not relish due to General Spikers' reputation as a strict commander who did not like any sort of spy activities or other horsing around.

Bozeman was jolted from his daydreaming by Staley, who said, "We'd better get going, the Commandant doess not tolerate tardiness!"

Bozeman was startled as Staley bolted away from the house that Ivan had entered. Bozeman quickly followed and the pair of hedgehogs darted through the grass and into the back yard of a house next to the one that Ivan had entered. They stayed close to the wooden fences of these yards so they would not attract the attention of the host of dangers that surrounded them, from hawks, owls and eagles in the sky, to cats, dogs, and humans on the ground.

They crossed several yards and streets and eventually came to a house that was under construction. They clamored into the house through one of numerous crevasses. Sounds were heard coming from a room in the rear of the building and they rounded the corner to see something that Bozeman found incredible.

There were seven hedgehogs there, none of whom Bozeman recognized. They were not an impressive looking crew. They looked unkept, a little slow on the uptake. There was something about them that Bozeman could not quite get a fix on. One by one, they glanced in his direction, but went on with their conversations. The amazing thing, though, was that the room was full of insects! There were mainly cockroaches, but also some crickets, a few grasshoppers, and an assembly of ants in one corner. In another corner were two large praying mantises standing upright and stock still, looking around, as if acting as monitors.

Bozeman whispered to Staley, "Umm, how come these guys aren't chasing those bugs around?"

"Forbidden by the Commandant," said Staley. "In this war against the Bigss the insectss are our alliess. We are fighting the Bigss together."

Bozeman wondered to himself if he was hearing things. Even though he was no big fan of the hedgehog military, he did know something about it, and the reputation of the Commander, Major General Spikers. Bugs as allies? This was something that he thought the old general would never permit. Sure, bugs were sneaky—and small, but had been the natural enemies of the Order Insectivora—of which hedgehogs were a member—for millions of Springtimes.

Staley interrupted Bozeman's train of thought, "Ssay, you don't sseem like you're with it, man."

"Umm," Bozeman answered almost absentmindedly, "how come you talk with all these 's's' in your speech, anyway?"

"Boy, you are really not with it," answered Staley, "it'ss sso we can recognize one another, dummy. You musst have not learned anything in the introductory courrsse."

"Well, I was tired most of the time. Had to travel a long way to get there," Bozeman said, beginning to think that something was very, very wrong. Where was he, anyway? What's with all these insects? We can't understand insects. How can they be our allies? Well, except for the big mantises, and we can barely understand them, what with all of their hiss . . . hissing.

Bozeman's train of thought was again broken, this time by one of the giant mantises that sort of tottered up to them in that strange way they have of walking. The praying mantis was tall, terribly skinny but very tall, but with sharp, powerful jaws. The mantis spoke, "Ssstaley, I sssee you have brought SSDunggarrssee with you. The Commandant Anthrosss will be here sssoon and will be pleasssed."

Bozeman just stood there trying to take all of this in.

Staley replied, "He wasss just where he wasss sssupposed to be over on that sssstreet where the Dowagersss place is."

"Important we are clossse by," hissed the mantis, "thossse dowagersss mean trouble with their peacssse talk with Bigssss. That Grand Dowagerss isss the worssst. And now that this Spikersss old fool hasss arrived, Anthrosss will have to deal with them before he ssstopss the Bigsss."

As the tall mantis cast a look at Bozeman, Bozeman just sort of stammered "Ssssure."

By this time, now after interacting a little more with Staley and two of the mantises, he knew he was in the wrong place and was supposed to be somebody that apparently looked like him. Dungeness or something, Funny a hedgehog would be named after a crab. Whoever these guys were, they seemed to hate not only the Bigs, but also the Dowager hedgehogs. They seemed to be even more hostile toward General Spikers and Bozeman wondered why. Given that Bozeman was tapped for a so-called "intelligence" role, maybe he should play the game and pretend he was this "Dungeness" guy. Bozeman had played it fast and loose all of his life, and he loved it. He loved being the comedian and the escape artist, as well as the actor. So he started grinning and wandering around the room hissing at some of those in attendance.

Staley soon waddled up to him with a nervous expression on his face, "Dungarsseee! What are you doing? Are you crazy? You been ssmoking ssomethin'? Thessse guysss will kill you!"

"Ohhh," muttered Bozeman, "can't take a joke, huh?"

"NO!" Staley shouted.

One of the mantises clanked up to Staley, and hissed in his ear, "Who isss thiss foolisssh thing SSDungarssseee? The Texasss recruiter Bowlsss sssayss he trained him. What isss hiss problem?"

N . . . n . . . nothing," gasped Staley, "he is jussst a little dizzy from the long trip and breathing in the gasoline fumesss that the Bigsss produce," realizing that he, himself, was in danger. Staley had seen what they had done to that naive, young hedgehog north of town, and what was left of him was not a pretty sight. He had been skinned alive by six mantises, their razor sharp jaws working so fast he could not believe it.

"SSee to it he behavesss himsself, thiss iss no laughing matter," hissed the mantis.

"Of coursse," stammered Staley.

All of the banter was suddenly interrupted by a mantis making an announcement: "The Commandant hasss arrived!"

The multitude of insects suddenly stopped what they were doing and lined up in straight rows. The hedgehogs that were there, nine in all, also arranged themselves in a row. The mantises stood erect in the back of the room. Bozeman stood in the row of hedgehogs and wondered what he was going to see next. In his wildest dreams, he was not prepared for what he saw.

Through the door rattled about fifteen mantises, seemingly larger and more menacing than those at the back of the room. Then, walking stiffly into the room, with an awkward gait Bozeman had never before seen, was a hedgehog. The hedgehog looked almost sickly. His skin hung loosely about him and his eyes were sunken. This guy looked like he had been through he mill, but there was something about him that gave him a menacing look, something Bozeman could not place.

All of these observations were cut short by a mantis at the door saying, "The Commandant, Anthross, hasss arrived!"

The hedgehog went to the platform that had been prepared for him and began to speak in a halting, hissing tone. "Thank you all for agreeing to become part of the forcesss that will dessstroy the Bigsss. All of usss creaturesss here represssent the oldesst creaturesss on earth. You all know how these latecomer Bigsss have dessstroyed thisss Earth with their greed and their plunder and their lack of ressspect for othersss. We all know they mussst go. Now. All of them. And we have a way to do it."

Bozeman sat there messsmerized, er, mesmerized. "Who IS this guy?" he asked to himself. "He sure has a big following and seems to have brought together hedgehog and insect alike, although a little heavy-handed in his methods."

Anthross continued, "I am asssking you all to help me to see that these Bigsss dessstroy one another. Given their mutual ssusspicionsss of one another, it will not be difficult. But I need both hedgehogsss and inssectss to do it. Are you with me?!"

Throughout the room, legs and paws went up in the air, including Bozeman's. A big hiss emanated from the group.

Anthross continued, "The plan isss thiss: The hedgehogss will act as a diverssion for the Bigs at the North American misssile ssites while the sspecially trained roachesss and carpenter antsss infiltrate the misssile consolesss. They will sshort circuit and launch the misssiles at targetss around the world. You hedgehogss presssent here have been selected for the diverssion. The roachesss and antss have been in training for over a year. Once thessse misssiless are launched, the Bigsss will desstroy one another. You hedgehogss will sstart training right away. I need a volunteer to sslip into the camp of the Grand Dowager to report what they are speaking of."

Silence.

Suddenly, Staley spoke up, "What about this Dungareesse here? He is sso ssilly they would not sssusspect."

Anthross stood motionless looking down, as if in thought.

One of the mantises, seemingly a personal assistant, came up to Anthross and whispered "Not a bad idea, for if the fool isss killed, it is no losss. He looksss like he would be hard to train anyway."

"I wonder what Bowlsss wass thinking when he sssent him, Archniss," whispered Anthross.

"I do not know, but it is hard to find hedgehogsss willing to buy into our ideasss. We get the dull, the gullible oness," replied Archniss.

Anthross raised his head and announced, "Yesss, we think it isss a good idea. You, Dungaresse will infiltrate the place of the Dowager and her minionss and report back. They oppose our planss. Find out what they are going to do about it. Esspecially find out about what that obnoxiouss Sspikerss iss up to."

Bozeman just sat there and blinked a few times.

Finally, he said, "Y . . . y . . . yes, er, yesss, of courssssssse."

Archniss whispered to Anthross, "Lissten how the fool exaggeratesss."

Anthross spoke up, "That ssettled, we beginning training the diversssionersss tomorrow. Dissmisssed!" The cockroaches all sprang to attention. A little slower on the uptake, so did the hedgehogs. Well, with the exception of Bozeman, who was not at all used to military precision. Bozeman just sort of jumped straight up in surprise, only adding to his appearance as a hapless klutz.

As the Commandant was leaving the room, the mantis Archniss veered over to Staley's side and whispered "Be ssure to esscort that fellow Dungareesee, or whatever hess called to the Dowager place. We would not want him to get lossst."

"Of courssse," said Staley.

CHAPTER 13

DUNGAREE RIDES THE BUS

Dungaree, A Disciple of Anthross

CHAPTER 13—DUNGAREE RIDES THE BUS

As all of the insect activity was going on in the house under construction, Dungaree the hedgehog was sure he had missed his stop, for the city bus was now empty and had rolled to a stop. The driver exited and Dungaree heard some clanking noises. She was pumping fuel into the bus. Not a good sign for Dungaree, who had a really bad trip all the way from Texas. He wasn't even sure he was in the right town! Never good on directions, Dungaree wished he had never let himself be talked into this "war against the Bigs" stuff.

It all started out looking pretty good when the recruiter came around. Big guy named Bowls. "Death to the Bigsss, who have ruined the whole place for everyone!" he had said. All animals were going to join together to get rid of the Bigs. Dungaree didn't have anything to do anyway. He had been "turned loose" by a bunch of Bigs that never treated him well anyway. He was always in a dirty place and never had enough to eat. When Bowls found him he had nearly frozen to death three times. What Bowls said really made sense.

Bowls got him to a feed store where they also sold pet animals, including hedgehogs. He finally got something to eat. Bowls said he'd return for him when it was time to go north to begin the fight against the Bigs.

Several weeks later, Bowls returned in the middle of the night and helped all four hedgehogs in the feed store escape. This was not difficult as they were all being kept in a small ten gallon aquarium. From there they went to a run down house in Dallas where the training began for the elimination of the Bigs. Bowls was in charge, but also introduced a tall praying mantis. Although this seemed to go against almost all he had been taught, much of which was instinctive, it made sense. It especially made sense to Dungaree himself, who had always been badly treated by the Bigs.

Bowls had begun the training: "We are all going to die at the handsss of the Bigsss! Look what they have done to thisss place with their greed. Thisss whole planet isss almost not fit to live in any more. The old hedgehog leadersss talk about letting the Bigsss in on the Original Instructionsss! But those Instructionsss were handed down over fifty million wintersss ago! These Bigsss cannot understand thossse!" Bowls shouted. "The Bigs must be eliminated and our leader, our Commandant Anthross has devisssed a plan to have them get rid of eachother! Thisss plan will call for we hedgehogs, just a few ssselected hedgehog warriorss to join with our alliess the insectsss to win this battle. The Bigsss will be gone forever."

Dungaree liked what Bowls had said. "Gee," he thought, "a world without Bigs."

Bowls went on to explain how to alter one's speech to imitate that of the mantises, so the hedgehogs that had joined forces could be recognized by the allied insects, and also by one another. They would also be recognized by their strident stand against the Bigs. Then there was a long indoctrination about how nothing must come between them and their mission to set the Bigs against one another. This battle was also against hedgehogs that were sadly trying to adhere to the old ways of doing things.

"The Original Insstructionss," said Bowls, "were a couple of million yearss outdated. Hedgehogss sstill believing that the Bigss can be taught to be lesss greedy and take care of the earth are foolss and musst be done away with."

The final plans would be laid out by none other than Anthross himself, the Commandant of the insects and hedgehogs, to whom it seemed even the mantises paid homage, according to Bowls. There would be a meeting in a town north of Denver in several months. The location was critical, because their work against the Bigs would be in that area of the country. Also, if there was going to be any resistance by traditional hedgehogs, it would come from there as well, since that was where the hedgehog Grand Dowager had taken up residence.

Dungaree and the three other hedgehogs were taken back to the feed store by Bowls before daybreak. Back into the ten gallon aquarium they went, where no humans were any the wiser as to where they had been.

Getting to the small city north of Denver proved to be more difficult, not to mention distasteful, than Dungaree had ever imagined. Normally, Dungaree was not a confrontational pog. He only went along with Bowls' tales of conquering the Bigs because of all the bad things that had been done to him in his short lifetime.

Dungaree thought back upon his life. The woman Kirsten, who had purchased him from a pet store in Austin, was having trouble with her boyfriend, Jeb. Jeb seemed to despise both of her pets, Dungaree the hedgehog and Jesse the cat.

One day, after a particularly vicious argument between Kirsten and Jeb, Kirsten grabbed Jeb's keys from the top of the bookcase and took off in Jeb's brand new pickup truck. Enraged, Jeb gathered up and threw both Jesse and Dungaree out the back door. The orange tabby cat and the Algerian chocolate hedgehog just sat there in the weed-choked, junk strewn back yard for a few moments. Under other circumstances, the cat and the hedgehog may have seen each other as competition. But here, because of Jeb's frequent abuse (he liked to kick the cat or throw hedgehog to punctuate his arguments with Kirsten), both Jesse and Dungaree saw themselves as fellow travelers on a perilous path. Besides, Jesse simply considered Dungaree as a strange sort of small quilled cat. At least Jesse knew Dungaree was not a rodent. Rodents he could smell, so if Dungaree was not a rodent, then he must be a cat. He certainly was not a dog, which exhausted Jesse's entire list of four legged critters. A worldly cat Jesse was not.

Jesse leaned over toward Dungaree and squinted with that "closed face and hooded eyes" look of his, something common to Texas cats. He then said "Y'know, Bud, that's the third time this here week that 'ol Big Jeb has throwed us outta the house."

"Yeah, I been countin' too," said Dungaree forlornly. "I'm gonna hit the road. Some day that guy is gonna kill me the way he throws me around."

"I dunno, Bud," Jesse replied, "this place ain't much, but it might be better'n out there."

"Guess I'll take my chances. Been good knowin' you, Jess," said Dungaree.

"Gonna miss havin' somebody to get beat up with, Bluejeanman," said Jesse playfully. "Keep yer head down and yore quills up, Bud."

Jesse and Dungaree briefly touched paws as Dungaree waddled off into the night. He was found several days later by Bowls, skinny and hungry. But his close calls with death were the cold nights when he could not get warm enough and each time had drifted off into a fitful numbing sleep. Dungaree knew the dangers of cold, for he had been taught as early as he could remember, that he was one of only two kinds of hedgehog among all fourteen species that could not hibernate in cold weather. Seems that Algerian and Central African hedgehogs had lived too long near the equator, over 20 million Springtimes, and over time had lost their ability to store the brown fat necessary for those healthy long sleeps in cold weather.

But Dungaree's problems were not over even after he had joined Bowls' seemingly optimistic campaign against the Bigs. From the feed store, he was taken into a "rescue" for hedgehogs by a woman named Heather. He began to get confused about Bigs, since Heather was not cruel like Jeb nor neglectful like Kirsten. Heather was really very kind and had several hedgehogs there she treated with a great deal of love—and all of the food they wanted. Pretty good food, too. There was an old female hedgehog there called Blackberry and she seemed wise and calm.

But Dungaree had been trained to his new role of fighting the Bigs, so he dove into that with dedication. It annoyed him that Blackberry never got upset with him and when he mounted his usual tirade against the Bigs, all Blackberry would say is "Now, now."

Then this big hedgehog called Spikers showed up, and he sure was bossy. He wore kind of a funny round iron hat with a couple of stars on it. He seemed too big and old to argue with, but Dungaree put on his best show, thinking that maybe this Spikers was one of the hedgehogs that Bowls said was going to go fight the Bigs. Spikers did not seem to like Dungaree, snarling at him to keep out of the way.

Dungaree was glad to get out of there, especially with Spikers eyeing him so suspiciously. He was glad he was leaving a day before Spikers, so he would not have to go to the airport with him. Dungaree was placed in a small carrier with a door at the end. He was driven to the airport air freight terminal by Heather's fiance, who apparently had no love for hedgehogs. Sorta reminded him of Jeb.

At the air freight counter Heather's fiance bid Dungaree a not-so-fond farewell: "Good riddance to you!" he exclaimed, as the clerk logged in the carrier and its passenger.

As it turned out, it was too hot to fly animals according to airline regulations that day, so Dungaree stayed in the carrier overnight at the air freight terminal. The next morning he was delivered to the cargo staging area for boarding. He was greeted by a rat named Gnarley, a rather grizzled old rat that identified himself as the Loadmaster.

"Care to stretch your legs?" asked Gnarley as he opened the carrier door, which was latched from the outside.

"Don't mind if I do," answered Dungaree, "those Bigsss have kept me cooped up in thiss thing all night long. But they will pay for thiss, all too ssoon!"

"Well, don't get too uptight about it," Gnarley commented, "typical behavior. Bigs, you know, only looking out for themselves."

As Dungaree stiffly exited the carrier, Gnarley continued, "I'll show you up the ramp into the pressurized compartment. The Bigs won't look into your carrier when they load it, just be sure you are in it when they unload you in Denver. Can't let them get suspicious, you know."

As they were scurrying up the ramp, the craziest thing happened. Seemingly out of nowhere, hundreds, maybe a thousand or two cockroaches appeared, as if from nowhere. They swarmed and attacked Gnarley, fiercely biting him over and over. Dungaree stood there frozen and did not know what to do. Gnarley tried to fight them off, but there were far too many and he looked like nothing more than a huge pile of swarming, biting cockroaches.

Then, so suddenly that it caused a very cold chill to shoot straight up Dungaree's back, he heard a metallic voice come from just behind his left shoulder.

"Jussst be ssstill. The roachesss know what they are doing."

Dungaree jumped. There, within paws length at his back was a giant mantis looking at him with steely eyes.

The mantis continued, "Thessse ratsss do not permit insects to fly. Bigottssss! SSo we mussst overcome them when many of usss need to travel at once."

Dungaree winced and felt a little sick at the spectacle. As soon as Gnarley the rat was unable to move due to his injuries, the mantis shrieked out a sound that Dungaree did not understand. The cockroaches abandoned Gnarley and all ran for the pressurized cargo hold. Some of the roaches who were killed were drug away by the others. With hundreds of bleeding bites all over him, Gnarley looked delirious and sort of stared at Dungaree. But no words came as he lay there on the cargo ramp.

"He isss finisshed," hissed the mantis. "Quickly, get into the hold with my troopsss before the Bigss come."

The commotion alerted several of the other rats working the cargo staging area that day. They ran to the ramp just as it was near time for the Bigs to finish their "break time," which was fairly predictable, and enabled the rats to do most of their transport work unimpeded.

Chauncey, the lead rat in the staging area, exclaimed "I say, 'ave a look at poor Gnarley there, mates! A bloody mess, what?"

"The Bigs are comin' back, boss!" Bottomsley, one of the crew, said. "Better get 'im out of 'ere."

The rat crew picked up the limp and bloody body of Gnarley and headed back through the tunnel-like channels into the terminal, straight to Dr. Snout, the very old mole who served as the animal airport physician.

As the aircraft was buttoned up after the freight was loaded, Dungaree hid between the containers, keeping a healthy distance from the hoard of cockroaches and their leader, the rather menacing and self-assured mantis. He located his carrier and scooted inside, slamming the door, not wishing to associate further with his new "friends." Dungaree wondered what he had gotten himself into.

The cockroaches did not seem to want to have anything to do with Dungaree, either. They kept to themselves at the far back end of the cargo hold. Dungaree could not understand them when they spoke. It all just sounded like different pitches of hisses. At one point a small group of cockroaches wandered over to his carrier and began crawling up the grated metal door. Dungaree began to worry, asking himself why he had slammed the door behind him, because now he could not get out, escape not being high on his list of skills.

He wondered if the cockroaches could kill him if they wanted to. It certainly looked like they did that to Gnarley the rat. But now they were coming over to his carrier, and this got Dungaree pretty nervous. As the 20 or so cockroaches crawled through the spokes on his carrier door, Dungaree sat quietly at the back of the carrier wondering what was going to happen. The roaches milled around at the front of the carrier seeming interested in a small food container. They gnawed at the dry kibble cat food in the container, grunting and hissing as they went.

Suddenly, there was a shriek similar to the one that Dungaree heard the mantis make when he called the roaches off of Gnarley. Immediately, all 20 roaches abandoned the food dish and scurried away toward the main body of hundreds of roaches milling about at their end of the cargo hold. As Dungaree inched forward to have a look, he thought he understood why the roaches obeyed the mantis with such speed. Before the roaches helping themselves to Dungaree's food could rejoin the others, the mantis positioned itself between them and the main group. Then, with lightening speed, the mantis swooped down and, like some fierce, gnawing razor-sharp machine, ripped the entire party of 20 roaches to shreds, spitting their remains over the deck of the cargo hold. The mantis then reared back up to its full height and shrieked again, causing the entire body of roaches to back a little further into the corner of the hold. It all happened so fast that Dungaree could not believe it.

Dungaree slinked back to the rear of the carrier. He knew he was supposed to be an insectivore and all that, but, after all, he had become used to commercial hedgehog and cat food. In fact, he really did not like the flavor of insects all that much. Now this. He again wondered if the cockroaches, with their huge numbers, could kill him as they did Gnarley the rat. Of course, Dungaree had some defensive abilities the rat did not, like his quills and the ability to roll up into a spiky ball. Still, he wondered if the roaches could get down in between his quills and bite him. Or even slowly eat his quills, as he has heard some rodents, like gerbils, can do. Then he wondered about the mantis with those razor sharp jaws. He was glad he apparently did not have to test any of these questions at the moment.

As the plane was coming in for a landing, the mantis came over to Dungaree's carrier and briefly said, "Remember, Dungassree, you are to meet with our Commandant Anthross a week from today at the lassst sstop on Conifer Ssstreet of the busss on route number eight. There a hedgehog named Ssstaley will meet you and walk you to where the meeting isss."

"OK," said Dungaree, "a week, Ssstaley, busss, route 8, lasst sstop, Conifer ssstreet. Got it."

When the cargo hold opened, the roaches filed off in a silent line right down the conveyer ramp, unnoticed, and the mantis stayed hidden in the hold until there was a lull in activity. Dungaree was taken off in his carrier and transported to the air freight office where a human named Art came for him. Art was a student who arranged to take in Dungaree over the Internet through corresponding with Heather. Unfortunately for Dungaree, Art lived one entire town south of where he was supposed to go to meet with the Commandant, Anthross. This only meant one thing: Dungaree could not simply disappear for a few hours in the night. He had to escape. Permanently.

The local mice filled in Dungaree on the transportation options. He could catch a bus called "Foxtrot" to take him to the next town north, but then he had to catch the Route 1 bus to take him further north to get to where he could board the Route 8 bus. The buses did not run after dark, either, so he had to sneak on in daylight, which was risky. He figured he had to escape the night before the meeting and spend the next day traveling north. Dungaree had no trouble getting out of Art's ground floor apartment. A window was open and after he tipped over his lightweight plastic container, he was out the window and on his way. He had no problems asking local mice along the way to send him to the places to catch the buses. The "Foxtrot" bus was pretty easy, as he was able to climb in a woman's large canvas shopping bag that she laid down while waiting for the bus. However, he had to lay low at the terminal and almost got caught boarding the Route 1 bus. He made it into the bushes just in time as a passenger saw him and yelled "What was THAT?"

But even though he eventually got on the Route 8 bus, he had trouble counting the stops because the driver stopped for other things, too, like stop lights and stop signs. He knew he was supposed to hop of at the 13th stop, which the mice told him was the last stop on Conifer, but he lost count. After all, it is difficult to count stops, especially when the driver skips stops where no one wants to get off or on when you are hiding under a seat! And now he was still on the bus as night was falling and he was about to be locked in the bus in that place wherever buses sleep at night.

CHAPTER 14

BOZEMAN'S ROUNDABOUT JOURNEY

Grumpy the Chief of Staff (after promotion)

CHAPTER 14—BOZEMAN'S ROUNDABOUT JOURNEY

Staley and Bozeman waddled out of the meeting and across the street. No words were exchanged until they reached the oppostie curb and were well into the grass when Staley let loose.

"Were you trying to get uss killed in there?!" Staley wailed.

"Watcha' mean?" Bozeman said evasively.

"Those guys are killerss, sseriouss killerss, kill you ass ssoon ass look at you!" Staley exclaimed.

"So why are you hanging out with 'em?"

"Dungaree!, err, Duggarsseese, or whatever, I don't undersstand you! Are you with uss or not?" Staley demanded.

"Oh, I dunno," answered Bozeman. "These guys seem a little pushy."

PUSSHY!" Staley exclaimed. "Aren't you interessted in ssaving the planet from thesse desstructive Bigss?"

"Well, yeah. But I'm not convinced these guys, oh, I'm ssssorry, thessse guysss, have all the answersss. I mean, since when have we taken orders from a bunch of cockroaches?"

"The bosses aren't cockroaches!" Staley shouted.

"OK, mantisssssses," said Bozeman.

THE COMMANDANT ISS A HEDGEHOG!" Staley screamed.

"Well, OK, but you gotta admit that is one weird hedgehog. Never saw anything like him." Bozeman then stopped cold as he felt something strange come over him. As they were treading through the grass in the second back yard they were crossing, Bozeman sniffed in the air that something was imminent.

Bozeman instantly hit Staley broadside and forced him into the wooden fence, under the fence's horizontal support. Bozeman flung himself into the fence, but a substantial part of him still hung out from under the support. There was a scream.

"Screeeeee"

Huge talons ripped into Bozeman's side, and he felt the owl recoil but then come back for a second attempt. Once again the talons ripped into Bozeman, as he tried to flatten himself against the fence and under the horizontal bar. The second attack brought humans and a dog out into the yard.

"Whut's thet varmint want?" Jethro Flum shouted to no one in particular.

Jethro's son, Kial shouted, "Prolly got 'em some rats by the fence, I reckon," as he released the leash on Bohungus the dog. The dog bounded across the lawn.

Bohungus let out a mighty series of barks that were connected into a series "aroooooo, arrrooooooo" sorts of sounds. This was sufficiently disturbing to send the marauding owl off in search of other potential prey.

Bohungus, no novice at pooch field work once he got out of the house, smelled Bozeman's blood. He edged toward the fence finding not one but two hedgehogs crouched there.

"How-dee-do!" Bohungus exclaimed. "Got yerself a close call there."

"Ummm," groused Bozeman, "looks like we've been getting close calls all day!"

"You don't look like no rats I ever seen," said Bohungus. "You ain't from around here, are ya?"

"No, we're hedgehogs," explained Bozeman, "from a long way from here, like twelve thousand miles! Brought here from Africa."

"Go 'way!" Bohungus howled. "Whut brings you 'round these parts?"

"Usual stuff," said Bozeman. "Kidnapped by humans, brought here in the pet trade, now tryin' to sort out ourselves."

"Well," sniffed Bohungus, "you don't get no trouble from me. That durn owl been dive-bombing me and my food dish all week. Nasty gashes you got there, fella. Oughta have 'em looked at."

"Yeah, I know. You know a good mole around here?" Bozeman asked.

"Kinda hard to find a good one, what with humans building all these houses around here. But go to the prairie dog town just west of here and ask for ol' Mole Kleeber. She'll treat you right."

"Well, Staley, I guess I'm off." Bozeman said. "We'll meet up again at the . . . the . . ."

"Commandant'sss Hall" Staley offered. "Where the diversssionary training will be."

"Yeah, same place we just, er, jussst, came from," said Bozeman, now seeing Staley as a definite drag.

"OK," said Staley, "are you ssure you can get back to that place where I found you?"

"Yesss, of courrsse." Bozeman answered in the best hiss he could muster.

"Well, alright," said Staley a little skeptically. "I don't want those guys getting mad at me."

"Not to worry," assured Bozeman, "but first I've got to get these wounds looked at. Infections I don't need."

As Staley waddled off, now keeping pretty well under the lower fence crossbeams, Bozeman heard a nervous, low, "And thanks, Man," as Staley disappeared into the night.

#

The trip to the prairie dog town was easier than expected, as Bozeman, now free of Staley's awkward companionship, could dart and run as he saw fit. The human subdivision seemed like a maze, with all of the look-alike houses and exactly-sized back yards. As he picked up speed and bolted under fences and through gates, across streets and front yards, Bozeman came suddenly to a screeching halt.

Big yellow eyes peered down at him. Bozeman immediately rolled up into a ball and rattled his customary hedgehog warning.

"PhugggPhugggPhuggg-phuggg-phuggggggggggg."

"What kind of cat are you?" Moshe, the pride and joy of the Silverberg family, asked.

"PhugggPhugggPhuggg-phuggg-phuggggggggggg."

"Oy, I know, 'Phuggg' already. Now, what kind of strange cat are you?" Moshe continued on. "What's the matter, dog got your tongue?"

Bozeman unrolled a little, let loose with a few more little "phugggs" and stuck his snout out toward the large gray, meticulously groomed cat. At the same time he did that, a trickle of blood ran onto the ground from his side.

"Hi," said Bozeman, "I'm a Tasmanian quilled cat," offering the ridiculous explanation he had concocted to explain himself to cats. His thinking was that they would not know too much about Tasmania since it was about as far away from North America as one could get. Besides, he always liked the idea of the Tasmanian Devil, which seemed kind of fierce and merited being left alone. Bozeman had learned long ago, mainly through his escapades in running around in pet stores, that cats were convinced that the world revolved around them. They apparently had simplified the world into the following list of living things:

a. Cats.
b. Dogs.
c. Humans.
d. Rodents.
e. Small things with too many legs to count.

    f.   Slithery things that could be dangerous.
    g.   Peculiar armored things.
    h.   Flying things of two types:

        (1). Big annoying flying things.
        (2). Small tasty flying things.

    i.   Big (trees) and small (grass) things that could not move.

Going down the list, Moshe took inventory and about the only place Bozeman fit was into the category of some kind of strange cat. Then he saw the blood.

Moshe turned and meowed toward the shrubs of the perfectly tended yard, "Nellie! Come quickly."

A second cat, this one with light and dark orange stripes, trotted up to the pair.

"Nellie is much more street wise than I am," Moshe offered. "She knows almost this whole town. She was a professional alley cat before she came to live with us."

"Oh-oh," thought Bozeman, "she might see through this 'Tasmanian quilled cat' business."

But Bozeman needn't have worried, as Nellie, looking every bit as "spic and span" as Moshe trotted up and said "Oh! She's hurt. Or he's hurt. Or you're hurt, whatever kind of cat you are."

"I was on my way to the prairie dog town," Bozeman offered.

"Wise choice," replied Nellie. "See Kleeber the Mole there. She's a great doctor. I'd bring you in to see my humans, but that would make life more complicated for you."

"Yeah," offered Bozeman, "the fewer humans I see right now, the better. Besides, the dog Bohungus a few blocks over also mentioned this Kleeber."

"Oohhh, Bohungus!" Nellie exclaimed. "Great guy, for a dog, that is. Real live-and-let-live fellow."

"Oy," groused Moshe, who was now crouched down in the grass. "Nellie, when are you going to stop fooling around with these nuts?"

"Well," replied Nellie, "you can take the cat our of the alley but you can't take the alley out of the cat. Besides, you know you love hearing about all of my adventures!"

"Sheesh!" Moshe grumbled.

"OK!" Nellie exclaimed, brightening and straightening up. "Go straight through our front yard, across the street, under the boat trailer and through their yard and under the back fence. Do not go to either side. Weird humans on one side, really mean dog on the other side. Next yard no problem, friendly cat there. Cross that flatblack and go west two yards and go through the yard two doors down, south. When you come out under the fence, take a sharp right and do not go near the big humming thing with the fence around it. Humans call it 'lectical transformer. It'll kill you. Got a Foogermizer in there."

"Foogermizer?" Bozeman asked.

"Yeah," said Nellie, "big thing that hums until you get near it, then 'ZAP' comes a big blue streak that lights you up and kills you. Named after the late Foog Hoskins."

"Oh," said Bozeman respectfully.

"Now," continued Nellie, "if you follow the sidewalk west you will cross another flatblack and go by a human building. It is long and low and will be on your right. Lots of old humans live there. There are a lot of them, but they are very much alone. Strange, huh? Anyway, you're almost there."

"I think I've got it," answered a concentrating Bozeman.

"OK," continued Nellie, "cross the street at the long low building, going south. That's the prairie dog town. Just ask for Kleeber."

"Thanks! I'll get on over there."

"Go quickly, you need some care for those slashes," said Moshe, "and come back when you can. We can slip you out some of the best knishes you have ever tasted!"

"Will do!" Bozeman exlaimed as he speedily limped off, thinking that he certainly would return to these hospitable cats, perhaps even to use their place as a safe base of operations if needed. The place of the Grand Dowager and especially the intimidating General Spikers was still a very unknown thing. Bozeman sped off into the night looking for the prairie dog town.

Nellie's directions were excellent, as should be the case coming from a professional alley cat. The 'lectrical transformer was certainly a menacing sight, huge and humming in the moonlit night, stretching up into the sky with it's strange pointed towers. He went west and encountered the long low building with all of the old humans in it. As he went to cross the flatblack he saw a group of prairie dogs huddled in a circle by the side of the black strip. They were all chattering that fast prairie dog chatter that is almost impossible to understand. They were clearly distressed.

As he approached the circle, he saw that the prairie dogs were clustered around a dead prairie dog that had been ripped open. Fresh blood was all over the pavement. One of the members of the circle looked around as Bozeman approached.

"Akkkk!" screeched the prairie dog, and all of the others turned to stare at Bozeman.

Then another roared at the top of his lungs: "TENNNnnn-HUUUUH!"

With that command, all of the prairie dogs stood at attention. The prairie dog rendering the command said, "SIR, First Sergeant Muldraugh, Jr., Company A, 1st Battalion, 2d Hedgehog Marine Regiment (Infantry)(Prairie Dog), reporting!"

Bozeman waddled up with an air of military dignity he did not even know he had. He managed a wave of the paw and quickly added that he had been wounded in battle and needed to be directed to the aid station.

"Yes, SIR!" Muldraugh, Jr. shouted.

"What's going on here?" Bozeman asked.

"Another of our number met with tragedy, sir!" Muldraugh replied. "Roller traffic. The prairie dog town is built on two sides of a human flatblack, Sir. They do not even slow down. We try to watch but their rollers are too fast for many of us."

"We know about the rollers, Muldraugh," replied Bozeman, "our English and European cousins have terrible problems there."

"Yes, Sir," Muldraugh replied. "But you are seriously injured yourself. You'll be wanting to see Doc Kleeber, I reckon?"

"Yes, indeed." Bozeman replied.

"I'll take you to her, Sir," replied Muldraugh.

"Thanks. Losing blood is not my favorite pastime."

"Right this way," said Muldraugh. "We'll have to cross the flatblack, so watch both ways."

"No kidding," said Bozeman, as they scurried across the street, heading south into the main part of the prairie dog town.

Instead of their usual chirping an alarm, the seemingly endless line of prairie dogs standing guard over their burrows simply stood up tall and waved.

Along the way, Bozeman asked about all of the military formality.

Muldraugh was quick to respond, "Well, Sir, we were recruited by Colonel Grumpy to assist in the formation of the Second Hedgehog Marine Division (Mechanized). She told us about the dangers that face us. She said that normally the division can handle its peacetime mission to combat animal abuse by humans, but this time it's different. This time, she said, an army of insects is rising up to destroy the world. Since the hedgehogs are the oldest of us mammals, we believe them and follow their leadership, Sir."

"Well, I don't know if we're all that smart," replied Bozeman.

"The Dowagers and the Seekers are," Muldraugh said confidently. "We prairie dogs aren't much on grand strategy. Why, just look at where we put our towns! But we do fight a good battle, and we are loyal. We might love having a good time, but we are good troops. Disorganized, but good."

"Well, I've been asked to report to Major General Spikers," Bozeman said. "But I keep getting sidetracked. What's with all of this 'sir' business anyway."

"As hedgehogs are the oldest mammals and we look to them for leadership, all of you or almost all of you have assumed the duties as officers of the Legions Of Small Mammals," Muldraugh continued. "If you are reporting to the Commanding General himself, you probably occupy an important position, even though you may not know it right now."

"Hmm," answered Bozeman, "from what I've heard of General Spikers, he just wants to chew me out. I hear he has no use for those of us who have been recruited into 'military intelligence.'"

"I dunno," Muldraugh replied. "Colonel Shakespeare is our regimental commander. Wiry little old guy, even older than General Spikers. But, he is a good, fair commander. Never met a finer hedgehog."

"I guess this division is more organized that I thought," answered Bozeman. "General Spikers must have been hard at work putting all of this together."

"A lot of it was Colonel Grumpy's doing before the General arrived," continued Muldraugh. "She had four regiments lined up for his approval and he approved of and bought the whole works. Pretty clever if you ask me, keeping all of the species of rodents together rather than splitting them up. They work better together. Colonel Grumpy is the Chief of Staff, so you might be working for her."

"Who wound up in charge of the regiments?" Bozeman continued, ignoring the mounting pain in his side.

"Of course, there is us, the 2d Hedgehog Marine Regiment (INFANTRY)(PRAIRIE DOG)," Muldraugh explained. "Colonel Shakespeare is a seasoned old man, and very serious. Does not put up with the antics from us prairie dogs. We need the discipline. The 6th Hedgehog Marine Regiment (INFANTRY)(MUSKRAT) is commanded by Colonel Louise, a desert hedgehog, who is known as a feminist. She's just what they need to keep those muskrats in line as they are pretty hard to handle and like to roughhouse. Colonel Prickles commands the 8th Hedgehog Marine Regiment (INFANTRY)(FIELD MOUSE). Her steady and calm manner makes her ideal to deal with that frantic bunch that is always getting into mischief and is so active that it would drive almost anyone nuts. Finally, there is Colonel Grouchy (not to be confused with Grumpy), who is a very substantial hedgehog commanding the 10th Hedgehog Marine Regiment

(ARTILLERY)(MARMOT). Marmots are easy to manage and are very reliable. They roll the heavy guns very well."

"I know a few marmots, myself," added Bozeman. "Pretty close to hedgehogs in their outlook."

"Yes, Sir!" Muldraugh continued. "Good artillerymen, too. The fact that they live at high elevations does not hurt, either. Anyway, Sir, here we are, the dispensary burrow, and Doc Kleeber."

"Thanks, Muldrau . . . . , er, ... First Sergeant," said Bozeman, "just in time. These wounds are getting annoying."

Muldraugh scurried down the burrow as Bozeman followed. It was a large burrow with several tunnels leading off from the main corridor. "Where's Doc?" Muldraugh asked of a passing prairie dog.

"Straight down and take the third left." Minerva the prairie dog nursing supervisor replied. "Sure hope the trail of blood won't bring that fox back tonight. Might have to call your company out again to run her off. She's got three hungry cubs."

"We'll keep a lookout, Minerva," said Muldraugh as he continued down the tunnel. They rounded the turn to find Kleeber, the resident physician finishing up treating the sore throat of a prairie dog that had been squeaking a few too many alarms.

Kleeber turned and squinted at Bozeman, her eyesight about as bad as it gets for mammals. "Oh, my," Kleeber said, "what on Earth did you have a run-in with? Big bird, I would imagine."

"Yes, Ma'am, owl," said Bozeman, suddenly feeling very tired.

"Well, feel glad you're not a human," offered Kleeber. "We'll fix you right up. A human would be dead by now filling out insurance paperwork and HMO stuff. Fortunately we don't have currency. Saves lots of time."

Minerva entered the room and began cleaning Bozeman's wounds. Upon close examination she observed that were three very deep gashes in Bozeman's side.

"Lucky that owl didn't get anything important," said Kleeber as she inspected the wounds. "We'll have you sewn up in no time, but first let me rub these numbing leaves on you and clean up the inside of the wounds. You've been running around with these for a little too long a time."

Bozeman, now sewn up with a long strip of some sort of leaf pasted to his side, thanked Kleeber and the dispensary burrow staff, then stepped out into the cool night air just in time to look into the very large jaws of a surprised red fox.

"Aw, great!" Bozeman exclaimed as the fox lunged for him, but was quickly repelled by a bloody nose when the fox collided with the ball of sharp quills that Bozeman had suddenly become.

As the startled fox galloped off whimpering, Muldraugh, who was waiting in the shadows, offered "Well, our local foxes don't know what to make of you guys on this side of the pond. Just as well, too."

Bozeman, unrolling, said "Yeah, and I hope it stays that way. Our European cousins have enough problems with foxes. An animal with more answers than they have questions makes me reeeel nervous."

"Sir, it was good to be able to help," said Muldraugh. "Good luck in your new assignment."

Bozeman thanked Muldraugh and threaded his way back through the prairie dog town, keeping an eye out for the fox. And the cars. And the HMOs, whatever, on Earth, THOSE were.

Bozeman had come full circle from the time he had escaped from Ivan's automobile. A field mouse stood watch near the front of the house and offered to take Bozeman inside. They climbed up under the plastic exterior siding common to tract homes and waded through layer after layer of suffocating pink insulation before coming out into a room on the main floor.

"Mr. Ivan is going to be surprised to see you," squeaked the mouse, who identified himself as Blevins. "You've been gone a pretty long time."

"Don't I know it," said Bozeman, "It's a long story."

"We'd better go see the Chief," said Blevins, "she asked me to have you see her as soon as you arrived."

The mouse led Bozeman around a corner and squeaked a code in front of a kiddie gate. In an instant, Grumpy appeared from under the blank papers on the floor and eased through a wide gap in the gate.

"Bozeman, I suppose?" Grumpy asked rather curtly. "Follow me, please."

Grumpy waddled to the far side of the kitchen, stopped, and listened intently for noises. Once satisfied that she would not be disturbed, she began: "We've been waiting for you for a long time. I hope you have not been clowning around out there. However, from the looks of you, it seems like you've been through the mill."

All Bozeman could say was "Yes, Ma'am." He then told Grumpy the entire story in an abbreviated fashion, but did provide details of his being mistakenly identified as Dungaree and his experiences with Anthross, the mantises, and the cockroaches.

Grumpy remained silent for a moment and then spoke again: "Well, Bozeman, you seem to have earned your keep already. You have been appointed a major in the Hedgehog Marine Corps and assigned here at Hedgequarters as the Assistant Chief of Staff, G-2 (Intelligence). As you know, I'm the Chief of Staff and the other staff members are Lieutenant Colonel Thembekele the G-1 (Administration), Lieutenant Colonel Xena, the Adjutant General, Colonel Clyde the G-3 (Operations), and Colonel Tiggywinkle the G-4 (Logistics). There are also others that you will meet. I'm glad you got done what you did so far. I'm also glad you got wounded in battle, too."

"Oh, great!" Bozeman said, dejected. "All I need is a boss that is glad I get wounded!"

"Please understand," said Grumpy, "your case is a very hard sell to the General. He does not like 'intelligence types and assorted spies,' as he puts it. Getting yourself in harm's way and getting injured in battle goes a long way with the Old Man. He admires courage. I'll have a few words with him before you meet him. We can do that tomorrow. For now let's make some noise and rouse Ivan, so you can get a bath."

CHAPTER 15

THE GATHERING

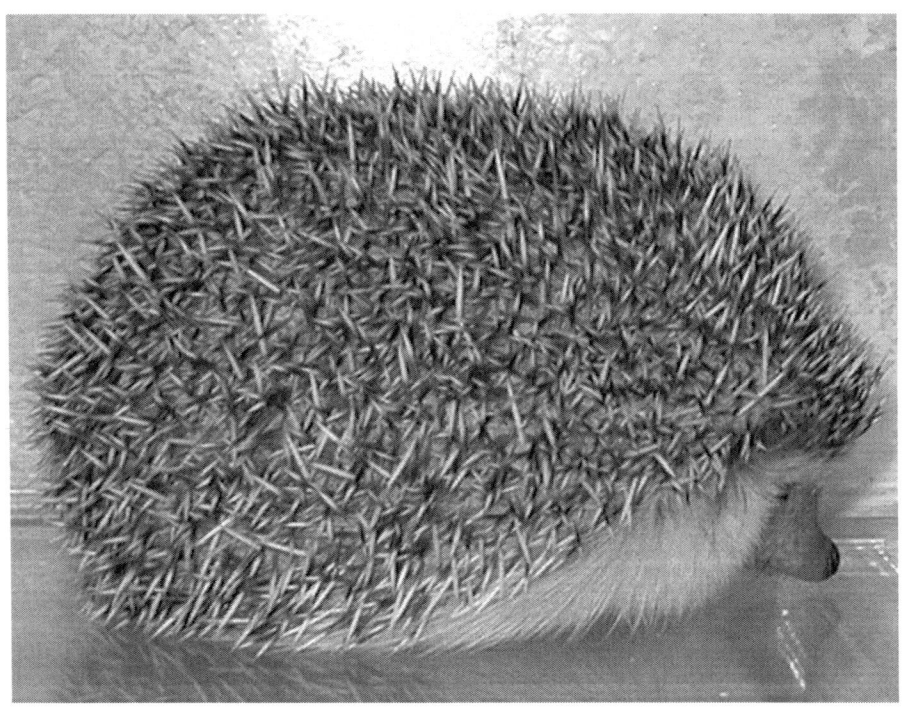

Roscoe the Recon Commander

CHAPTER 15—THE GATHERING

As Major General Spikers was finalizing the organization of the Second Hedgehog Marine division (Mechanized), he was satisfied that he had most of the bases covered. He was especially pleased that so many other animals not only wished to join up, but also would readily accept hedgehog leadership.

"We realize the importance of saving our earth from almost certain destruction," offered Axel, a field mouse that had signed on with the 8th Hedgehog Marine Regiment.

Although several of his units would have to remain unstaffed and inactive, General Spikers did his best to fill each unit. Finding enough qualified hedgehogs to fill leadership positions, however, continued to be a problem. Finally, he sought assistance from the Dowagers on a particularly difficult staffing matter.

"How may we be of assistance, General?" Thelma asked, as a special meeting of the Dowagers and the General got under way.

"I have most of the Division leadership staffed, with one glaring exception," General Spikers reported. "I am missing a commander and an able deputy for the Light Armored Reconnaissance Battalion. I need the special skills of this unit due to some of the unknowns we will be facing. They can be very fast and mobile and we will need that."

"And you can't recruit the type of leadership you need from the pogs you have assembled?" Little Flash, the Dowager-in-Training asked.

"I could," responded Spikers, "but the very best in the business are a couple of hedgehogs by the names of Roscoe and Bill. I knew them in their younger days, some years back. They're swift and absolutely fearless. They are on our reserve rolls, but I can't get them here without a lot of commotion."

"And commotion is what we don't need," commented Thelma.

"What sort of commotion?" Little Flash asked.

"Well," responded Spikers, "short of going into where they are confined with a task force to hognap them, there is little hope of getting them out of their locked down condition."

"How badly locked down?" Little Flash continued.

Roscoe is confined in a locked aquarium in a third floor apartment that is secured with deadbolts." General Spikers said. "Even the field mice can't get in there."

And Roscoe has been unable to get himself out of there?" Little Flash continued.

"Tried. To no avail." Spikers said, and then added, "Roscoe's a female."

"Hmm," said Little Flash, "another case of human gender misidentification, I see."

"And the other hedgehog?" Thelma asked. "Bill?"

"Bill is kept in a large, luxurious home," said Spikers, "with security alarms and a closed circuit television surveillance system."

"I guess I can figure out what you wish us to do," Thelma responded.

"Yes, Ma'am," replied Spikers. "Dowagers and Seekers or those potentially with those qualities are the only hedgehogs that can subliminally communicate ideas to humans. But we are at the end of our rope and I need to get those two out of those places."

"Of course, you know the risks of subliminally communicating ideas to humans," continued Thelma.

"Yes, Ma'am," Spikers replied. "Humans are so flighty and unpredictable that the idea subconsciously sent to them can get twisted, and disaster can result."

"So have Roscoe and Bill consented to this approach?" Thelma asked. "We cannot place them in danger against their wishes."

"Yes," replied General Spikers, "we have communicated with them and they are itching to get out of their confined places. Roscoe's been locked up for about three years! They are willing to take the risks."

"Very well, then," said Thelma, "we will set the human minds in motion. I will go myself. I will need to get within ten to fifteen feet of the human in order to communicate an idea."

"Thank you, Ma'am," said Spikers. "If this were not such an important assignment, I would not ask that it be done."

#

Dungaree thought he had bought the farm, so to speak. Locked up in a cold bus overnight, with no way to escape that he knew of. Freeze to death for sure, he thought. But it did not quite happen that way. He gathered up scraps of paper, rolled up, and hunkered down. Little did he know that at 5AM the next morning, things would get considerably worse.

"There's a THING in there! Some sort of WILD THING!" Mae Booth, the very best bus maintenance worker the transit line had ever had, exclaimed.

The entire maintenance crew was supervised by Beulah Washington, a woman that was not rattled by much of anything.

Beulah said, "Well, let's go see what kind of critter done got into one of our buses." She brought along a long stick she used to repel dogs and went to the spot that Mae had told her about. Beulah poked around and elicited a few pops and hisses from Dungaree. "Whutevah it is, it don't look dane'grus!" Seems to be more scared of us that we is of it! Let me go get a towel and corral that little bugger." And off she went, leaving Mae sort of on "guard duty" over the little bugger, whatever that bugger was.

Dungaree did not like the sound of any of this, but there was not much he could do.

Beulah returned with a large towel and within a few seconds Dungaree was rolled up in the towel and being transported to places unknown (to him, anyway). The destination was reached in only a few seconds and Dungeree was plunked into a large metal sink, and the towel was unfolded. Two early schedule bus drivers, Sheila Knudsen and Joe Morales, joined the spectators.

Dungaree sat there humiliated while the foursome tried to figure out what he was.

"Looks to me like a baby porcupine," offered Sheila.

"Naw," said Joe, "I seen plenty of them in the woods 'an they don' look nothin' like that. This little guy sorta looks like a porcupine with a crew cut. I just wonder how he got on the bus."

"I bet some kid left him there, a pet he don't want no more," Beulah said. "I just don't know what folks is teachin' these kids today. You know last week we found that little kitten on the Route 1 bus."

"Not teachin' 'em nothin'" scowled Mae, "that's the problem. Kitty's doin' fine, though. Gets along great with my dog."

"Say, Joe," asked Beulah, "why don't you head out a little early and stop by the Animal Shelter with this little critter, it's jest around the corner?"

"Sure, Beulah," said Joe, "then at least we can find out what it is. They won't kill it will they?"

"Naw," answered Beulah, "they's good folks. Mae and me got us some fine ol' dogs over there."

"See if it'll drink some water?" Sheila asked.

Beulah filled a cut-off paper cup with water as Dungaree, now a little more relaxed, looked up at the rainbow of colors of the four staring human faces way up there beyond the greasy walls of the deep sink. The cup with water was lowered down to him. "Well, he thought to himself, if I'm gonna die I might as well not die thirsty," as he dived into the cup and drank heartily.

"Hey, looky there!" Beulah cheerfully exclaimed. "The little feller's thirsty."

Heh heh," intoned Mae, "he looks a little more normal now that we know he's got a face."

"Awright, ladies," said Joe, "gotta go mount up if I'm gonna drop this whatever-he-is off at the shelter."

Fortunately for Joe, Ed Lukens was not patrolling but in the office at the Humane Society, which was also the agency contracted for animal control in the county. He looked up as the bus pulled in to the parking lot. Joe ambled off the bus with Dungaree wrapped in the towel inside of a cardboard box.

"Looks like some sort of stray somethin' on the bus!" Ed exclaimed.

"You 'bout got that right," said Joe, "'cept we don't rightly know what it is." Joe unwrapped Dungaree there in the parking lot.

Ed took one look and said "African hedgehog."

"Do what?" Joe asked. "How'd he get here from Africa?"

"Imported as pets some years back," offered Ed, "now I guess all of 'em are born here. Y'know, fad pets, popular for a while. People get tired of 'em and toss them out. We got a local guy here that takes 'em in."

"Are there a lot of these things around?" Joe asked. "Never seen one before myself."

"Ah, there's a few," answered Ed, "people collect the strangest animals. Takes all kinds, I guess."

"What're you gonna do with him?" Joe asked, once again exposing his soft spot for animals. "Wouldn't want him hurt or nothin'."

"We'll put him in the Wildkind Department," said Ed, and call that fella that takes 'em in. He treats 'em real good, special food and all, even their own special kind of exercise wheels. Heard they ain't too sure-footed and can break their legs on the rodent wheels."

"Sounds good," said Joe, as he returned behind the wheel of his bus. "Just don't hurt him."

#

Becky and her husband Eddie were having an argument: "Look, I don't want to get rid of him, either, but all he does is just sit around and hiss at me." Eddie said. Eddie had somehow suddenly decided that they needed to get rid of their pet hedgehog.

"He's been here for THREE YEARS!" Becky shouted.

"He's just a stupid hedgehog," countered Eddie.

"He's not stupid, and he's sick!"

"We can't afford vet bills for a rodent," said Eddie.

"He's not a rodent, but I agree we cannot afford vet bills. What'll we do?" Becky asked.

"Well whatever he is, this big lump on him does not look good," said Eddie.

Roscoe the hedgehog was not feeling at the top of her form and thought the golf-ball sized tumor just to the rear of her left front leg was a definite hindrance. Roscoe had not been enjoying life for nearly all of it—now four years. Three of those years had been here with Becky. During the first year with her, things were much better since she got to run around the apartment most of the time. Then Becky married Eddie, and all of that changed.

She longed for the time when she was young and thought often of her hedgehog friends back then, especially the spirited youngsters who were going to make all things right in the world. She fondly remembered that young fellow Spikers, who wanted to join the Marines and stamp out animal abuse, and that nutty guy Bill, who would take on anything.

She would have escaped years ago had she known where to go or even how to get out of the apartment she lived in. Eddie and Becky argued much of the time and Eddie would have nothing to do with Roscoe. Becky fed Roscoe and cleaned the small 20 gallon aquarium she was trapped in most of the day and night. On rare occasion, she would get to run around on the floor, but those events were few and far between, always when Eddie was not home.

Several months ago, Roscoe felt a lump growing under her front left leg. It grew very rapidly and became more and more uncomfortable, but not very painful. She worried what Eddie and Becky had in store for her.

"Look, Tod has a gun," suggested Eddie, "he can just put him out of his misery, no fuss. You don't have to come along."

"You JERK!" Becky shouted.

"OK, ok," said Eddie, "just a suggestion. If we bring him anywhere, they're just gonna kill him anyway and charge us for it."

"Let me call the Humane Society," said Becky, "maybe they can tell us what to do."

"I KNOW what to do," retorted Eddie, "animal's got cancer, lump as big as a golf ball. Put him to sleep!"

Becky looked up the number of the Humane Society and dialed it.

"Humane Society, Connie speaking," answered the intake volunteer on the front desk.

"Wow, pretty impressive, no answering machine!" Becky exclaimed, surprised.

"We try," responded Connie, "how can I help you."

"Do you take in hedgehogs?" Becky asked, not mentioning the tumor. "We are moving and cannot take him with us," she lied.

"Yes, we do," replied Connie. "In fact we have one here now, but if you are looking to adopt him, we can't do that because we don't have the USDA license needed to adopt one out.," ignoring what Becky had said.

"Oh no, we don't want to adopt one," replied Becky, "we are moving and cannot take ours with us."

"Oh," replied Connie, "well, when it rains it pours. Sure, bring him on in, what's one more. No hedgehogs for a year and now we get two of 'em. Well, there's a local guy with a license that takes 'em in."

"I'm going to take Roscoe to the Humane Society," said Becky to Eddie, and she quickly grabbed her purse and Roscoe's aquarium and exited the apartment.

For the first time in four years Roscoe smelled the fresh outdoor air and wondered what a Humane Society was. In any event, she thought she knew it was better than going to meet Tod and his gun.

Becky and Roscoe arrived at the Humane Society on the south side of town in just a few minutes, as their apartment was close by. She struggled a bit with the aquarium on the front seat of their Saturn and walked quickly into the front office of the Humane Society. Deep down, Becky was quite attached to Roscoe, even though he was fairly prickly and seemed irritable most of the time. Despite this, she often preferred Roscoe's company to Eddie's. She wanted to get this over with quickly, before she changed her mind. She was ushered into a small room with a desk and two chairs.

The intake volunteer was Melinda Worth, an animal rights advocate who had little use for these creeps who gave up animals when they became inconvenient. Melinda often let her scorn show, and today was no exception. Hard up for volunteers, the Humane Society was marginally tolerant of Melinda's attitude, but she had been warned that if one more complaint was received, she was going to return to cleaning kennels, a clear demotion among the volunteer crew.

Melinda began with her reading of the release agreement and handed Becky the form to fill out. Given Melinda's apparently condescending and borderline hostile attitude, Becky said little and tried as quickly as possible to fill out the form. Roscoe, in the meantime stayed rolled up in a ball, not wishing to take any chances in this strange new environment, with its strange scents and howling noises. Melinda poked at Roscoe with a pencil, which caused Roscoe to roll up even tighter.

Becky decided, especially since Roscoe was rolled up tight, not to mention the tumor.

The transaction was over quickly and, feeling ashamed and a little sad, Becky climbed back into the Saturn for the all-too-short ride home.

Roscoe was taken back into the Wildkind Department and placed in a cage that had heavy metal bars. It was a larger enclosure than she had ever seen, but that was not really a big deal since all she ever knew was the 20 gallon aquarium. The glass water bowl was a very pleasant surprise after all of those years of trying to get water out of that water bottle and tube. Food looked pretty good, too. Not bad for starters, she thought.

Roscoe looked around and did not believe what she saw through the bars in the next cage—a hedgehog! Another hedgehog!

Dungaree blinked a few times and said "What are you doing in here, sweetie... err, I mean, Sssweetie?"

"Hmm," Roscoe thought to herself, "what a strange way of talking. But then what do I know, never having even seen another hedgehog for most of my life since I was a kid."

"Hello," Roscoe communicated rather formally. "I was given up by my human caretakers. But that's Ok, because there was not much care involved. Just lucky to be alive."

"That'sss the problem with those Bigsss," Dungaree began with the rhetoric he had practiced from his training days with Bowls. "They need to go."

"Humphh," sighed Roscoe, "maybe they do but I do not see what I can do about it. I'm just trying to keep from being killed."

CHAPTER 16

BILL THE BOMB

Critical Bill

CHAPTER 16—BILL THE BOMB

Elsewhere in town, another couple seemed to be having a different problem with a hedgehog, this one being a little less emotionally charged than with Becky and Eddie. Jadran and Stefia, recent immigrants from Bosnia, had suddenly been given a hedgehog "as a pet" by one of Stefia's employers where she cleaned houses for extra income to make ends meet. For Roscoe and now Stefia's new acquisition, it seemed that Thelma had put her subliminal suggestions, however potentially dangerous, to work.

Jadran sadly put it to Stefia, "What are we to do 'vis that thing, whatever is it?"

"I don't know," Stefia said, "the man says he gives to us as pet, but really I don't think he wants. But what can I say when I need the work?"

The couple tried very hard to speak English in front of their son, Kresimir, who had just turned 15. Kresimir, now known as Carl, Stefia and Jadran felt, needed to blend into his new country as fast as possible. So they practiced their English constantly.

"We cannot afford to feed ourselves," groaned Jadran, "let alone animal."

"Also animal not friendly," offered Carl. "Not a good pet animal."

"We take out and leave by side of road," offered Jadran. "Maybe somebody pick up."

"No," replied Stefia, "maybe we bring to better place where somebody can find."

"Why not bring to a school," suggested Carl. "Lots of kids there, maybe one wants a pet."

"Good idea. OK, we bring to school, to playground," said Jadran. "Kids there can look and maybe take home."

Stefia called up her friend Marija, who had lived in the USA several years longer and had a car. She explained the situation and Marija understood the delicate circumstances. Marija also had to work at the pleasure of wealthy Americans and be ingratiating in order to keep her job. It was not long before Marija showed up in her aging Toyota, and she and Stefia set off with Bill the hedgehog in a large brown bag. They brought the telephone book along, which contained local road maps and a listing of public schools with their addresses.

Bill, among the more grumpy hedgehogs on the face of the earth, prided himself on how fast he could roll up into a protective ball. He considered that he had had a pretty crummy life so far, as he was handed off to more humans than he could count. He could not understand these humans. What did they want, anyway? "I mean, hedgehogs roll up and they have quills," he thought to himself, "what else was there to explain? You don't want quills? You don't want roll up? Then do not get a hedgehog. Simple as that."

But now new things were in motion and he looked forward to the adventure. Thelma, the Grand dowager herself, accompanied by that crazy Bozeman and an alley cat named Nellie showed up in the middle of the night asking him if he wanted to be "sprung." Thelma subliminally put the "hint" of giving away the hedgehog into the mind of the rich man who kept Bill confined.

He wondered what was happening in this latest excursion. He did know that he was not wanted in this new home, and here he was in a paper bag and could not see where he was going. The women were talking very rapidly now in Serbo-Croatian, since they were out of earshot of their children.

They pulled into the parking lot of the first school they had noted in the telephone book. It was a high school, but there was no one present. Stefia and Marija decided they would not drop the hedgehog off at either of the schools where their own children attended. They wanted to find a school playground where there were some children present that could maybe see the hedgehog and take him home. They talked about how they did not want him to get run over by a car, like happened a lot to wild animals in the old country. They were also careful to disguise the automobile license plates by smearing mud on them.

At the third school they tried, it seemed like an ideal situation. It was a middle school and the parking lot came right up next to a playground that had a low fence around it. At the far end of the playground there was a small group of children, too far away to run to the car before the car could get out of the parking lot.

Stefia acted quickly and exited the car with the bag containing Bill, walked hurredly to the playground fence, and up-ended the bag over the fence. Bill fell unceremoniously to the ground. She scurried back to the car and the pair sped out of the parking lot, disappearing into neighborhood streets.

Gayle Sanchez, 7th grader, had seen the whole thing. "Did you see that?" She asked her friend Robin.

"See what?" Robin asked.
"The car over there that just left."
"Well, yeah. What about it?" Robin asked.
"Somebody got out of the car and dumped something out of a bag onto the playground," said Gayle. "See it over there? That white thing, sorta round."
"Well let's go see!" Robin said as she trotted off, with Gayle right behind her.
As they approached the white thing, their pace slowed. They looked curiously at it as they drew closer.
"What is it?' Robin asked.
"I dunno." Gayle said. "Never seen anything like it. It has all these spikes on it."
"Let's go get Miss Monahan," offered Robin, referring to the activities teacher that was supervising this summer class at the school. Both girls, now running at top speed, darted into the school to find Miss Monahan.

Patricia Monahan was enjoying a leisurely Summer contract that was a welcome respite from the hectic pace of the normal school year. She calmly greeted the two out-of-breath girls, who were, by now, quite excited.
"M . . . M . . . Ms. M . . . M . . . M . . . onihan," squealed Gayle, "there's a THING in the playground!"
"A THING?" Miss Monahan queried.
"YES, a round white THING with sharp POINTS!" Robin exclaimed.
"Well, I guess we can use a little excitement for today," said Miss Monahan calmly, as she got up from her desk and followed the girls outside. "And how did this white thing get there?"
Gayle repeated her story about seeing the car drive up and someone from the car dumping the thing onto the playground from a paper bag, and the car speeding off.
The trio approached Bill, who was still rolled up in a ball in this strange environment. As he heard and felt the vibrations of the approaching footsteps, he rolled up tighter and let our a few warning hisses.
"My goodness!" Miss Monahan exclaimed. "What IS that?"
"WE DON'T KNOW!" Shouted both girls together.
The sudden racket caused Bill to roll up even more and hiss all the louder.
"PhugggPhugggPhuggg-phuggg-phugggggggggg."
"It's making NOISE!" Gayle shouted, as all three turned on their heels, as if rehearsed, and made a beeline back to the school building.

Wilson Turnbull, principal at Westwood Middle School, like Miss Monahan, was enjoying a relaxed, light summer. He was working on curriculum changes for the coming year. It was, therefore, very startling when a very tense Miss Monahan and two seemingly hysterical students burst into his office.

"There's a THING out there!" Robin screamed.

"And it's making a HISSING NOISE!" Gayle yelled.

"And it's round and white with barbs all over it!" Miss Monahan added.

"Come, now," said Mr. Turnbull calmly, "let us go and see what sort of terrible thing you are speaking of," as he jauntily strolled out of his office with the three females at his heels.

On the way out to the playground, the story was retold about how the "thing" got to be there.

"Thrown over the fence, eh?" Mr. Turnbull droned. "Car sped from the lot. Hmm."

As the group neared him, Bill sensed the voices and the vibrations and rolled up again.

"PhugggPhugggPhuggg-phuggg-phugggggggggg."

Mr. Turnbull stopped dead in his tracks about ten feet from the huffing Bill. The color drained from his face and he started backing up. "Oh, my God!" he half whispered. "M . . . M . . . Miss Monahan, g . . . g . . . get all the children off the playground and into the building." Mr. Turnbull walked as fast as dignity and supposedly being in charge would permit. He hurried back to his office and nervously sat down at his desk, picked up the telephone and dialed the numbers 9-1-1.

Teresa Johnson, Emergency Center operator, immediately answered the call: "Emergency Center, how may I assist."

Th . . . th . . . this is Wilson Turnbull, principal at Westwood Middle School. W . . . w . . . we h . . . h . . . have a b . . . b . . . bomb that is hissing in the school playground. It was thrown from a car."

"Yes, sir," responded Ms. Johnson, "I am connecting you with Hazardous Materials Emergency. Are there any structures on your school grounds or near your school that are over two stories?"

"N . . . n . . . no." Turnbull replied.

"Other than what you reported, did you notice anything else that seemed unusual—sights, sounds, smells, people, anything?" Ms. Johnson continued.

"No, nothing."

"Buckleton, HAZMAT here!" Tom Buckleton roared, the Hazardous Materials Emergency supervisor, retired from 25 years with Army Explosive Ordnance Disposal units. "Tell me what you've got!"

As Turnbull was relating the incident to Buckleton, Ms. Johnson was busy on a couple of other radios: "Echo Charlie to Engine 6, Chemical 2, Battalion Chief 2, HAZMAT report Code 2 at Westwood Middle School. Tower One stand down."

"Engine Six rolling," came a reply over the radio.

"Chemical Two on the way," came another broadcast.

"Get a DOT sand truck and send Engine 3 also. This is Battalion 2," said another voice.

"Echo Charlie, ten-four," Teresa said, and turned to another radio and said "Echo Charlie to Patrol Zone South, HazMat report Code 2 at Westwood Middle School, Buckleton and FD on the way."

"Unit 266 ten-four, on the way," responded Police Officer Matt Conway.

"South Supe 34 responding," said Police Sergeant Ken Paxton, the South Patrol Zone patrol supervisor.

"Patrol Commander 5 responding," reported Captain Charles Woodley, also on the air and in his police vehicle.

"Unit 260 responding," added Police Officer Kevin Reichard.

"Patrol Commander 5 to South Supe 34," radioed Captain Woodley, "better get about five or six units in there and the motorman. We'll need traffic control and may have to evacuate."

"Ten-four, PC 5," said Paxton, "Units 261 and 263, report to Westwood Middle School."

"Motor 2 on the air, will respond," said Motor Cycle Officer Jake Hamlin.

"Ten-four, Motor 2, thanks!" Paxton responded.

Teresa addressed another set of radios, "DOT Emergency, over."

A voice crackled back, "Department of Transportation Emergency."

"Need a sand truck ASAP to Westwood Middle School, HAZMAT report code 2," said Teresa urgently into the radio.

"Whatzat HazMat Emergency 2 thing? I don't have my code book here," said Chuck Bungg, the DOT equipment yard supervisor.

"HAZMAT 2 emergency is suspected active but as yet undetonated bomb." said Teresa, "Fire Battalion Two Chief requested a sand truck."

"Oh no!" Bungg replied. "All my dump trucks are in for summer major maintenance and the one that is here has its dump on stilts. Tell ya what, I'm going to get our emergency contractor, Bubba Treesler over there with his truck. Now, I dunno how long it'll take Bubba to get there, so if you see a dump truck full of sand or a cement mixer, just pull 'em over and comandeer their services. DOT will pay for the materials."

"Cement mixer?' Teresa asked.

"Yeah, could serve the same purpose of smothering some active ordnance in an emergency. Stops flying shrapnel," replied Bungg.

"OK, will do," replied Teresa, while repeating this information back to both the police and the responding fire department vehicles.

By the time Teresa had dispatched Engine 3 in accordance with the Battalion Chief's instructions, almost all of the hardware was rolling toward Westwood Middle School and Bill the Bomb.

Engine 6 and most of the police units arrived first and cordoned off the area. Police officers evacuated the school and then began to evacuate neighborhood houses. Traffic control points were set up. Bill was impressed. Somehow he knew that all of this activity involved him, probably at the request of that very scared and nervous man that had been looking at him in horror a short time ago.

Sherman Bolduc, the Fire Battalion Chief, arrived to take charge and immediately asked over the radio where the sand truck was. Teresa relayed the instructions from Chuck Bungg, including the recommendation to commandeer either a dumptruck full of sand or a cement mixer. Chief Bolduc looked up just in time to see a large cement mixer stopped in the heavy traffic slowed by the emergency. The chief told the officer on Motor 2 the situation and asked that the cement mixer be commandeered.

"Can do!" asserted the Motor 2 officer as he rode off toward the traffic jam and the cement mixer.

"Big Al" Emerson was cussing the heavy traffic and was glad he was through for the day hauling lumber and other supplies in the back of his truck. At 6'7" tall and weighing in at a little over 350 pounds, Big Al was a fairly formidable figure, and his long, gray beard added to the appearance of someone not to be messed with. He and his Vietnam War pal, Otis Driggs, who was almost as tall and heavy as Big Al, owned adjoining parcels of property in Wyoming, just over the Colorado border. They were both reclusive men who, when asked to list their occupations, answered "biker." Both Big Al and Otis considered themselves to be "old time bikers." Indeed, they never used any means of transportation other than motor cycles unless some heavy hauling was needed.

Big Al was finally having to make some major repairs to his log cabin and figured that the only way to get the lumber and materials up there was to get him a four wheeled vehicle. So he shopped around, and got a hands down great deal on a very old used truck. OK, so it had a little bit of a strange configuration, but it was one helluva bargain! But now he sat in traffic and was getting increasingly irritated.

As Big Al was sitting there fuming, he heard a rap on the door of his truck. It was the knock of a police officer, only this time he did not appear to be serving an arrest warrant.

"Good afternoon, Sir," said the police officer.

"Afternoon yerself," Big Al answered. "What kin I do fer you?"

"Well, sir, it has been ordered that we are going to commandeer your vehicle," said the officer.

"Whut're you talking about?" Big Al asked.

"Your cement mixer has been commandeered for emergency hazardous materials neutralization," came the voice, having to shout over the clatter of the diesel engine in the huge, seemingly very old yellow Autocar cement mixer that only had two words lettered on the side of the door: "Big Al."

"Whatchoo goin' to do with it?" Big Al squinted.

"I don't know!" Officer Hamlin hollered. "I guess they need it to pour cement on some hazard or somethin'."

"Not this cement mixer, pal." Big Al said.

"You don't have a choice!" Officer Hamlin yelled.

"Naw, it's you that don't have no choice!" Big Al roared.

"Well, we'll see about that!" Hamlin said as he requested backup on his radio.

"Yep, we'll shore see." Big Al responded.

Additional patrols, fire apparatus, and the HAZMAT truck arrived. Four officers responded to Officer Hamlin's radio call and now had Big Al's cement mixer surrounded.

As soon as the additional officers were in place, Officer Hamlin ordered Big Al from the cab, "Real slow like!" he added.

In his aging years, having picked up 50 to 60 pounds somewhere, Big Al was not very much into speed anyway. He climbed slowly from the truck and just stood there looking at the officers (over their heads) with a sort of humorous contempt. "OK, boys, whut now?"

"We are going to commandeer your cement mixer!" Officer Hamlin ordered.

"Commandeer away!" Big Al said.

"Anyone here know how to operate a cement mixer?" Hamlin asked.

No one volunteered.

"Will you drive your cement mixer over to that school yard, please?" Officer Hamlin, exasperated, testily asked Big Al.

Big Al, no lover of official authority figures, especially smartmouth cops that saw fit to push him around, in sort of miming a hangdog helpless expression, groaned "Awww, whut kin ah do? Th' mixer's been commandeered, 'an I ain't got no commandeer license." Big Al then ambled to the side of the road where a nice, shaded bus stop bench offered a cool place to sit.

In the meantime, traffic was backing up. Especially in the lanes immediately behind the commandeered cement mixer.

Officer Hamlin was beside himself with anxiety. First he had heard this emergency call to commandeer a sand dump truck or a cement mixer because the DOT could not respond. Then, lo and behold, he lands this cement mixer, but the driver will not cooperate. He evaluates the driver as a very large antisocial dirtbag. Now he has an abandoned cement mixer in the middle of an evacuation highway with traffic backing up for several miles.

Hamlin radioed his concerns to Teresa. Teresa, an experienced dispatcher accustomed to doing many things at one time during an emergency, had also called paramedic units at the local hospital, who were on the way but were now being slowed by traffic. The Flight For Life helicopter was also on standby if needed.

"Echo Charlie to Motor 2," radioed Teresa, "let me get working to get a driver for that mixer."

"Ten-four," replied Hamlin, as the traffic situation worsened.

Over on the far end of the Westwood Middle School playground, where a wide circle of "no man's land" had been staked out with POLICE LINE DO NOT CROSS yellow tape, Tom Buckleton conferred with his two Explosive Ordnance Disposal colleagues, Peter Waldron and Nancy Charles. They were a little nonplussed. Buckleton had already approached the hissing white ball of spikes to within some dozen feet or so and had also used field glasses, to little avail. "What do y'all reckon?" Buckleton asked.

"Beats me!" Waldron answered.

"Never seen anything like it in all of our manuals," offered Charles, "do you suppose it is some kind of new weapon from the Middle East?"

"Well," said Buckleton, "I'd wonder why any terrorist organization would pick this town, but we can't rule anything out. What's holdin' up the X-ray real-time thing?"

"Umm, Tom," replied Waldron, "you know it's on loan to Denver."

"Yeah, but they were sposta return it today," said Buckleton.

"They broke it, remember?" Charles said. "In for repairs."

"Aw, JEEZ!" Buckleton bellowed. "That's right! MAN! Helluva time for this to happen!"

"Want to try to detonate in place?" Waldron asked.

"Yeah, if we knew what it was." Buckleton said. "But we don't and I do not want to set off some kind of dirty device that might have chemicals, germs, viruses, whatever. Rather dump cement on it."

"By the way," offered Charles, "EC says she's got a cement mixer but they are having some trouble getting it over here. Driver not cooperating."

As the house by house evacuation was being conducted by police, Teresa Johnson was on the telephone to Chuck Bungg at DOT explaining the difficulties Officer Hamlin was having with Big Al.

"What company is it?" Bungg asked.

"It's an old yellow cement mixer with only the name 'Big Al' printed on the doors," replied Teresa.

"Beats me," replied Bungg. "Look, there's a retired DOT driver that knows cement and sand real well living on that side of town. Bill Creasey. Let me give him a call."

"Great!" Teresa replied. "If he can come have him call 911 and ask for Teresa and I'll alert the other operators. The situation is getting pretty bad there."

As soon as he hung up, Chuck called his old friend Bill Creasey, who sounded a little agitated. "Yo!" Bill said as he picked up the phone.

"Yo, yourself, Bill!" Chuck said good-naturedly. "Chuck Bungg here, ol' bud. Seems there's a little excitement over in your neck of the woods."

"Tell me about it, pal!" Creasey answered. "There's two cops here telling me I'm gettin' evacuated. Some kinda terrorist bomb or somethin'!"

"Well, Bill, they may be able to use your help," responded Chuck. "Seems they need a cement mixer real bad and there's a truck over there but no one to drive it."

"What?!" Bill exclaimed. "Whose truck is it, one of Lafarge's?"

"Guess not," replied Chuck, "no name I recognize. Probably some independent."

"Well, be glad to help," said Creasey.

"Put one of them cops on the line," said Chuck, "and I'll tell 'em to escort you to the truck."

"Officer Dempsey," said one of the police officers into the telephone handed to him by Creasey.

Chuck Bungg explained the situation to the officer, and Dempsey agreed to escort Creasey to the truck, as he had been keeping up with the radio traffic on the difficulties Officer Hamlin was having with the cement mixer.

"OK," said Buckleton, "I'm going to go up to the thing with a shield and see if I can spot anything further. Get everyone back. See what's holding up that cement mixer."

"Will do!" Charles replied.

Officer Dempsey and Bill Creasey threaded their way through the swarm of police and fire personnel, around the school playground with the yellow tape, and east two more blocks to the main traffic jam. They were walking directly toward the front of the cement mixer, a large, yellow looming hulk sitting in the middle of the snarled traffic.

"Creasey eyed the mixer with skepticism, but was distracted by the throng of vehicles, officers, and emergency equipment on site. There was also the noise, sirens, horns, and the familiar "bap-bap-bap-bap" overhead—a helicopter.

The helicopter, one of the few unusual vehicles at the scene that Teresa the dispatcher did NOT call, bore the large words EYEWITNESS NEWS on the side.

Bill Creasey was escorted up to the front of the cement mixer as he thought to himself "old ten yard Autocar. Wonder where THAT came from?" He was immediately surrounded by police officers, with Jake Hamlin as the spokesman.

Hamlin explained the situation to Creasey and asked him to drive the truck west two blocks to the school playground and stand by for instructions from the Explosive Ordnance crew. Bill immediately agreed, as this was the most exciting that had happened to him since that hair-raising day 18 years ago when his DOT dump truck slid sideways down a two-story high sand pile when the supports gave way.

The old diesel truck shuddered and roared to life, idling surprisingly well for what Bill estimated was a truck manufactured in the early 1950s, although it was real hard to tell age with Autocars, known as durable old workhorses with amazing driver loyalty. The truck easily shifted and rumbled slowly toward the school playground as police officers cleared traffic ahead.

Big Al stood up and ambled after the truck, taking his time and wondering what the "commandeers" were going to do with his truck.

News stories began to abound on local radio and television stations, and news blurbs began to show up on national networks. Reporters plugged in speculation where there were no facts. Buckleton's remark about not detonating in place due to the possibility of a "dirty" weapon was overheard by a school official and casually repeated to a news reporter. The possibility of a terrorist chemical or germ weapon quickly made its way into the broadcast media.

As Big Al's truck lumbered up to the cordoned-off playground, Tom Buckleton walked up to the cab as Bill Creasey shut off the engine and climbed down.

"Thanks for bringing this over," said Buckleton, "we're gonna need you to back this up to that curb over there," pointing to a distant curb nearest to the round white object of everyone's attention, "and stand by ready to dump cement down the chute onto that white thing over there."

"OK," said Creasey, "let me check the load." As he looked toward the rear of the cement mixer for the first time, a thought again crossed his mind that he had absentmindedly noted as he first approached the truck, but lost track of as he became surrounded by police officers. The mixer drum was not rotating.

Now, as Creasey walked toward the rear of the truck, he noted another interesting fact: The truck did not have the "booster" typical of trucks of this size thus enabling a ten square yard load. More interesting things presented themselves as Creasey walked to the rear of the mixer, the most profound being that there was no chute. Indeed, the back of the drum was open and there was no cement inside.

By this time Big Al had caught up with the truck and stood there in amused silence.

Creasey turned to Buckleton and his escort, Officer Hamlin, and said, incredulously, "There is no cement in the drum. Even if there was, there would be no way to get it out. All of the equipment has been removed from the rear of the truck."

"What, on earth, kind of cement mixer IS this, anyway?" Buckleton asked.

"Durned if I know." Creasey said. "Never seen anything like it."

"WELL!?" Officer Hamlin screamed, as he turned to Big Al.

"Well, what?" Big Al asked calmly.

"WHAT KIND OF CEMENT MIXER IS THIS!?" Hamlin screamed, exasperated.

"Usta be a cement mixer. Now it's my personal ride." Big Al answered.

"WHAT?!" Hamlin hollered, apparently not believing what he was hearing.

"P-e-r-s-o-n-a-l r-i-d-e." Big Al articulated the words very slowly.

"You mean to say that this is what you use for a car?" Bill Creasey asked, flabbergasted.

"Yep," Big Al said, "gas mileage ain't worth a damn, but it has its advantages."

"Advantages?' Tom Buckleton asked curiously, momentarily distracted from all the activity of the day. "What advantages?"

"Park where ya want, fer one thing," answered Big Al, "folks figure if a cement mixer's there, it needs to be there. Nobody gets in yore way, fer another."

Buckleton quickly recovered and commanded: "Somebody get on the horn and get us a real cement mixer, and get this piece of junk out of here."

Officer Hamlin immediately radioed to Teresa about the order for a new cement truck, and then ordered Big Al to be on his way.

Big Al did not move.

Hamlin ordered Big Al again to get the truck out of there.

"Can't," Big Al said stoically, "it's still commandeered."

"WELL IT'S NOT COMMANDEERED ANY MORE!" Hamlin screamed.

Big Al, remaining maddeningly calm, softly said "Have a nice day," and climbed up into his personal ride, started the engine, and slowly lumbered down the street.

Buckleton, regaining his composure, said "OK, until a real cement mixer arrives I am going to try to get a little closer to that thing to see what I can see. Everyone stay back."

Buckleton's foray back onto the playground yielded no new information. The thing seemed to begin hissing the closer he got. The hissing started and stopped, as if triggered by air waves or currents.

Through all of this, Bill the hedgehog was getting a little weary of all of the agitation, noise, and the strange vibrations. "When are these Bigs going to go away?" he thought to himself, "especially that clown that keeps creeping up to me with that board in front of him," referring to Buckleton's shrapnel shield. "I wonder if he thinks he's hiding?"

Finally, a real cement mixer arrived from a local company and Buckleton ordered it into place, backing up to a position where the chute could deliver fresh cement to cover up Bill the Bomb quickly.

As the chute was slowly lowered, Buckleton crept back up to the "thing" with his shrapnel shield, inching ever closer. Sweat poured down his face as he got closer and closer: Seven feet . . . six . . . five. He constantly stared at the round white object, straining to see any kind of sign. Four feet . . . three. The chute lowered and hovered over the object and the shadow of the chute extended across the object, which up until that time had been in direct sunlight.

Bill the hedgehog felt a cool relief from the sun as the chute was positioned overhead. A drop of watered down wet cement fell on his quills and he jumped and popped.

Buckleton nearly fainted and jumped right along with Bill the Bomb, smashing his head on the shrapnel shield. The tension had built so consistently, that Buckleton was convinced he was having a heart attack. After a few tense seconds, he relaxed, and then saw the most amazing sight.

The bomb had feet!

He could not believe his eyes. The bomb had FEET! The bomb started moving! MOVING! But that was not all.

THE BOMB HAS A NOSE! Buckleton looked on in disbelief as, there in the cool shadow of the cement mixer chute, this little nose was snuffling around, moving in a rapid-fire, twitching fashion.

Buckleton fell backwards and sat on the ground with his shrapnel shield at an odd angle and his head between his knees. Upon seeing this, police sharpshooters stationed at three points inside school classrooms carefully took aim at the white object through their scopes.

Buckleton began to laugh hysterically, and finally, between giggles, managed to gasp into the radio handset: "Somebody call the dogcatcher!"

Buckleton staggered back to the yellow police line dragging his shrapnel shield behind him. "It's an animal!" he exclaimed, "some sort of weird little animal. It's got a face and a bunch of little feet and a twitching nose. Call the dogcatcher."

#

Sandra delVecchio, the Humane Society's manager of the Wildkind Department thought she had the best job at the shelter. Contracted with the county for animal control, euthanasia of mostly dogs and cats was a process that Sandra and most of her fellow employees despised. In the Wildkind Department, which consisted of only her and a volunteer or two when needed, exempted her from dealing with the euthanasias. Euthanisia was not permitted for those animals designated as "wild," unless they were in unrelenting pain and could not be rehabilitated. Even for those wild animals not able to return to the wild, Sandra had a network of legal and appropriate shelters willing to take them in. The local university had an excellent raptor program for big birds that could not be returned to their natural habitat. There was even a squirrel rehabber. And now, a hedgehog rescue had been formed by a local professor. Sandra was rightly proud of the connections she had made and, accordingly, the lives of all the animals she had saved.

Sandra recalled when the issue of hedgehogs had first come up at a Humane Society staff meeting. Eleanor Wikulski, the Society Director led a discussion about hedgehogs: "So now we have a hedgehog!" she exclaimed. "Where, on earth, do we put THOSE critters?"

Wanting to keep as many animals as possible from the mainstream processing, Sandra immediately piped up: "Wildkind!"

"Wildkind!?" The Director exclaimed. "Those are sold in pet stores and are not even found in the wild in the USA!"

"Yeah," continued Sandra, "but they are still recently from the wild in Africa and still act pretty wild."

"Well," said Eleanor, "can't argue with that. They all look just like little pincushions to me. You want 'em, Sandra, you got 'em!"

And that was that, Sandra got the hedgehogs. There were few hedgehogs to arrive at the shelter, only about one or two per year. Now there was this guy Ivan that took them in. That was good news to Sandra, for she had just found out that hedgehogs were a protected species under the federal Animal Welfare Act, and that a special USDA license was needed to "transfer" a hedgehog anywhere. Fortunately, this Ivan guy had such a license. It was especially fortunate today, for the third hedgehog in 24 hours was now making its way to the shelter in the HAZMAT truck, no less.

Sandra had been following the news accounts on TV with all of the other shelter employees. Imagine, a bomb in a schoolyard right here in our town! All had sat glued to the screen for most of the afternoon. Then, when Tom Buckleton collapsed against his shrapnel shield and began hysterically laughing, the whole thing was captured from the Eyewitness News camera in the hovering helicopter.

With his words, "call the dogcatcher," the collective jaws dropped on all of the faces of the Humane Society TV audience. However, the on-duty animal control officer, who was also watching the TV news station, received a message that there was no need to respond. HAZMAT was going to deliver Bill to the animal shelter personally. The "Bomb," somehow named "Bill the Bomb," or more lately "Critical Bill," got his name because, according the commander of the HAZMAT team, the event had reached "critical" proportions several times during the day.

Indeed, Critical Bill was a famous hedgehog, and all of the Humane Society crew was there at the front door to greet him as the brightly colored HAZMAT truck pulled up. Everyone stood and applauded. Eleanor, at the head of the shelter queue, stood ready to accept Critical Bill from Tom Buckleton, who suddenly felt very, very tired. Eyewitness News recorded the entire grand event.

Eleanor brought Critical Bill inside the shelter and handed him off to Sandra. Sandra cuddled Critical Bill for a few moments and thought that he was not so bad, after all. The shelter had an old department store glass display case that was set up in the second office/lobby back from the main lobby. This second office held the two bookkeeper/cashier cubicles, an adoption cubicle, two small couches and a few chairs. The display case usually held small animals for adoption, but, Critical Bill, being a local celebrity, was immediately set up there, complete with an exercise wheel and an extremely beaten up little wooden house that looked like hamsters had gnawed on for a few years. He took to the little house right away and settled in.

As soon as the excitement died down, Sandra called Ivan and informed him that the Humane Society had not one, nor two, but three hedgehogs for him to take in. Ivan was a little nonplussed by all of this and told her that he did not have room at the moment for three new male hedgehogs, but would come over and take a look. Ivan took food and hedgehog exercise wheels, and headed for the shelter.

Ivan's arrival was met with greetings from numerous shelter staff members and volunteers. Normally his arrivals gained no attention, but now a local celebrity, a hedgehog named Critical Bill was in residence. Ivan explained to Sandra his perceived space problem, and asked to look at the hedgehogs. Examinations of Dungaree and Critical Bill went without incident. Both males were apparently in good health, although pretty feisty and mostly rolled up in balls of quills. Back in the Wildkind Department, he bathed each hedgehog and got to look at them in good detail as the hedgehogs suddenly cared more about not drowning than staying rolled up. Then it came time to examine Roscoe.

As it turned out, Roscoe, who had spent four years being misidentified as a male by humans, was really a female. Moreover, it was discovered that she had a golf-ball sized tumor just to the rear of one of her front legs. Given this evidence, Sandra wondered if it would not be better to "put her down." Ivan offered that they really did not know what the problem was, and so a trip to the veterinarian was in order. He agreed to take in Roscoe, since she was a female, but asked to wait a while on the other two until he could decide on adequate space. Little did he know that the hedgehogs already had that figured out.

Roscoe was bundled up for a trip straight to the veterinarian. Ivan did not hope for too much in Roscoe's case, given the size of the tumor. Roscoe was feeling a little uncomfortable herself, and wondered what was next in store for her.

CHAPTER 17

THE TACTICAL DRILL

Wumpling the Dowager

CHAPTER 17—THE TACTICAL DRILL

Roscoe's arrival at The Flash Memorial Hedgehog Rescue, or simply "Hedgequarters" (the names affixed to Ivan's place now that numerous hedgehogs lived there), was met with excitement. The staff of hedgehogs tasked with developing the tactical plan for dealing with the legions of hostile insects were especially glad to see her arrive. After three days at the veterinarian's, Roscoe was feeling very much better and more energetic. The freshly closed incision where her tumor had been removed was the only thing that bothered her, and even that was not too bad. Indeed, on an outing for the houseful of hedgehogs, while Ivan trained his attentions on those hedgehogs known to run, Roscoe used the opportunity to zip under the wooden fence and scout the neighborhood. Exasperated and looking through the entire area, Ivan spent a little over two hours hunting for the hedgehog he thought could not move very fast after major surgery.

After the outing, a meeting was held between Roscoe and Grumpy. Grumpy, the no-nonsense "Old Lady" of the Second Hedgehog Marine Division (Mechanized), otherwise known as the Chief of Staff, laid it on the line for Roscoe.

"Look," said Grumpy forcefully, "there are a lot of details we have not solved in this insect business. The Old Man has a great military mind, but he's up to his ears in problems. Even though he hates spies and "military intelligence," he knows he will have to recruit the best MI pogs in the business. Major Bozeman is on board, and he's the best. Crazy, but the best."

"You gotta be crazy to be the best in that business," Roscoe offered.

"I know," Grumpy continued. "We also need commandoes: Fearless hedgehogs that can carry off raids with minimal support. That's where you and Critical Bill come in."

"Well, fear is not in my vocabulary, nor in Critical Bill's," responded Roscoe. "Didja see where he just stood his ground and did not even flinch there when they were ready to pour ten cubic yards of cement on him?"

"Yeah," said Grumpy, "nerves of steel."

"Looks like we're your pogs for the desperate missions," Roscoe said. "I never figured I'd get out of that aquarium alive, so everything from here on out is an adventure—on borrowed time."

"OK," said Grumpy, "I'd like to put you in charge of the 2d Hedgehog Light Armored Recon Battalion, as a lieutenant colonel."

"Can do!" Roscoe immediately replied. "But what about Critical Bill? We all know how much of a rebel he is. Why, he can't stand even being an officer in the hedgehog military. Insists that he 'works for a living' and wants to be a sergeant."

"Now where have we heard THAT before?" Grumpy sighed.

"That would be shades of Sergeant Gunney, now the Acting First Sleeve in Company A of the outfit I'm going to. It'll be good to see that old hardhead again. Claims he taught the Old Man everything he ever knew."

"Heh heh," continued Grumpy, "well, the General gives ol' Gunney all the credit for teaching him escape and evasion. But, back to Critical Bill. I think we have him under control. He said he'd be willing to work for you in the 2d Recon as a Warrant Officer, which is what we offered him when he turned down a commission. We explained to him that a warrant officer is a sort of 'working officer' and he bought it. Bill is definitely not an elitist!"

"Oh, good!" Roscoe exclaimed. "Bill is the very best and bravest!"

"I've briefed the General on all of this and he's ready to see you," said Grumpy.

"Then let's do it!" Roscoe answered.

The audience with her old friend Spikers, now a Marine major general, impressed Roscoe very much. The "Old Man" came up to her and saluted even before she could gather herself, "It is an honor to have you with us!" Generals saluting lower ranked soldiers was pretty much unheard of in the military.

Spikers continued: "We are up against a fierce and worthy adversary. Much worse than the humans, for the humans are not particularly smart when it comes to warfare. They are good at organized warfare once in a while, but we study them more for why they fail. But they cannot wage a total war effectively. This is why we are so concerned about this latest effort by the insects. They outnumber everyone, and if they figure out how to pull this off they will kill every living thing on this planet. Including themselves. The insects have numbers and power, so we must out-soldier them."

"From Major Bozeman's reports, we know they are going to try an experimental strike," continued Spikers. "We only know vaguely how and we really do not know where yet—just that it's going to be in Colorado. I will have to send Bozeman back in there on another mission to find out the details. But the story is getting complicated, because our adversaries think Bozeman is someone else, and that someone else is sitting right now in the local lockup."

"Lockup?" Roscoe asked.

"Yes," said Spikers. "The place from where you just came. It's that character Dungaree. He's a loose cannon on the deck and may get some of us killed. If we can't head him off somehow, Bozeman is going to be history. The Chief and I are working on it."

"Yes, sir," replied Roscoe. "Looks like you've got your work cut out for you."

"Looks like WE'VE got OUR work cut out for US, Colonel," said Spikers forcefully as he saluted again, "and I'm glad to have you on the team, my old friend!"

"One final question, General," as Roscoe began to leave. "I've been around military hedgehogs for some time now, and I have never known a senior officer to salute juniors. Can I ask why you do that?"

"The salute is a soldier's greeting," General Spikers said without hesitation. "It is exchanged only among soldiers. It is a greeting that recognizes the mutual sacrifices of a soldier's life and the perils that are jointly shared in the defense of one's homeland. It is a greeting of honor among honorable souls. To me, it's not a show of deference to superiors, but rather a greeting and an honor to bestow upon a fellow soldier. 'Sides, after a while the troops begin to enjoy trying to get the drop on me and see if they can salute first. Then it's no longer a chore."

"I'll always remember that, General," said Roscoe appreciatively as she finally retired after a very long set of encounters.

#

Next on the General's agenda was the meeting with the newly minted Major Bozeman, United Hedgehog Marine Corps (UHMC). Bozeman was not thrilled to be finally facing the "Old Man." He saluted smartly but clumsily as soon as he was escorted into the General's presence. "Sir, Major Bozeman reporting to the Commanding General."

"Relax, Major," Spikers said a little gruffly and began right away. "Major, we already know one-another pretty well. If you did not know my command style and likes and dislikes you would not be much of an intelligence officer."

"Yes, Sir," Bozeman replied.

"You know I do not like your kind," continued Spikers with brutal honesty, "and have little use for sneaks and deceivers. I prefer an honest and straightforward battle."

"Yes, Sir."

"However, the Chief and I have agreed and decided that this situation calls for extraordinary measures, and the judicious use of intelligence will help to win this battle and save the lives of our Marines."

"Yes, Sir," Bozeman said, now sounding to himself like a broken record.

"I understand that you are the best there is in military intelligence, escape and evasion," said Spikers, "and therefore we do have some serious and dangerous jobs for you. I must admit that I was very skeptical at first, but your initial intelligence gathering effort and your battle wounds were very convincing."

"Thank you, Sir." Bozeman replied, a little relieved.

"How do you plan on solving this Dungaree mess, Major?" Spikers asked forthrightly, catching Bozeman completely off-guard.

"Dungaree mess, Sir?" Bozeman asked, naively stepping into it.

"DUNGAREE MESS, MARINE!" Spikers said, irritated. "That misguided fool Dungaree is at this moment LOCKED UP in the CAN at the Humane Society and is about to be turned over to Ivan for transport HERE! And here YOU are pretending to be HIM in front of all of these BUGS that want to BLOW UP THE WORLD!"

"Oh," whispered Bozeman, encountering a momentary lapse and forgetting the customary "sir." Then, regaining some composure, Bozeman continued, "Uh, Sir, couldn't we just lock him up here until this is all over?"

"We could," replied a slightly calmed down Spikers, "but what if Staley gets to him first and Ivan bungles again, as he did with you? No, the Chief and I have come up with an idea that will serve our mission and hopefully keep you from getting killed."

"Thank you, Sir," Bozeman replied. "I appreciate it that you do not want me to get killed."

"Nothing personal," groused Spikers, "we cannot afford to lose good Marines, even if they are spies."

"*Sheesh!*" Bozeman thought to himself.

Spikers continued: "Here's the drill. You and this Dungaree look strikingly like one-another. When Ivan brings him here, you be outside to be sure that Staley is not there and/or that Dungaree does not take off. You explain to Dungaree how you covered for him at the first meeting and that they would have smoat his butt if he had not showed. Come to him as an ally, a helper. Tell him the truth about the whole meeting and tell him about the double agent bit. After the next meeting, you can let Dungaree go to the meetings after that and have him feed the information back to you. Imply that you are on his side. Even speak in that silly hissy way they use."

"But, Sir, what about letting Dungaree in here as an agent for the insects?"

"No problem," continued Spikers, "we'll just treat him very cordially and tell him nothing except what we want him to know. Then he will feed back to his insect friends exactly what we want them to hear."

"Ingenious," said an amazed Bozeman, "no wonder you're the General."

"A combat division is a team, Major," Spikers said quietly but deliberately. "It eats, works, plans, and fights as a team. I did not come up with this idea by myself. Don't you forget that! The Chief, Colonel Grumpy, and The Ops, Colonel Clyde, had a lot to do with cooking this up."

"Yes, Sir!" Bozeman said, impressed, leaving the presence of his Commanding General with a new respect.

#

Bozeman returned that evening to the meeting of the insects and their leader, the hedgehog Anthross. He was met half way there by Staley, who thanked him again for saving him from the owl attack and remarked at how well the wounds on his side had healed. Bozeman brushed it off as no big thing. Sounding a little worried, Staley asked how Bozeman's intelligence gathering efforts had gone in the camp of the enemy.

"Not much to report," replied Bozeman matter-of-factly, "they are very disorganized, so, err, ssso I don't think we have anything to worry about from them."

"Oh, good!" Staley said, relieved. "Anthross will be glad to hear that."

"Yeah, there aren't very many of them," Bozeman continued. "They are relying upon prairie dogs, of all things, to fill the ranks."

Bozeman made his report at the meeting and Anthross stared at him intently the entire time, as did the several mantises that were standing behind Anthross. Bozeman could not put his paw on it, but there was something almost surrealistic about Anthross. Maybe he was one of them Far Eastern hedgehogs or something, but he had never seen such a stare. It was almost as if it had no depth, no soul. His eyes were sunken and he looked very different.

This time Bozeman behaved himself, finally realizing that these guys were not a bunch to clown around with. He listened intently as the plans were discussed. First there would be an experimental mission at a missile silo in eastern Colorado. There would be three bailywogs of cockroaches and two megahills of carpenter ants. They would strike at dawn on a particular day in August, with the main attack to be carried out two weeks later by three times the original experimental force at three locations in Wyoming. The next meeting was scheduled in three days.

Staley accompanied Bozeman back to Ivan's place, although nervously looking up at the sky every few seconds.

"Bozeman stopped two backyards away from Hedgequarters and told Staley, "Look, these guys at Ivan's are getting suspicious and so it's dangerous to get too close to the place. I have a hard enough time sneaking in and out as it is. Those durn field mouse sentries are all over. I'll leave you here and you can meet me at this spot 20 minutes before the next get-together."

"OK," said Staley, completely unaware of the switch Bozeman was planning for the next meeting.

Bozeman scurried back inside Hedgequarters and briefed Colonel Grumpy and the G-3 operations chief, Colonel Clyde, a big, no-nonsense old hedgehogs of few words. It was said that Colonel Clyde was very much into meditation and Zen, and had rigged up a small waterfall where he slept. He was not much for small talk and disliked those who wasted time . . . and breath. Bozeman kept his briefing short and businesslike.

When he got to the strength figures, Bozeman admitted that he did not know what a "bailywog" nor a "megahill" was.

Colonel Clyde clarified the question: "Insects organize militarily in different ways than we do. We organize along human historical lines, but they, because of their small size, organize in far larger numbers to get their jobs done. A 'bailywog' of cockroaches is some ten thousand members and a megahill of ants numbers about forty thousand. Any way you cut it, that's a lotta bugs."

#

The atmosphere was a little tense when Major General Spikers and the staff met in a circle to discuss strategy. The four General Staff officers were there, Lieutenant Colonel Thembekele, who, until the arrival of Bozeman, had acted as both the G-1 (Administration) and the G-2 (Intelligence). Thembekele, no slouch in the area of escape and evasion himself, seemed a little disappointed to give up his intelligence role and devote full time to what he considered the less interesting administration job. Colonel Clyde, the G-3 (Operations) sat stock still and silent, which was pretty typical for him. Colonel Tiggywinkle, the G-4 (Logistics), an aging chocolate Central African hedgehog, seemed a little on edge, for it was in her area that things were the most unsettled. The newest and by far the youngest member of the staff, Major Bozeman, sat in silence and somewhat in awe of this assembly of senior veterans.

Also in attendance was, of course, Colonel Grumpy, the Chief of Staff, and the diminutive, old brown hedgehog that was the commander of the 2d Hedgehog Marine Regiment (INFANTRY)(PRAIRIE DOG), Colonel Shakespeare. Among the senior hedgequarters officers, only Brigadier General Pickles, the Assistant Division Commander, was absent. According to The Chief, General Pickles was off training troops.

As Major General Spikers entered the hedgiehut designated as the War Room, Colonel Grumpy called "TENNNNN HUHHHHHH!" All of those gathered stood at attention.

"At ease!" General Spikers said, and everyone attentively hunched over some maps drawn by the G-3. Pointing to an "X" drawn on a map of northeastern Colorado, Major General Spikers said "Here is where they are going to hit in their preliminary, experimental strike. According to Major Bozeman's report it will be three bailywogs of roaches and two megahills of carpenter ants. Clyde, what do you need to roll it?"

Colonel Clyde, ever the pragmatist but not a hedgehog to "beat around the hedge," so to speak, laid it on the line. "No one knows. Insects have never massed in this way before. This exercise will be as much of an experiment for us as it will be for them."

"Thanks for that optimistic report, Colonel," said Spikers with a tinge of sarcasm.

"Any time, General." Colonel Clyde said, unruffled. But then he continued, "General, we are up against a potentially overwhelming force. There are endless multi-legged resources available to these insect commanders. They rule by fear and their smaller brethren seem to quickly and fearfully obey. There are billions of them. We are but one division of Marines and the troops we have managed to recruit have the highest esprit de corps, but we are few."

"The few, the proud . . ." echoed Lieutenant Colonel Thembekele.

"I think I know what you are telling me, Clyde." General Spikers said. "Whatever we do for this experimental mission, we must only use an expeditionary force of a fraction of the Division."

"Yes, Sir, regretfully," Colonel Clyde replied, somberly.

"Shakespeare, you agree?" General Spikers asked.

"Yes, Sir!" Colonel Shakespeare said. "Unfortunately. Clyde's always right."

"Roger that!" Colonel Grumpy affirmed, uninvited.

"Tiggywinkle!" General Spikers called. "Give us more bad news."

"You know it already, Sir," Colonel Tiggywinkle, the G-4 said. "Logistics nightmare. We are going to need some human assistance."

"I was afraid of that," General Spikers groaned. "We will have to request help from the Grand Dowager. The Dowagers and Seekers are the only ones who can solve these kinds of problems. Alright, I thank you for your wisdom and vision. There has never been as fine an outfit as this division. I will consult with the Grand Dowager and we will reconvene at this same time tomorrow. Dismissed!"

The inevitable "TENNNNNN HUHHHHHH!" came from The Chief and all stood at attention as the General exited.

On the way out of the meeting, Bozeman was, to say the least, confused as to what had taken place. He considered himself a fairly good spy and a pog of action, but this high level mumbo-jumbo had him perplexed. He sidled up to Lt. Col. Thembekele, with whom he felt he sort of identified, and asked a battery of nonstop questions.

"What was that 'fraction of the division' stuff?" Bozeman hurredly asked.

"Those guys, the General and his full colonels go back a long way. They've studied a seemingly endless history of the battles that have been waged," Thembekele began. "They study the Bigs and any other animals that have engaged in organized warfare. They know that this thing we are facing is new in the history of the world. If all of the insects of the world organized and rebelled, no one would stand a chance. Our effort of a single little hedgehog combat Marine division is a courageous but tiny effort in the face of what these insects can do. We know that they have an experimental mission and a main mission, thanks to your intelligence gathering. If we throw all we have against the experimental mission and we fail, there will be nothing left to combat the main mission. If we commit a representative portion of the division to this experimental mission and we are whupped, then we can learn what we need to learn to do better battle next time. Then we will learn from our errors and have the resources to hopefully thwart the main mission of these bugs."

"Whew!" Bozeman gasped. "I think I see the reasoning. What about the logistics thing?"

"Well," continued Thembekele, "we are going to have to move massed troops to these battle sites. Insects can travel fast and light, but our troops, save perhaps for the field mice, will need some heavy transport. Moving three to four thousand muskrats or prairie dogs will require some heavy equipment. We do not look to the Bigs for much, but there are a few that can speak with us. Most of us cannot communicate with the Bigs. The Dowagers and the Seekers know about these things and know how to speak with Bigs, those one in a million Bigs that can communicate back. I think the General was going to ask about this."

#

Major General Spikers's meeting with The Grand Dowager, Thelma, went very, very well. He explained the various predicaments the Division was facing, and she agreed with his judgment and supported his contentions as to how things were shaping up. She also had a welcomed surprise.

"I know of a Dowager that is ready to come here. She will find the human for you to solve your logistics problems," Thelma said. "She is being retired as a Mom hedgehog by a breeder and has made known her desire to come here. She's from the same community as Grumpy and Angel. Ivan will bring her here. She will find a human she can speak with to address the logistical problems. We Dowagers know these things. Her name is Wumpling. She started out as a pet hedgehog in Omaha, Nebraska, and it was intended that she be named Dumpling, but her human teenage caretaker hit the wrong key on her computer and the name 'Wumpling' was broadcast to her Internet friends. As is typical, the teenage caretaker became involved in 'sports' and 'boys' and Wumpling lost her importance as someone to be cared for. Ahh, how the Bigs abandon their souls so trivially and quickly. Wumpling was sold to a breeder, but after a few births, the breeder became ill and could no longer care for her animals. Wumpling was part of the entourage that came to Colorado. Now, Wumpling is being retired, and she can come here. She is, indeed, a magical Dowager. She will make it happen."

"It's amazing how you Dowagers and Seekers can influence the minds of these Bigs!" Spikers exclaimed, astonished. "They are so powerful in their momentary cleverness."

"Well, the way they are going they will not last long. We can only communicate with them in a limited way," explained Thelma, "and then only to Bigs that are open to subconscious suggestion and communication. They have to have open, kind, and sympathetic minds in the first place. Then our ideas come in as if they thought of them themselves. That is about the best we can do with Bigs. Most are so full of themselves that our thoughts and subconscious suggestions never get through their self-absorbed skin, let alone into their brains. It worked pretty well with Roscoe and Bill, although things with Bill were a little dicey for a while. Then, of course, there is the one-in-a-million among the Bigs that can communicate back with us. Wumpling knows of one and she will steer Ivan to him."

#

Wumpling was the largest hedgehog Ivan had ever seen. She weighed just at 2 and a half pounds, about 1,000 grams. She was labeled as a retired breeding Mom, coming from the same population as Grumpy and Angel, Marilyn said when she called.

"Want to give 'er a good 'ome," said Marilyn over the telephone. She's given me some fine babies, she 'as, but she's gettin' on up in years and needs to retire. Too big for a pet store, y'know. Might not treat 'er right."

It was early enough in the day when Ivan returned to stop off at Cilla's veterinary clinic for her to have a look at the newest member of the Flash Memorial Hedgehog Rescue.

"My, she's a big girl!" Cilla exclaimed. "About the biggest African hedgehog I've seen or even heard about. But she's very long and big boned, so she carries even this much weight pretty well. Could do to lose about 200 grams, though."

Cilla prodded and poked Wumpling, who tolerated the ritual pretty well, even to the point of letting Cilla examine the inside of her mouth and her ears without objection. The short examination completed, Cilla gave Wumpling a tentative clean bill of health, and the pair were on their way to the Rescue.

On the way, it "suddenly" dawned on Ivan to stop at John's Harley-Davidson to pick up a motor cycle part he had ordered some time back. The employees at John's, especially the women who worked the clothing and accessories sales counters in the front, all knew of the hedgehog rescue. They were continally trying to get dibs on Grumpy, their favorite, "when Ivan died."

Ivan walked into John's with Wumpling and introduced her around to the sales staff. He then went to the parts counter and plunked Wumpling on the counter, where she took an immediate interest in the Master Parts Catalog. As the parts man was back checking on the order, an enormous countenance appeared at the parts counter. It was Otis Driggs, half of the huge, bearded, Vietnam Vet pair that operated their "Old Time Biker Repair Shop" in Wyoming. The other half of the pair, of course, being Big Al Emerson, of Cement Mixer Personal Ride fame.

Otis stared down at the large ball of quills on the counter and bluntly asked, just as the parts man returned, "Whut th' hell's that?"

The parts man, a typical old time biker being a man of few words, uttered "Hedgehog."

Otis looked a little quizzical and asked further: "Part, accessory, or weapon?"

"Animal," said the parts man.

"Whut the hell you mean, animal?" Otis continued, perplexed.

At that time Wumpling decided to explore another part of the counter and ambled over to sniff at a set of head gaskets.

"What's it got, wheels!?" Otis exclaimed, startled.

"Naw, it's got FEET! It's a animal!" replied an exasperated parts man.

"I don't see no feet!" Otis replied.

"Well, this here's a biggun' and you cain't see the feet," responded the parts man.

"I'll be damned!" Otis said.

At that point, Wumpling, tired of sniffing at the head gaskets, ambled down the counter toward Ivan and Otis.

Ivan called "Come here, Wumpling," a command which Wumpling completely ignored.

"Haw haw!" Otis roared. "It don't do like it's told, just like bikers!"

It was then that Wumpling turned and walked straight toward Otis, stopping just short of 18 inches from him and looked straight up into his eyes.

Otis looked back at Wumpling and the look of mirthful entertainment departed from his eyes. "Uhh, whut th' hell?" Otis muttered, as he shook his head slightly and scratched his beard.

It seemed as if time was suspended for a few moments . . . minutes . . . five minutes? No one moved, not Ivan, not the parts man, not Wumpling, not Otis. The seeming trance was broken as Otis vigorously shook his head from side to side, and Wumpling turned and waddled back to the Master Parts Catalog.

Otis, a bit shaken, leaned over toward Ivan and said in a quiet voice, "Hey, Man, kin I talk to you outside when yore through?"

"Sure," said Ivan, "soon as I get rung up."

Ivan gathered up his purchase and Wumpling and went outside with Otis ambling along not far behind. As Ivan put Wumpling in the truck, Otis said, again in a quiet voice, "Uhh, Man, that is some kinda weird animal you got there. Whut do you do with a animal like that?"

"Well, I run a rescue for 'em," replied Ivan. "Seems people don't know how to take care of them. We have several now at our place."

"They sure are interestin'," continued Otis. "You mind if I come see 'em some time?"

"No, not at all. You're welcome to."

"Driggs' th' name, Otis Driggs. Me and my partner Big Al run a bike repair shop north of here. We fix old bikes like Shovels, Pans, Flats, an' Knuckles. Business been pretty good since John quit fixin' the old timers. Work on yore bike, if ya want, even though you ride Evo."

"How'd you know I ride Evo?" Ivan asked.

"Not hard to figger," Otis replied. "Them's Evo parts you jest bought."

"Anyway," said Ivan, "like I said, come by any time."

"Howsabout now? Then if I follow you there, I don't need to get d'rections."

"Er, why, uhh, sure," Ivan replied. "Just follow me."

The small entourage of Ivan in the truck and Otis on his old Harley panhead threaded their way back to where Wumpling was to meet with the assembled court of concerned hedgehogs. Ivan placed Wumpling in with the main group of female hedgehogs, whereupon Wumpling immediately disappeared into the hedgiehut. Otis was given a tour of the rescue and he and Ivan sat around for acouple of hours and discussed everything from the hedgehog rescue to the Viet Nam war, of which both were combat veterans. At the end of their discussions, Otis asked if he could have a few moments alone with "Wumplin'."

Ivan said that he had not seen Wumpling since she had disappeared into the hedgiehut, but he'd be happy to go look. A few minutes later he emerged with Wumpling, and handed her, rather speculatively, to Otis. Ivan need not have been concerned, as Wumpling glided into Otis' hands and stayed there. Otis walked out onto the back patio and sat down. He held Wumpling at arms length and then let her down on his lap. Much to Ivan's amazement, both Wumpling and Otis sat there, almost transfixed, for seemingly an endless period of time. Actually, it was about two hours.

As dusk began to set in, Otis came back inside the house and deposited Wumpling into the corral of hedgehogs. He then asked Ivan if he could come back and volunteer at the Rescue.

"Yes, I'd like that!" Ivan said. Otis seemed to have a special relationship with the hedgehogs. Little did Ivan know!

#

"It's all set," Wumpling told the assembled hedgehogs. "This Otis fellow is as trustworthy a human as you'll find. He and his friend will help us with the big transportation problems. He knows how important it is to keep quiet about this."

"We are all now assembled," added Angel.

Little Flash looked up and quietly remarked, "The Great Adventure begins."

"The Great War, I fear," whispered Rosie. "Nothing like this has ever happened before. Open, organized, large scale warfare between nonhuman species."

"And all of it concealed from the Bigs, no less." added Grumpy.

"Can we prevail, General?" an anxious Rosie queried.

"I'm afraid we must," a somber Spikers replied.

Thelma took in the entire circle. "Over sixty million Springtimes of life and living must not fail us now."

Made in the USA

Original title:
Frostbitten Shadows

Copyright © 2024 Swan Charm
All rights reserved.

Author: Olivia Oja
ISBN HARDBACK: 978-9908-52-632-4
ISBN PAPERBACK: 978-9908-52-633-1
ISBN EBOOK: 978-9908-52-634-8

Winter's Perpetual Echo

Snowflakes twirl in joyous flight,
Laughter dances through the night.
Candles glow with warmth so bright,
Hearts uplifted, pure delight.

Children play with gleeful shouts,
Bundled up, they twist and flout.
Sleds glide down the snowy route,
Echoes of joy, there's no doubt.

Fires crackle, stories shared,
Cocoa sipped, all hearts prepared.
Gifts wrapped up with loving care,
Winter's magic fills the air.

Stars shine down, a dazzling view,
Every moment feels so new.
Beneath the sky, a lively hue,
Winter's echo, bright and true.